Praise for the Haunted Bookshop Mysteries

"Jack and Pen are a terrific duo who prove that love can transcend anything."   —The Mystery Reader

"I highly recommend . . . the complete series."
                    —Spinetingler Magazine

"A charming, funny, and quirky mystery starring a suppressed widow and a stimulating ghost."
                    —*Midwest Book Review*

"The plot is marvelous, the writing is top notch."
                    —Cozy Library

The Ghost
AND THE
Bogus Bestseller

CLEO COYLE

BERKLEY PRIME CRIME
New York

BERKLEY PRIME CRIME
Published by Berkley
An imprint of Penguin Random House LLC
375 Hudson Street, New York, New York 10014

ISBN: 9780425237458

First Edition: September 2018

Printed in the United States of America
1 3 5 7 9 10 8 6 4 2

Cover art by Catherine Deeter
Cover design by Lesley Worrell and Natalie Thompson

This book is dedicated to our readers,
who have waited nearly ten years
for Jack to come back.

ACKNOWLEDGMENTS

It is fitting that the authors of the Haunted Bookshop Mysteries be acknowledged in print, in their own work. Alice Alfonsi, in collaboration with her husband, Marc Cerasini, created and began writing this series in 2003. Their first Haunted Bookshop Mystery, *The Ghost and Mrs. McClure*, was published by Berkley Prime Crime in 2004 under "Alice Kimberly," a pen name that Alice and Marc also dreamed up. Alice and Marc's subsequent books in this series include *The Ghost and the Dead Deb* (2005), *The Ghost and the Dead Man's Library* (2006), *The Ghost and the Femme Fatale* (2008), *The Ghost and the Haunted Mansion* (2009), and—after a nearly ten-year hiatus—this book, *The Ghost and the Bogus Bestseller* (2018).

Alice and Marc gratefully acknowledge their readers, to whom this book is dedicated, for their long-suffering patience. Their enthusiasm for this world and these characters is what inspired this work. The authors also sincerely thank their new editor, Michelle Vega, for having the faith to bring Jack back. A final tip of the fedora goes to literary agent John Talbot for his longstanding support. To find out more about Alice and Marc and the books they write, under their pseudonym Cleo Coyle as well as their own names, visit these online addresses: cleocoyle .com and coffeehousemystery.com.

CONTENTS

"A terrible book," said the Bishop.

"Who wrote it?" asked Cyril. "Does anybody know?"

"The author prefers to remain anonymous," intoned the Bishop, "and I for one am not surprised . . . In fact, I have written to the papers suggesting it should be withdrawn from publication."

"A sure way to increase its sales."

—*The Ghost and Mrs. Muir* by R. A. Dick
(aka Josephine Aimee Campbell Leslie)

PROLOGUE

I been shaking two nickels together for a month, trying to get them to mate.

—Raymond Chandler, *The Big Sleep*, 1939

New York City
April 1, 1947

"I NEED YOUR help, Mr. Shepard," the woman said. "You
are Jack Shepard, aren't you?"

Jack would have pointed to a nameplate, but his desk
didn't have one. There was a phone that jangled several
times a day, and scuffed filing cabinets he opened and
closed on a regular basis, a beat-up desk, a couple of chairs,
an electric fan that didn't work and a flyswatter that did.

Because his name was already painted on the door, right
above the words PRIVATE INVESTIGATOR, a desk plate made
about as much sense as a polo pony on skid row.

"Sure, I'm Shepard," Jack said, swinging his long legs
off the desk.

French perfume followed the dame in like a lovestruck
floral arrangement, the cloying bouquet bringing an intentional whiff of money.

Her pearls looked genuine, her tailored togs the latest style. The pair of stuffed foxes draped over her shoulders might have testified to her social standing—if their dead eyes could do more than stare. But mostly Jack knew the dame was flush from her uptown expression, the one your average Alvin gets in too-tight shoes. Lips pinched, nose held high, she spoke his name like she'd just eaten a bad oyster.

Opening conversation had to take a back seat to the Third Avenue El, now playing a rumba on their eardrums. Waiting out the racket, they eyed each other like an exhibit at the Museum of Natural History, each wondering who was on the wrong side of the glass.

Finally, the glass cracked, and Jack saw the flicker of nervousness cross the matron's proud face. She wasn't an old woman, but she wasn't young, either, her wrinkles betraying hard years. Reaching down, he freed the bottle from his bottom drawer.

"You like it neat?" he asked, pouring. He slid the glass her way. She scowled at the shot of rye as if a dead fly were floating in it.

Shrugging his wide shoulders, he poured one for himself and sat back. "Okay, I give. What's a dame like you want with a guy like me?"

"My chauffeur, Williams, recommended you."

"Name don't ring a bell."

"I'm surprised. He told me you're both members of the same private gentlemen's club."

"Gentlemen's club?" *Sure*, he thought, *and the Bowery Boys are taking tea at Oxford.*

"Oh yes. I forgot. Williams said I should mention a Mr. Benedict."

Jack covered his smirk with a sip from his glass. Roscoe Benedict—alias Bennie the Bookie—had a lot of suckers in his "club," and all of them played the horsies.

"How can I help?"

With that question, some of the hot air left her skirts. "Honestly, I'm not sure . . ." Frowning, she settled herself in the chair opposite his desk. "The truth is, Mr. Shepard,

I have no experience with private dicks. That's what they call you, isn't it?"

"Among other things. Why don't you tell me your problem?"

"Yes. The problem. Well, you see . . ." She tried to go on, but her voice went shaky, her lower lip quivered, and her eyes filled with tears.

Jack reached into his breast pocket for a handkerchief, but she waved him off, pulling her own lace-edged hankie from her purse.

That's when the Grand Hoover broke. Not crocodile drops, either. Jack let her go, until he feared drowning. If this went on much longer, he'd have to consult Noah on building an indoor ark.

"Please, ma'am, slow the waterworks. If I'm going to help, you've got to stop bawling and *tell me* what ails you."

Jack's firm voice seemed to help. The matron nodded, swiping at her wet cheeks and eyes. The disdain in her expression was wiped with it, leaving a shaky, broken look. That's when she reached for that glass of rye, drinking the shot like a sailor on shore leave. One loud gulp and down the hatch. Still gripping the glass, she leaned forward.

"Oh, Mr. Shepard. I'm a victim of a horrible crime."

"Go on." He brought his glass back to his lips, but went still when the dame blurted—

"Someone kidnapped my baby!"

Jack set down his drink. "Ma'am, that sounds like a job for proper authority, not a gumshoe for hire."

"I talked to the police. They refused to help. Not even after I told them who the kidnapper was!"

"You're telling me you know the identity of your baby-snatcher?"

"Henri Leroi, my soon-to-be ex-husband. When you bring my baby back, I'm sailing us to my sister's home in London, where that horrible man can never bother us again."

Jack rubbed his square jaw. He could use the work. His bank account was flatter than a pancake under a bulldozer. But custody battles were no cakewalk.

This matron looked a little long in the tooth to have an infant, but for all Jack knew, her "baby" could be fifteen— or adopted.

"Look, Mrs. Leroi—"

"Mrs. Armitage, if you please. I've gone back to my former name. Captain Armitage, my late husband, died at Anzio."

Another war-widow. Jack felt for her. He'd seen far too many men gasp their last breath Over There.

"So, this Mr. Leroi is—?"

"My second husband and former hairdresser. You know Leroi's Trés Jolie Casa de Beauty on Lexington, don't you?"

"Not by personal experience."

"Henri owns it. When I was his customer, he was always so kind. Then the Captain died, and . . . well, I admit, I was lonely, and too easily taken in by Henri's Continental charm and impeccable manners."

"Continental charm, eh?" Jack smelled a rat. "Did your baby come along while you were married to your first husband?"

"Oh no, the Captain wasn't interested in that sort of thing. He thought of it as my silly hobby . . ."

Jack shifted. He wouldn't have used those particular words, but he knew the Captain's meaning.

Long ago, inner demons assured Jack that a wife and kiddies were not for him. As a husband, he was certain he'd make a woman miserable, probably screw up the offspring, too. But on moonless nights, Jack's pillow knew his dreams: a curvy redhead for a partner, smart and feisty but decent, too, the kind of dame he could trust. She'd have a backbone but be soft where it counted, like the sweet idea of home. There'd be a rough-and-tumble boy with half a brain and plenty of gumption. And a pretty little house in some quiet little town . . . these were what heaven was made of.

Jack never said this out loud, of course, barely admitted it to himself. To the client across from him, he merely said—

"So, ma'am, let me get this straight. Henri Leroi is your baby's—"

"We adopted her together. From a distressed family in

Europe. Her name is Arianna . . ." Mrs. Armitage gestured toward Jack's bottle. He slid it over, and she downed a second shot.

Jack felt a twinge of sympathy for a little girl who was obviously a war orphan. But that didn't change the misgivings he had about jumping into the middle of a custody brawl.

"Why did Mr. Leroi kidnap Arianna?"

"He intends to sell her, Mr. Shepard. Can you imagine such a thing?"

After four years fighting through the same bloody mess as Captain Armitage, Jack could imagine plenty of things too terrible to share with this poor grieving woman. He downed the rest of his rye instead.

"And how old is Arianna, Mrs. Armitage?"

"Three."

Jack's temper went from simmer to boil. The flesh trade was shocking enough, but to sell a toddler as if she were some sack of potatoes? That made him burn.

Meanwhile, the matron rummaged through her handbag for a thick envelope and handed it over. "Here you are."

"What's this?"

"A copy of Arianna's papers."

Jack studied the documents and scratched his head. "I don't get it."

"I simply want to assure you that recovering my baby is a worthy case. You can see that from her lineage, can't you? It's all right there in the pedigree."

"But this pedigree is for a Pekingese."

"So?"

"You mean to tell me your 'baby' is a plain old dog?!"

"Mr. Shepard! How can you be so insensitive? There is nothing 'plain' about my Arianna. She's best of breed in her category, and one of the top show canines in the world!"

CHAPTER 1

Girl in the Store

Some people make no effort to resemble their pictures.

—Salvador Dali

"EXCUSE ME, MISS. Do you have the new *Girl* book?"

The question came on a busy Saturday afternoon. My inquisitive customer tapped me on the shoulder while I was restocking Erle Stanley Gardner's Perry Masons (in order), *The Case of the Velvet Claws* through *The Case of the Postponed Murder.*

The woman was about thirty years my senior—early to mid-sixties. Fashionably slender, she wore designer jeans at least three sizes smaller than my curvy figure. Her lilac cashmere sweater was an elegant choice for the early-autumn chill, along with her matching beret, which she'd jauntily pinned to her sleek silver bob. A fine leather jacket was draped over one arm while the other balanced a stack of books from our shelves.

Judging from her posh clothing and late-September tan,

I assumed she was a holdover from the summer people who had second homes in nearby Newport. I'd noticed her a few times, strolling through the streets of our little town, but I'd never seen her in Buy the Book, and I welcomed this chance to make her a regular customer.

After grabbing a basket, I helped her load it with her selections—while trying to decipher her enigmatic request.

"About the new *Girl* book, were you referring to *The Girl with the Dragon Tattoo*? Are you looking for one of its sequels?"

"No, no! That's the *Millennium* series!" The woman shook her head so vigorously I was afraid her pastel beret might Frisbee off and bean another customer. "I'm talking about the other *Girl* series."

"I see. The one written by . . . ?"

An impatient exhale followed—as if to question whether I knew *anything* about the books I was selling. "I forget the author's name, but the first was *Gone Girl* and then came *The Girl on the Train*. I'm simply asking if the third book is out."

"That's not actually a series," I gently replied. "More of a literary trend, written by two different authors."

"You're telling me the *Girl* in the title is not the same girl?"

"Uh, no. *Gone Girl* did not divorce her husband, move from Missouri to London, acquire a drinking habit, and see something she shouldn't have while riding the British rail system."

By now, I was smiling good-naturedly. My chic customer was not.

A strand of auburn hair escaped my ponytail. Curling it around an ear, I tried to read the woman's eyes behind her heavily tinted glasses. I couldn't. But her long silence told me she was not amused.

Aw, tell her to go pound sand!

The impolitic voice in my head had a familiar gruff ring.

I ignored it, along with the sudden cold emanating from our shop's fieldstone wall. The chill penetrated the thin material of my pleated brown slacks and simple white blouse, sending shivers from the nape of my neck to the tips of my toes.

Pushing up my black-framed glasses, I pressed forward in the only way an eager bookseller (or Mafia don) knows how—I made the customer an offer she couldn't refuse.

"If you liked the *Girl* novels, I'm sure you'll enjoy this!"

With the speed of a Treasury press minting money, I handed her a copy of the hottest-selling book of the fall season, a spicy thriller called *Shades of Leather*.

The woman set down her basket and accepted the weighty hardcover (six hundred–plus pages). A lift of her tinted glasses revealed high cheekbones and azure blue eyes that appeared quite striking against her tanned skin and silver bangs.

"Jessica Swindell? I've never heard of this author. Has she written anything else?"

"It's her debut. The reviews are mixed, but the general public is raving. A major movie contract is in the works, and sales are through the roof. It's far outpacing the trade's last big book, *Bang, Bang Baby*."

Her hand fluttered dismissively. "I heard that novel was nothing but tripe."

As she spoke, she studied the front cover, an artfully done side-shot of a nude woman stretched catlike across a red leather couch. The muscular arms of two strong men gripped the sofa on either side, ready to haul the furniture and the woman out of the picture.

I tapped the tome. "The publisher came up with a clever idea on the packaging. They issued three dustcovers, identical except for the color of the upholstery. That's the red couch edition. We've already sold out of the black leather and blue suede covers."

Clearly curious, the woman flipped over the book—and gasped.

Frankly, I couldn't see why. The author's photo was as artfully done as the cover. Jessica Swindell appeared young and attractive, her face partially veiled by a curtain of wild black hair, her nudity concealed tastefully behind a bedsheet—sure, the silhouette created by the diamond-shaped window in the background gave the *impression* of nudity. But the portrait was far from salacious enough to elicit the woman's extreme response.

Swaying as if she were about to faint, my new customer stepped back and spilled the basket of books on the floor. Gripping *Shades of Leather* with two trembling hands, she stared harder at the author's photo.

"I don't understand," she rasped. "How can this be? HOW?"

She looked up at me so suddenly her tinted glasses dropped back over her eyes.

"This picture. It's ME! But I'm not the author! I've never even heard of Jessica Swindell!"

I blinked, too confused to cross the gulf of silence between us. At last, I gently inquired whether her vision might be the issue. "Now that your glasses are back on, why don't you take another look—"

"MY EYESIGHT IS FINE. I KNOW MY OWN PICTURE WHEN I SEE IT!"

A few nearby customers were staring now.

Obviously, this woman was not Jessica Swindell, which meant, of course, she wasn't right in the head. *Maybe she needs her medications*, I thought.

Or maybe she's had a few too many!

Pipe down, I warned the gruff voice. *This lady is in some kind of distress. The reason doesn't matter. What matters is . . .*

"Ma'am," I said carefully, "why don't you sit down? I'll bring you a drink of water, unless you prefer—"

Another bottle of giggle pills!

"—some nice hot tea."

While I suggested more (*non*-alcoholic) remedies for her delusion, I began to pry the offending book from her hands. Her response was instant. Jerking the novel to her chest, she glanced from side to side as if searching for answers. Finding none, she bolted, shoving aside customers as she raced down the aisle.

Before I could stop her, the old girl was gone.

CHAPTER 2

Girl on the Run

Nobody steals books except kleptomaniacs and university students.

—Mark Helprin, *Freddy and Fredericka*

"SAKES ALIVE!"

The store's anti-theft alarm brought my aunt, Sadie Thornton, out from behind the cash register, hands covering her ears. "What on earth just happened?"

A little larceny, I'd say . . .

The unspoken reply didn't come from me. The unapologetically masculine presence belonged to Jack Shepard, the spirit of a murdered private eye from the 1940s who'd been haunting me since the new renovations to our old bookstore disturbed his eternal rest.

Either that, or he was my own special kind of crazy.

Whatever he was, Jack had become a source of . . . well, many things: comfort and advice; aggravation and exasperation.

Was he really a ghost? Or some kind of alter ego, created by a girl weaned on her late father's collection of *Black Mask* boys? Whatever he was—to me, Jack felt as real as death and taxes. And ever since I began "dialoguing with him" (as an online therapist once suggested), I'd felt better able to cope with the stresses of life.

Bottom line: I couldn't get rid of Jack. But at this point in our relationship, I honestly didn't want to.

Hurrying to the alarm box, I told my aunt about the mystery lady who ran off with our twenty-nine-dollar hardcover—

"The magnetic tape inside is what triggered the alarm."

"She didn't pay for it?" Sadie cried in surprise. Not because of the theft itself. Petty pilfering was nothing new to a woman who'd spent decades in retail. The whole town could recite the story of the local college kid who'd tried to shove a Hammett first edition down his pants. Sadie had put a stop to that with one sharp Patricia Cornwell to the head.

What astonished my aunt was the blatant grab-and-dash by an elegant older woman. It surprised me, too. And I had no explanation except to say—

"She seemed disturbed." As I danced my fingers over the alarm's keypad, the deafening racket ceased.

"Why in heaven was she so upset?"

"I don't know. She insisted the author portrait on the back of *Shades of Leather* was really *her* photo. Then she spilled her basket of books and ran off."

"My goodness me. It certainly doesn't sound like your average store thief. I hope that poor woman is all right."

Sadie's forehead furrowed with concern, an expression I'd seen many times, including on that day a few years back when I'd arrived at her shop feeling as confused and upset as my mysterious fleeing customer.

Shortly after my husband died, I packed up my son, moved away from my wealthy in-laws in New York City and back to this little Rhode Island town where I'd been born and raised.

When I turned up on Sadie's doorstep—a weary young widow with a son unable to comprehend the suicide of his father—my stalwart aunt took our burdens on her diminutive seventy-something shoulders without breaking stride.

There was no judgment, no inquisition, and most importantly no implication of fault, which I couldn't say about my toxic in-laws, who wanted someone to blame for my husband's end.

From Sadie there was only love, support, and the practical matters of settling us into her place, helping us move beyond death and get on with the business of living.

My grateful response was to pour all of my husband's insurance money into rebuilding Sadie's failing business, from the restored plank floor to the new awning and paint job.

Sadie's father had opened this shop decades ago, and (unfortunately) the interior showed it. I replaced the dented metal shelves with polished wooden cases, added throw rugs, comfortable chairs, and standing lamps. I even bought the storefront next door to create our Community Events space. But the most important improvement was to the core of the business.

My years in New York publishing had paid off with connections in the book trade. For the first time, our little family store began to host author appearances and signings. We'd cosponsored festivals, fostered reading groups, and closely monitored and refreshed our stock, adorning our windows with big bestselling hardcovers as well as trade paperbacks from local authors. Finally, I introduced Sadie's expertise (in used, rare, and first edition publications) to the twenty-first century's World Wide Web of customers.

The result of all this was a new, improved, and *profitable* Buy the Book. A store that prided itself on knowing its business and its customers—

Ahem!

Okay, Jack, with the exception of today's embarrassing incident.

You can say that again!

"I've seen the woman around town," I told my aunt, "but I don't know her."

Sadie returned to the shop counter, glasses swaying on the chain around her neck. "Let's tuck her selections into a reserve nook, in case she comes back to shop again—"

Don't you mean shoplift?

Don't be snarky, I told the ghost while retying my ponytail—that's when the phone rang.

"Is it Spencer?" I asked hopefully.

My young son had won a scholarship to attend a special weeklong computer seminar for middle schoolers, and he wouldn't be back from Boston until the middle of next week. He hadn't been gone long, but I missed him terribly.

Sadie checked the caller ID and shook her head.

"It's Chief Ciders. He's probably calling to find out why the alarm went off."

"This citywide security system is starting to bug me. It's a big time-sink for the police and a dubious added cost for the small businesses. We've had three false alarms this month—one in the middle of the night!"

Sadie sighed. "I felt bad for Bookmark. The poor little cat didn't mean to trigger the motion detector. She just likes to roam the store at night."

"I wonder if the burglar alarm goes off every time someone samples a grape at Koh's market?"

Sadie handed me the phone. "Ask the chief. He's been pinching produce for years."

"Buy the Book. May I help you?"

I answered in a cheerful tone, even though I knew it would annoy Quindicott's top cop. Pretty much everything bothered Chief Ciders, who'd been talking retirement since before Sadie and I revitalized her once-failing business. Unfortunately, he never got around to actually retiring.

"That you, Penelope?" Ciders griped. "You gonna tell me why the heck my computer lit up and disturbed my busy Saturday?"

"A book set off the door alarm."

"Does that mean I have to arrest some church lady for slipping a Mickey Spillane into her girdle?"

"And that would be a problem because—?"

"Deputy Chief Eddie Franzetti is running security at the high school football game with Deputy McCoy. And my new deputy is out on the highway working traffic duty for Dr. Ridgeway's funeral. Which means I'm way too short of officers for a Saturday, the very day punk kids, who don't care about football, gather on the town commons to cause trouble. So what do you want me to do?"

"Not a thing, Chief. Let's call this a false alarm—you're free to police the teenage flash mob to your heart's content."

Ciders grunted a reply.

"Chief, you really ought to drop by the bookstore. I know you love Mike Hammer, but there *are* mystery authors *besides* Mickey Spillane—"

"Not to me," he said and hung up.

With a sigh, I returned to the aisle to finish gathering up the contents of our book thief's spilled basket—an array of newly published mysteries and thrillers.

Sadie seemed convinced the lady would return to apologize and pay us, not only for *Shades of Leather* but also for the basket of books she'd taken time to pick out.

I had my doubts—until I found the game changer among the scattered volumes. The mystery woman had left something else behind.

"She should at least come back for these," I said, waving a pair of expensive driving gloves.

As the fine leather flapped in the air, I detected a sweet, familiar scent. Could it be? Putting the gloves to my nose, I carefully inhaled—then smiled.

"Cinnamon!"

Male laughter filled my head. *Good job, baby. Now that's what I'd call sniffing out a clue.*

CHAPTER 3

Girl in the Bakeshop

I had gotten a taste of death and found it palatable to
the extent that I could never again eat the fruits of a
normal civilization.

—Mickey Spillane, *One Lonely Night*, 1951

WHILE SADIE RETURNED to serving customers, I made
a local call.

"Cooper Family Bakery!" The fast, forceful greeting
came from Linda Cooper-Logan. She and her husband ran
the bakeshop she'd inherited from her parents, turning the
once-struggling business into the most popular place on
Cranberry Street.

"Good morning, Linda, it's Pen. Isn't Saturday cinnamon bun day—"

"Let me stop you there," Linda interrupted in her no-
nonsense manner. "The football crowd cleaned us out an
hour ago."

"Actually, I was calling to ask if you'd seen a particular
customer, probably in the last two or three hours?"

Give her the dope already, Jack insisted.

"She's an elegant woman, in her sixties. Blue eyes, lilac
beret—"

"It matched her sweater!" Linda interrupted. "I'd kill for that cashmere set!"

Kill? File that one away.

For goodness' sake, Jack, it's just a figure of speech.

"Do you know her, Linda?"

"No, sorry. I pegged her for a Newport holdover. And I remember her order exactly. She bought a single cinnamon bun, a coffee, and a one-dollar raffle ticket."

"Raffle ticket?"

"For the upcoming church festival. Milner and I are sponsoring a drawing for a week of free coffee and morning pastry plus a dozen of our new Boston Cream Whoopie Pies."

Whoopie, huh? My kind of pie!

Quiet, Jack.

With a cross of my fingers, I asked Linda: "Does the ticket have her name on it?"

"Sure does. Her address, too. She filled it out and stuffed it in the box. I know because I had to lend her my pen."

I sighed. "There are probably a hundred tickets in there, right?"

"Nope. This is the second box. We set it out this morning. She might have been the only one who bought a ticket today. None of those rowdy teenagers did, I can tell you . . ."

Never trust punk kids, said the ghost. *And never raise your hand to one, either, that's my advice—*

Good for you, Jack.

It's common sense, doll. Raising your hand leaves your thorax exposed.

Ignoring the ghost, I made my plea, the next half-truth flowing a little too smoothly out of my mouth.

"That customer left our store without her expensive gloves, and I'd like to return them . . ." (Okay, so I really wanted to check on her mental health, and maybe collect that twenty-nine dollars plus tax she owed the shop—but why take the low road?)

Linda was happy to help. She fetched the box and dug out the ticket. "There's no phone number, and she left the e-mail line blank, but here's what I've got . . ."

Mrs. Emma M. Hudson
1919 Pine Tree Avenue, Apartment 7
Quindicott, Rhode Island

I thanked Linda and tucked Mrs. Hudson's book selections and her gloves into a nook behind the counter. Then I went back to the selling floor, where I finished restocking the shelves with Perry Masons, replenished the scavenged Longmires, and happily signed for a delivery of Carolyn Hart's backlist.

That's when our front door burst open, and a hysterical Wanda Clark stumbled in. Wanda was the *usually* unflappable conductor of our church choir—but right now she was trembling, breathless, and pale.

"I . . . I thought I was going to die, Ms. Thornton!"

Sadie hurried to Wanda's side as the woman collapsed into one of our reading chairs.

"I was an inch away from death! That's how close it was!"

I brought her a paper cup of water, and Wanda took a giant gulp.

"Tell us what happened," Sadie urged.

"I was crossing the street down by Bud's hardware store when this steel blue sedan ran the red light and came at me. I just froze, right there in the middle of Cranberry Street. I would have died, too, but Mrs. Hudson must have seen me, because she swerved at the last possible second—"

"Do you mean Emma Hudson?"

Wanda nodded. "She was driving the Ford Fusion that Kent sold her a few days ago. The car still has temporary plates!"

"Kent" was *Mister* Clark, Stuckley Motors' top salesman. He'd sold half the folks in this town a vehicle, including me.

Kent Clark? And I bet I know his alias. Man Super.

Very funny, I told the ghost. Then I pressed Wanda—

"What happened next?"

"After she swerved, I lost my balance and fell on the street. Mrs. Hudson got out of the car to see if I was hurt. She was still clutching her smartphone to her ear—and the conversation must have been terrible, because she had a really nasty expression on her face. And she acted so strangely. Almost crazed!"

I took the empty cup. "How did you know? Did you speak with her?"

"That's just it . . ." Wanda shook her head. "She didn't say a thing to me. Didn't apologize. Didn't even ask if I was all right. She just kept talking on her phone—shouting, really. 'Sorry isn't enough!' she said with this beet red face. Then I got to my feet, and as soon as she saw I wasn't hurt, she slammed back into her car and raced west, right out of town. She never even looked back!"

Wanda sniffled. "Whatever is wrong in that poor woman's life, she's too distracted to be driving. I swear she's going to kill someone . . ."

As my aunt handed Wanda a box of tissues, she shot me a look. What began as a freakish occurrence was beginning to resemble a tragedy—the kind of tragedy I was all too familiar with.

"Well, *you're* alive, and you can thank God for that." Sadie laid a soothing hand on Wanda's shoulder. "Just relax until you feel better. Is there anything else I can get you? How about some tea? And something to read, perhaps?"

Wanda nodded and dropped her voice so low we had to lean closer. "Actually, there is a book I wanted to buy. It's called *Shades of Leather.* Have you heard of it? Everyone in my choir seems to be whispering about it. I noticed a copy on Emma Hudson's dashboard as she drove away."

Sadie smiled. "I'll be happy to get one for you, dear."

The front door bell signaled a cluster of arriving customers. While Sadie handled Mrs. Clark, I took care of the newcomers. Then Wanda departed, carrying off our last copy of *Shades of Leather*, a credit card purchase this time—

Yeah, instead of a five-finger discount!

Two busy hours later, the afternoon skies darkened as clouds rolled in. The turn in the weather was followed by a lull in business. That's when I made my move.

I unlocked the door connecting the main store with our
Community Events space, where I'd hung my coat and scarf.

The spacious room was shadowy. Most of the chairs
were folded and stacked, with the exception of a dozen or
so, which we set up in a circle for the Monday night meeting of the Quindicott Business Owners Association (better
known around town as "the Quibblers"). Buy the Book's
next event would be an author talk with Dr. Roger Leeds,
winner of the Bentley Prize for Literary Criticism. (We expected a huge turnout.)

When I returned to the shop, my aunt wasn't at all surprised to see me with my hair down, makeup refreshed, and
hands tightening the belt on my raincoat.

"I'm going to return Emma Hudson's driving gloves and
check up on her. If I can find out what's wrong, maybe I can
help the poor woman."

"Good idea."

"I'll try not to be too long."

With understanding in her eyes, Sadie patted my hand.
"Take as long as you need, dear."

As long as you collect that twenty-nine bucks plus tax!

Oh, give it a rest, Jack.

CHAPTER 4

Girl in the Wilderness

The meeting of two personalities is like the contact of two chemical substances: if there is any reaction, both are transformed.

—Carl Jung, *Modern Man in Search of a Soul*

OUTSIDE, THE STING of drizzle struck my cheeks as a rushing whoosh of briny wind battered my coat and ravaged my hair.

Shivering, I slammed the car door, tossed Emma Hudson's gloves onto the dashboard, and quickly finger-combed my reddish brown tangle. Then I scraped it back into a ponytail.

I like it better when it's down, baby.

"Tell that to the nor'easter."

While the real rain had yet to fall, clouds of angry purple and ominous gray were moving in quickly off the ocean. Gazing through my streaky windshield at the menacing sky, I now wondered—

"Should I reconsider this drive?"

I'm a spirit, not a weather vane. Check the forecast.

I flipped on the radio, and the local news assured me the

squall would pass soon enough, as opposed to the local traffic.

After pulling out of the alley next to our shop, I turned onto Cranberry, the main drag of Quindicott's shopping district, for a straight shot to the town's west side. Within two blocks, I ran smack into the jam-up Ciders had predicted—and predictably groused about.

The football game was over, and despite the coming storm, the streets around the town commons were clogged with revelers on wheels and on foot.

"Now what?"

When things stand in your way, you got two choices. You can stay still as a corpse. Or make your own road.

My ghost was right again.

One U-turn later, I was headed for the highway with a hasty plan to double back. This detour would add miles to my drive, but at least I was moving.

As I rolled off the highway near the burned-out barn that marked the edge of Prescott Woods, the deluge started. Fat raindrops splattered my windows as gusts from the cold Atlantic rattled my car. Then a boom of thunder shook the sky, and a lightning bolt bleached the swaying dark trees around me. With a loud crack, a branch broke off and tumbled through the air like a somersaulting high diver. When it slapped against my windshield, I jerked back in my seat.

Once more, a sky-flash turned everything ghostly white, and for a brief, disturbing moment, that ordinary fallen branch was transformed into my other ghost—the vision of my young husband sprawled on a Manhattan sidewalk.

A powerful windblast swept the large branch away, but not everything went with it. Leaves and twigs remained on the glass, beyond the reach of the busy wiper blades.

Just like those horrible memories, I thought, *forever clinging to my edges.*

Seeing a safe spot on the shoulder of the road, I pulled over, cut the engine, and listened to the storm battering the car windows.

It's no wonder I feel so compelled to help Emma Hudson...

The woman's unstable behavior reminded me of Calvin in those final weeks—paranoid illusions about people, places, and events, past and present; extreme shifts in emotion; sudden outbursts, all leading to tragedy.

I had no plans for singular heroics. If I found the woman in a disturbed state, I would simply notify the authorities. But I had to do something. I had failed—utterly failed—to help the father of my child. I wasn't about to make the same mistake with our new customer.

As my thoughts swirled, the brightest flash yet split the air, and I felt a shudder go through me like sparks of icy electricity. That's when he appeared, his long legs stretched out in the passenger seat beside me.

He had a rugged face and iron jaw with a dagger-shaped scar, as if the lightning had etched it on his anvil chin. His shoulders were broad, tapering down in a V to his trim waist. His strong body was clad in a double-breasted suit, and on his head sat a fedora of gunmetal gray.

Sitting next to me was the spirit of a dead man, but there was nothing lifeless about him. Energy pulsed around the ghost, crackling and exciting, as if the virility and vitality he'd possessed in life had been amplified in his afterlife.

In a frank and masculine gesture, Jack's gaze swept me up and down, and the tingling connection raced through me again, from feet to fingertips.

I closed my eyes, took a deep breath, and let it out.

When I opened them again, the vision was gone, but the electric presence remained.

Such a preternatural contact should have been unsettling, if not downright frightening. But by now, the unfathomable relationship I shared with my ghost was both familiar and welcome, especially on this turbulent afternoon.

You know, baby, there's something missing from your melodrama. Or maybe the thunder's so loud its drowning out the violins playing "Hearts and Flowers."

"'Hearts and Flowers'? Isn't that the sappy filler music they play during silent movies?"

Now you're catching on.

"Excuse me? You're likening my memories of Calvin's suicide to celluloid melodrama?"

Yep. Both are flights of fancy, ain't they?

"Calvin's death is a fact. He jumped from the bedroom window of our high-rise apartment."

And once again you're taking the blame for it. Telling yourself you had control over something you didn't. But listen, sweetheart, thinking like that is a dead-end road to nowhere.

"Except I still don't have any answers. Not for myself, my in-laws . . . or my son."

I've been in your head, baby. You have plenty of answers.

"Sure, I can tell you all about the succession of doctors and therapists Calvin gave up on. The medications he stopped taking. I can tell you about his mood swings— from his aloof silences to his verbal abuse. But none of it answers the most basic question of why. Why did Calvin McClure give up on life at such a young age? Why did he give up on me and Spencer? Why did Calvin kill himself?"

You're still breathing air, so you haven't figured it out yet.

"Figured out what?"

The mysteries that are hardest to solve are the ones in our own lives.

"Then how do I stop feeling guilty?"

You don't. But here's something you can do. Get off the mental merry-go-round. There are plenty of concrete problems to pound on in this mixed-up world of yours. And you've already got one ghost. Three's a crowd. Stop flirting with your phantom from the past, and focus on something real.

"Coming from you, that's not exactly self-serving."

Don't crack wise, honey. That's my jigger of gin. All I'm saying is hammer at the walls you can break, and dump all the other garbage. Today you've got actual business on your plate, a genuine, bona fide mystery to crack open.

"That's what I'm doing, Jack, although it's not much of a mystery. Just a lot of extenuating circumstances."

Don't be vague. In my business, thinking like a rube gets you nowhere.

"I'm not trying to be vague, just polite—"

And politeness will get you killed.

"Fine. What do you need to know?"

I already know the facts. What's your theory about this dame? She got a record?

"I doubt it, though she does appear to have some mental instability. When she fled with that thirty-dollar hardcover, I doubt she was even aware she was holding it. Today's so-called crime is no more than petty larceny."

Petty? In my day, three Hamiltons could buy you a month's rent. And I put my life on the line for that sum, more times than I can count. So remind me, please. Why didn't the local yokels follow up?

"They had other duties."

Where? The doughnut shop?

"According to the chief, it was a matter of prioritization."

Seems to me actual policing is as rare as the dodo bird in Cornpone-cott.

"There are too few officers here in QUINDICOTT, and too much to do on weekends. They don't have time for petty theft—"

Baby, there's nothing petty about theft when you're the victim.

"What's really bothering you, Jack? Are you bored because Spencer hasn't been around to turn on those old TV crime shows?"

Sure, I miss the snot-nosed little piker. But that didn't put the fly in my fedora.

"What did?"

That kooky klepto got under your sweet skin, right? So let's find a way to pry her loose—together.

CHAPTER 5

The Bird Is the Word

Live in such a way that you would not be ashamed to sell your parrot to the town gossip.

—Will Rogers

"HERE WE ARE, 1919 Pine Tree Avenue . . ."

Against a backdrop of dismal gray, the rambling, tree-shrouded Victorian had darkened windows, peeling paint, and all the grim foreboding of a Shirley Jackson novel.

What a dump.

"Thank you, Bette Davis."

Excuse me?

"Her famous line from *Beyond the Forest*, the film noir?"

Never heard of it. And don't get me started with your French euphemisms for black-and-white B movies.

I sighed, gazing at the run-down structure. "This place was lovely, once upon a time."

If you say so. Me, I'd prefer getting beyond THIS creepy forest. Not to mention the fright wig of a house . . .

I couldn't argue.

The expansive property was overgrown with weeds, ivy, and the old New England evergreens that gave Pine Tree Avenue its name. Amid this jungle sat the huge wooden structure. Its four sprawling floors would have provided more than enough space for a large turn-of-the-last-century family, live-in nanny, housekeeper, and cook.

But the past hundred years had been hard on Quindicott in general and this neighborhood in particular. Few Rhode Islanders lived the Gilded Age lifestyle these days—and certainly no one on the west side of our town. Over decades of decline, this once-great house had been divided into apartments for working people, and later for retirees and the unemployed.

Emma Hudson may have been impeccably dressed. She may have just purchased a brand-new car. But if she lived at this address, she had fallen on hard times, too.

A long sidewalk of rain-soaked concrete took me to a sagging front porch. I found a bank of mailboxes with peeling paint and a hand-scribbled note informing me that Apartment 7 had its own entrance at the rear of the property.

So around the building I went, following a narrow red-brick path with the house on my left side and an overgrown wall of pines on my right. I ducked a few swaying branches but couldn't avoid the post-rain drops, which splashed off the trees and onto my head.

As I approached the corner of the house, I heard a noise, coming from around the bend—rapid footsteps descending a flight of creaking stairs.

The sound was so close I stopped in my tracks for fear of colliding with the person, possibly a disturbed Emma Hudson herself. But the footsteps abruptly ceased, and no one appeared on the path, so I pushed forward.

When I finally made the turn, I saw no one.

The brick sidewalk ended at the wooden steps where I'd heard the creaking. The staircase led up to a dizzyingly high fourth floor. A check of the mailbox told me I was at the right place, so I began the ascent.

With the first creak, I again wondered about those phantom footsteps, and what happened to those feet.

"Maybe it was a ghost and this place is as haunted as it looks."

No way, Jack replied. *I have it on good authority that there's no such things as ghosts.*

Near the top of the stairs I heard an animated voice coming from inside the Hudson apartment. I paused to eavesdrop.

"One last dance! One last dance!"

The tone was high-pitched and a little hysterical. Whether the speaker was a woman or child, I couldn't tell. But it was certainly not the voice of Emma Hudson as I remembered it.

I waited for a reply, but none came.

"Is this a telephone conversation?" I whispered.

I don't think it's a conversation at all.

"One last dance . . . *Squawk!*"

"It's a talking bird!" I realized. "A parrot or maybe a mynah."

More like a stool pigeon—

"Huh?"

That bird has a pretty loose beak. You should pay attention to its patter.

"Do you think Emma Hudson is alone up there?"

Probably. Unless a pirate's shoulder is attached to the bird.

I finished my noisy climb. The stairs lead to a rickety widow's walk, which encircled the Victorian's highest floor. Branches of the tall pines hadn't been trimmed back in years. They'd grown so close to the house that they nearly blocked out the gray afternoon sky.

Reaching the shaky walk, I saw it served as a kind of front porch with a welcome mat and potted fern. Oddly, the apartment door stood wide open, so I called out—

"Mrs. Hudson? May I speak with you?"

The only reply was a flutter of wings and another high-pitched squawk.

"Hello?" I tried again. "Mrs. Hudson?"

"Hello, hello!" replied the bird.

Taking a deep breath, I stepped across the threshold—and nearly tripped over an open cardboard box packed with old photo albums.

The living room was small and modestly furnished,

with a worn floor of scuffed, poorly painted hardwood. The walls were once Victorian blue, but the color had dulled as much as the dirty white trim.

There wasn't much in the way of furniture—a matching set of folding chairs and tables, an old Singer sewing seat with embroidered upholstery, a pair of inexpensive standing lamps. There was no computer, television, radio, or even a telephone in sight.

There were, however, *books*. Hundreds and hundreds of them stood, neatly arranged, in alphabetical order on cheap pressed-wood bookshelves. Other volumes were piled on the floor in stacks, rising in knee-high columns. More books likely filled the sealed acid-free boxes stacked in the middle of the floor.

These weren't just any books. Most were protected by clear acid-free bags or swathed in Brodart book jackets, and my cursory glance revealed a treasure trove of literary booty.

In chronological order, I saw a string of signed Raymond Chandler first editions from *Farewell, My Lovely* to *The Little Sister*. Filed with the Fs I spied a first edition of Howard Fast's *Spartacus* and two autographed copies of Fitzgerald's *Gatsby*. I moved along to the Hs and found a British first edition of *Brave New World*; a pristine, personally inscribed copy of Hammett's *The Thin Man*; and a number of Hemingway signed editions, including *A Farewell to Arms*, *The Old Man and the Sea*, and *The Sun Also Rises*.

The shelved books ended at the letter M, with a first edition of Margaret Mitchell's *Gone with the Wind*.

There was no sign of my *Shades of Leather*, however.

Jack whistled. *Emma Hudson's got quite a stash. Do you think her light fingers lifted them all?*

"I doubt it. But it does beg a question . . ."

What?

"How can a woman who owns so many valuable books be completely unaware that big bestsellers like *Gone Girl* and *The Girl on the Train* aren't part of the same series?"

I eyed the sealed boxes, wondering what hidden treasures they contained. It was my ghost who pulled me back to reality.

Your eyes are bigger than a hooch hound at a hop joint. We're here to find Emma Hudson and your purloined pulp—not gawk at a pile of prehistoric publications. And maybe that's your answer anyway. The broad seems more interested in collecting the past than keeping up with the present.

"Okay, okay . . ."

Tearing my attention away from the fabulous collection, I stepped through a door to a dining nook—and bumped my head. Loose birdseed rained down on my flats, followed by a host of downy feathers.

"AWWWKKK!"

An agitated blue parrot glared at me from inside a faux-gilded cage. The bird's crest was up, wings spread wide.

"Sorry."

"Sorry isn't enough!" the bird squawked, followed by another angry whistle from its beak, and a preening of blue feathers.

That's one prickly parrot.

I called out for Mrs. Hudson again with silence as my reply.

"Emma's not here, Jack. What should we do?"

Keep looking around. That open front door should tell you something's hinky here.

The bathroom was empty, so I headed to the bedroom. Emma Hudson furnished her sleeping quarters with a French Provincial bedroom set and a queen-sized bed.

The spacious room included a balcony (of sorts), amounting to a metal-framed sliding door that led to another section of the railed widow's walk. In better times, I had no doubt the floor-to-ceiling window would have been beautifully framed by elaborate French doors. But these weren't better times. Not for this neighborhood. Or, apparently, this woman.

That flimsy sliding door stood open, allowing a chilly draft to billow the long drapes. Despite the earlier downpour and sopping wet pines around the house, I noticed the carpeting was dry.

On the bed, the lilac cashmere sweater that Emma Hudson had worn earlier that day lay beside her designer jeans.

Looks like she switched duds before taking a powder, Jack noted.

A second, smaller room contained a fold-out bed piled high with suitcases. The case on top was open. It contained women's clothing and intimates.

"Odd that Mrs. Hudson is still living out of her suitcase," I said.

There's no real furniture in the living room. These digs may be temporary for the dame. Maybe she planned a quick exit. Or maybe she's already gone.

"Certainly not for good. No one in their right mind would leave all these valuable books behind—"

Her "right mind" is what's in question, isn't it?

"She also left the front door wide open. And the sliding door in her bedroom, too. That makes no sense, either . . ."

Since when do candidates for the cackle factory act rational?

"Lack of rationality is one thing, Jack. I'm worried she's unhinged to the point of harming herself . . ."

And with those words, the vision of my husband's corpse returned with such power that I held my head.

Easy, baby, don't go back there.

But my husband's death leap was too vivid a memory. In this moment, it felt more like a premonition.

With dread, I hurried across the dry carpeting of Emma Hudson's bedroom, through the open sliding door, and onto the rickety widow's walk. I had to stick my head through the tips of wet pine branches to peer over the side, and that's when I saw her.

Emma Hudson, in a pink terry cloth robe, was sprawled on the rain-soaked ground. She lay facedown, and from the way her body was twisted, her head smashed like a burst pumpkin against a large rock, I had no doubt she was gone—

This time for good.

CHAPTER 6

Gone with the Windstorm

Suspicious? I should say I was; if my face ever betrayed anything, it betrayed it then.

—Carroll John Daly, "Three Gun Terry," *Black Mask*, May 1923
(cited as the first published appearance of a hard-boiled detective)

GRIMACING AT THE mangled corpse below, I speed-dialed the Quindicott PD.

Chief Ciders answered, and I described what I'd found. He told me he was on his way and ordered me to stay to answer questions. He also warned me not to touch the body or anything around it.

"Don't you disturb that corpse, Penelope McClure!"

Of course, he failed to say a thing about looking around Emma Hudson's apartment four stories above that corpse—as the ghost gleefully noted—

I doubt the deceased would mind if you snooped around. You do have stolen property to recover.

"You're a bad influence, Jack."

Maybe. But as a private dick, I'm the berries.

"Then how can you think of a stolen book at a time like this?"

Because that book is why Emma Hudson is lying among the pines, waiting for a pine box.

"You're right, in a way. I think that poor woman's delusion about the author photo drove her over the edge and she jumped."

And I think we're supposed to think she jumped. But in this PI's not-so-humble opinion, someone staged this scene like a Busby Berkeley extravaganza.

"Staged? Then you suspect foul play?"

No, I suspect homicide.

"Jack, it's obviously suicide. Just like my husband, Calvin—"

Emma Hudson is not your husband. Push the past out of the frame, or you'll miss the real picture.

"What real picture?"

Let's start with the facts, plain and simple. Tell me what happened here. Do it clean.

I scanned the porch and peeked over the side, cringing involuntarily at my second look at the dead woman.

"It's clear enough what happened, isn't it? Based on her behavior in my bookshop, I'd say she went into some kind of an emotional tailspin, became irrational, and—"

Skip the headshrinker stuff and tell me what gave her the big chill.

"She jumped from this widow's walk. Isn't it obvious?"

She dived headfirst, then? Like Johnny Weissmuller off a high board? Because that's the way she landed.

I stepped back and eyed the rail. Jack was right. To get over the rail cleanly, I would have to swing one leg, then the other. So my "jump" would have to be legs first, not head first, unless . . .

No "unless," baby. Most jumpers don't dive. They close their eyes, ease themselves off their perch, and down they go.

"Maybe she leaned over the rail as far as she could and let gravity take her down. Maybe she was determined."

If she was so determined, why didn't she use the bridge

*outside of town? That's a nice nosedive into a rocky creek.
Or how about that hundred-foot cliff by the railroad
tracks? Both sound more effective than four lousy floors off
your own bedroom balcony—why, that's sixty feet, tops—
yet she drove right past those prime places, to end her days
here?*

"Maybe she wanted to write a suicide note?"

Do you see one?

"No, but it could be in her robe, her hand, her pocket . . ."

And if it isn't?

"That doesn't mean a thing. My husband didn't leave a
suicide note."

*Okay, so not every jumper leaves a "good-bye cruel
world," but don't you think the dame would have something to say, even if it's how to care for her suddenly orphaned stool pigeon?*

I shivered. Not about Emma's corpse this time, but at
Jack's implication. "So, you think Emma Hudson was—"

*Murdered. That's right. And a suicide scene staged just
well enough to fool the local yokels. It's possible she was
dead before she went over the side . . .*

As Jack went on, I noticed an aroma in the air. "Do you
smell that?"

I do now. My Jimmy Durante picked it up with yours.

It took me less than a minute to locate the source of the
savory scent. A warm slow cooker sat on the kitchen counter, beside a half-empty bottle of Eclipse coffee syrup and
a spoon sticky with the sweet, delicious goo.

According to the digital timer, the cooker had been
working for many hours. The lid was hot, but I couldn't
resist the urge to lift it. Yes, Chief Ciders told me not to
touch anything, but I decided an untended pot was a potential fire hazard and should be checked out—

Put on your gloves first, Jack advised.

"Don't worry, Jack, I won't burn my fingers."

*But your FINGERPRINTS might burn evidence. PUT
ON THE GLOVES!*

"All right! For heaven's sake, calm down . . ."

Reaching into my pocket, I felt for my leather gloves—and suddenly remembered Emma's driving gloves, the ones I'd come here to return.

"I left hers in the car."

Forget it, doll. That dame don't need gloves anymore. What she needs is a coffin.

With a sad sigh, I pulled on my own gloves and lifted the lid on the woman's slow cooker. Simmering inside, I found a heavenly dinner of short ribs in red wine. I glanced around, found the empty bottle on the counter next to two untouched baguettes and a Cooper Family Bakery box. Inside I counted five cinnamon buns.

"If she was murdered, Jack, then the killer made a huge mistake."

Okay, how so? the ghost replied in a tone that told me he already knew the answer.

"Why prepare a magnificent last meal like this and not eat it?"

Good. Now you're thinking like me.

"If you're saying I have a completely jaundiced view of the world and everything in it, you're mistaken. But, I admit, something seems awfully suspicious here."

I agree. Leaving the pot cooking was sloppy work by a killer in a hurry.

"In a hurry . . ." Another thought occurred to me. "You know the sliding door that was left wide open? During the storm, rain would have come in and soaked the bedroom carpet. But that carpet was dry. Jack, whatever happened in this apartment happened *after* the storm passed, which means we just missed it."

You better hope the murderer doesn't remember that slow cooker being on—and come back to fix the scene.

"Why risk it?"

Why do you think criminals return to the scene of the crime?

"A guilty conscience?"

It's not guilt. It's fear that draws them back. The culprit can't shake the nagging suspicion that incriminating evidence was left behind.

"Now you're trying to scare me."

I'm trying to warn you.

"Jack, remember those footsteps we heard when we first got here? It's possible that was the killer fleeing the scene!"

It's also possible that the perp might be lurking around now, watching the apartment, waiting to see who comes by.

I shivered. "I hope the chief gets here soon—"

A loud creak, followed by another, silenced me. Outside, heavy boots began the long ascent to the porch.

"Someone's coming up the stairs!"

The local yokel?

"The chief's on the other side of town. Even with his siren, he can't get here this soon."

Another creak came, followed by a deep grunt.

"That's a man, and he's getting closer. Jack, there's no other way out but the front door—or over the rail of that widow's walk! I'm trapped!"

Keep a cool head. Just stall until the Keystone Cop arrives . . .

Jack kept talking, but I wasn't listening. Like a desperate woman who didn't want her son to grow up an orphan, I searched for any means to fight back.

When I spied a line of steak knives in a rack beside the sink, I snatched two of them. Then I ran to the front door and raised them above my head, ready to ambush the killer.

Meanwhile, those big, steady footsteps crossed the porch to the open door.

When the silhouette of a large man loomed into view, I screamed loud enough to scare the stranger into screaming, too.

Our delirious duet became a trio when the parrot joined in.

Jack was not amused.

Holy ghost! What are you tryin' to do? Raise the dead?

CHAPTER 7

My Baby Wrote Me a Letter

I get mail; therefore I am.

—Scott Adams, American cartoonist

"SEYMOUR!" I CRIED when our crazy choir went quiet. "What are you doing here?!"

Seymour Tarnish, my know-it-all childhood friend, blinked. "I'm the mailman, Pen. What do you *think* I'm doing?"

He nervously looked at the knives still raised above my head.

"Why the Jack the Ripper routine? I thought you were Norma Bates coming at me. I nearly filled my Underoos."

I lowered the blades. "A maniac dressed as his mother? That's some compliment."

The bird whistled. "Hello, Seymour. Hello!"

Seymour stuck his gawky, round face through the door and called back, "Hello there, Waldo!"

The bird talks to the birdbrain, Jack cracked. *Why am I not surprised?*

"Sorry about the knives," I told Seymour. "I thought you were a killer."

"Just what the heck is going on here?" he demanded.

"I've got a registered letter for Emma Hudson that she needs to sign for."

"Does she get many registered letters?"

"She mostly gets packages from PetMeds.com." His voice trailed off as the bird angrily ruffled its feathers. "That's one sick bird."

I slipped through the door to join Seymour on the porch.

"Emma Hudson seems to have jumped to her death."

The mailman grimaced in shock. Then he sighed, shook his head, and his gaze followed mine to the edge of the widow's walk.

"Did you call the cops?"

"Chief Ciders is on his way."

"Wait a minute! You said she jumped. But you also said something about a killer!"

Sharp as a bent nail, this one.

"I said she *seems* to have jumped to her death. But I'm not sure . . ."

Unfortunately, there was no time to elaborate further. Another set of heavy steps climbed the wooden platform. This time it actually *was* Chief Ciders, his gun belt half hidden under a paunch that appeared to have expanded since the last time I'd seen him. His hat was tipped back on his head, and his grizzled face was scowling.

Huffing and puffing, Ciders crested the final few steps and immediately fixed a suspicious eye on Seymour. "What are you doing here?"

"Chief, you *do* know there's a reason that United States Postal workers wear uniforms? It's for recognition purposes."

"So you were delivering mail?"

Seymour faced me with a smirk. "With insights like that, it's no wonder he's chief."

"The mailbox is at the *bottom* of the stairs," Ciders pointed out.

"Do you think I *wanted* to scale Mount Everest? I do enough walking on a given day. I didn't need this. As I told Pen, I have a registered letter the deceased was supposed to sign for."

Ciders' eyes narrowed. "How do you know Emma Hudson is deceased?"

"What kind of question is that? You think I croaked her?"

Ciders gave Seymour the kind of look he reserved for an undersized fish he had to toss back into the creek. Then the chief faced a bigger fish (metaphorically speaking)—me.

"Since I'm not convinced this widow's walk can hold our combined weight, we'd better step inside the apartment. Knowing your busybody ways, Mrs. McClure, I'm sure you've already made yourself comfortable."

As we all moved toward the door, Ciders blocked Seymour.

"Not you, Tarnish. You can wait at the bottom of the stairs like a good mailman. But stay away from the corpse. The medical examiner is on the way."

"I can't stick around," Seymour protested. "I have work to do."

"It won't take long."

"It better not. Neither snow nor rain nor heat nor pointless queries from uniformed authorities will stay this courier from the swift completion of his appointed rounds!"

"Stow it, Tarnish. And sit your butt on those steps. When Pen and I are finished, you're going to tell me *all* about that registered letter you're holding for the dead woman."

CHAPTER 8

Ciders' House Rules

"Cops are just people," she said irrelevantly.
"They start out that way, I've heard."

—Raymond Chandler, *Farewell, My Lovely*, 1940

"LISTEN, PENELOPE, I'VE known you for years. When you run that bookshop with your aunt, you act like a level-headed businesswoman. But right now, you're talking like someone who's been reading too many of those cheap thrillers you peddle."

"Please, Chief. You're not looking at the facts—"

"This is suicide, not homicide. You told me yourself that the woman was acting kooky . . ."

Ciders and I were sitting at Emma Hudson's kitchen table. By now, I'd gone through the events of my day, recounting the woman's odd actions. Ciders even phoned Wanda Clark and my aunt Sadie to corroborate my story.

When the calls were finished, I presented the chief with the evidence that Jack and I had found, from the footsteps on the stairs to the simmering stew.

"Uh-huh," said Ciders.

I then reiterated the reason for my visit.

"I came to return Emma Hudson's gloves—and get the

payment for *Shades of Leather*, the bestselling book she took. She was hysterical about it. Yet it's not here now. Someone must have removed it from this apartment, and I think that someone might have something to do with her death. At the very least, the person must be found and questioned."

"Uh-huh," Ciders replied again. "And where are those gloves you said you came to return?"

"I left them in my car."

"Well, maybe Emma Hudson left your book in *her* car."

I gritted my teeth. *This conversation is going nowhere! Sure it is, doll. It's going in circles.*

"Chief, if she was so disturbed by *Shades of Leather* that she wanted to kill herself, why jump here? On her way back from town, she would have crossed the Johnson Street Bridge. That's a two-hundred-foot drop to the creek below—"

Ciders grunted. "Who knows why she jumped where she jumped. Crazy people do crazy things. Wanda Clark called her 'unhinged.' And your aunt confirmed it."

"But—"

Suddenly, I was talking to the chief's hand.

"Until more evidence presents itself, I'm treating this as a suicide. We're only waiting for the medical examiner to make it official." The hand became a finger, and it pointed to the door. "You're done here, Penelope. You can go now."

I opened my mouth, but Ciders mimicked the one monkey in three who's always covering his ears.

At least he's got the species right, Jack said. *You're talking to a goon from Saskatoon—"*

"Huh?"

Your little town's top cop is thicker than a tree stump. Stop bumping your gums and use your peepers. Make like Norman Rockwell and paint a mental picture of the crime scene. And quick, before the long arm of the law tosses you out for keeps.

As I left Ciders in the kitchen, I heard him making a call to the still absent medical examiner. So I followed Jack's suggestion the twenty-first-century way—I took out my smartphone and started snapping digital memories. After quick shots of the two bedrooms, I returned to the main room.

As a bookseller, I couldn't help shooting some of the valuable titles Emma had collected. I noticed a handwritten Post-it note on top of one of the stacks, and I took a close-up.

Another note, written on a piece of lined white notebook paper, listed a dozen recently published books. I photographed that, too.

The absence of a smartphone or a computer seemed odd. In this day and age, who didn't have some kind of digital device?

Don't forget, it was the mug shot of the author on the back of your pilfered potboiler that set the dead woman off. Search those old photos you noticed when you came in. A trip down Emma Hudson's memory lane could provide a clue . . .

The box of old pictures and photo albums was still beside the door. With my leather gloves on, I rummaged through it. Some of the loose snapshots were black-and-white. Others were color Polaroids, and one caught my eye.

A young woman with wild dark hair stood facing the camera in a long flowered dress. Unfortunately, it wasn't a close-up. The colors were faded and the image was fuzzy, blurring the woman's features. But the diamond-shaped window in the background was a dead giveaway.

This cheap little "instant" Polaroid picture had the same background as Jessica Swindell's artfully done author photo on the dust jacket of *Shades of Leather.*

I flipped the picture. On its back I found a hand-scrawled date and nothing else:

May 19, 1972

Tuck that mug shot down your blouse, the ghost urged. *One five-finger discount is as good as another, and the Hudson dame owes you.*

"I can't, Jack. This is a crime scene, and I shouldn't remove potential evidence. But I can take my own pictures of the picture . . ."

And I did, front and back.

Handling the Polaroid, I noticed traces of a sticky, whitish adhesive on the back and deduced it had slipped out of one of the photo albums. That stack seemed promising. But as I reached for the album on top, a loud voice barked—

"Penelope Thornton-McClure!"

"Yes, Chief?"

"I thought I told you to leave. Now get a move on!"

I slunk out the door and down the steps, listening to Jack curse the whole time about the photo albums being a missed opportunity.

At the bottom of the staircase, I found an impatient Seymour.

"So what's going on?" he asked.

I lowered my voice. "Ciders believes the woman committed suicide. I don't. Any minute now, he'll be down to ask you about that registered letter. Do you know anything about it?"

Seymour grinned. "This mailman knows all, including the contents."

"Really? Let me see the envelope."

He handed me the thick legal-sized letter with the yellow registered sticker attached. It was sent from the law firm of Mitchell and Olivetti in Providence, Rhode Island.

"Seymour, how can you possibly know what's inside? It's sealed."

"We postal employees have our ways," he said. Then he lifted one eyebrow high enough to touch his receding hairline. It was a gesture he'd perfected back in eighth grade, a way to appear (as he put it) "enigmatic . . . you know, the way Mr. Spock looks when he's trying to explain to Doc McCoy something he's too stupidly human to understand." (Among other things, Seymour was locally famous for forming Quindicott's first official *Star Trek* fan club.)

Undeterred, I lifted my own eyebrow. "Spill it."

Seymour shrugged. "Thin envelope, pocket flashlight."

Jack laughed. *It's official. Cornpone-cott is packed with busybodies.*

"Okay, Seymour, what did you see?"

"Divorce papers, terminating Emma Hudson's marriage to Philip Gordon Hudson of Millstone, Rhode Island—"

"What are you two gossiping about?!" Chief Ciders bellowed from the top of the stairs.

"The stormy weather," Seymour shot back.

"Well shut your trap and get up here already." Ciders flashed us a sour look and went back inside.

"I'm worried about that parrot," Seymour confided.

"Why?"

"Waldo has a delicate condition—several, in fact."

"You know this how?"

"I deliver the PetMeds, remember? And did you see all those feathers? That poor bird is molting. I know birds. I grew up with them. My mom had more feathered friends than the Birdman of Alcatraz."

That gave me an idea.

"I think Waldo needs a proper home, don't you? Emma left no instructions, and you and I both know an animal shelter is no place for a parrot with delicate conditions."

Not to mention one that's a witness to murder.

Seymour was already nodding. "You're right, Pen. I'll convince Chief Ciders to let me take care of it. He knew my mom and her bird fetish. I'm sure I can win at least temporary custody, if only because the chief will be too lazy to drive Waldo to the shelter in Newport."

"I expect you to fill me in at the Quibblers meeting on Monday."

"Oh, I'll be there. With bells on." Seymour let out a cackle. "*Bells on*, get it?"

Of course, I got it. Everyone in town knew our mailman moonlighted as the owner and operator of Quindicott's only ice cream truck.

"Pen? Are you still here?" Ciders bellowed from above. "I told you to vacate the premises. Get out of here now or I'll have you arrested for trespassing! And *you*, postal worker—" He pointed at Seymour. "Stop jawing with the nosy book lady and deliver yourself to me. I've got my own questions for you!"

With a sigh, Seymour eyed the four-story staircase and shot me a look. "If I collapse from exhaustion, I'm holding Ciders responsible."

"Be strong, Seymour."

"See ya later, Pen," he said before addressing his feet. "Let's go, tired dogs. Make like Sir Edmund Hillary and mush me to the peak."

CHAPTER 9

Into the Woods

So into the woods you go again,
You have to every now and then.

—Stephen Sondheim

AS I WATCHED Seymour huff and puff his way up to
Emma Hudson's apartment, I faced the wall of pines.

"Well, Jack, now what?"

*You heard Chief Local-Yokel. He ordered you to go. But
you should have a look around first. That birdbrain mailman should confound the copper for at least ten minutes.*

"Okay, but what am I looking for?"

*Remember what the lawman said. He's treating this as
a suicide, until more "evidence" presents itself.*

"So we'll have to find some, won't we?"

Now that's the sort of sweet talk I like to hear.

"Where shall we look first?"

Remember those feet coming down the stairs?

"I remember they never came around the corner."

Then where did your suspect go?

"There must be a quick way out of here. Maybe a shortcut to a backstreet . . ."

Emma's apartment was at the rear of the house. To get

here, I'd followed a redbrick sidewalk, but the sidewalk ended at the base of the staircase. Beyond the steps, a wide dirt path took over where the bricks left off. The path hugged the foundation's perimeter, disappearing around the next bend. But (and this was a big but) the path was blocked by a crumbling six-foot trellis. Many of the wooden bars had rotted and fallen to the ground.

"Anyone trying to climb over that mess would have made a lot of noise. I would have heard it. But there's nowhere else to go . . ."

The overgrown evergreens effectively walled in the dirt path, and the trees appeared impenetrable. Drooping branches overlapped in an interlocking curtain of sharp needles with thick weeds tangled at each trunk's base.

"Nobody could get through all that without real effort."

And a hacksaw.

"I would have seen or heard someone struggling, and I obviously didn't."

It's a cinch. Your phantom perp disappeared into thin air.

"Gee, sounds like someone I know."

You think I'm a product of your imagination?

"I'm not crazy, Jack. I know you're real—to me, anyway. And I know what I heard."

Refusing to believe I'd *imagined* those footsteps, I continued looking for another way out. And I found it. Between two of the trees along the dirt path, just before the crumbling trellis, I noticed a patch of beaten ground covered in nettles. No weeds here. And when I quietly pushed a few low branches aside—

"Look, Jack!"

Behind the curtain of pine stretched a footpath.

Sweet and alreet, you've found the hidden trail! Okay, baby, let's blaze it.

Holding back the wet branches, I stepped between the trees and onto the path. The grove was heavily shaded, the scent of pine as powerful as the earthy smells from the fresh rain on the moss and weeds. Beneath my feet, the path was soft, but not muddy.

"I don't see any footprints. These pine needles are like wall-to-wall carpeting."

You're in the woods now, baby. Might as well look for bread crumbs . . .

As I walked along, the little forest grew taller and the shade deeper. Chilly breezes rustled the long branches, and the green giants moved around me, as if they were alive.

They ARE alive, doll, they're trees.

"They're creepy."

Maybe you only think they're creepy because you make a living selling their dead.

"What a thing to say!"

It's true, isn't it? All those blowhards whose daydreams you peddle print their petty parables on paper. Paper is pulped wood. Maybe these greenies can sense you buy and sell their stiffs.

"Don't be ridiculous! Trees aren't *that* sentient."

And ghosts don't exist.

"Most living people would agree with that statement."

So did I, doll, before my lead poisoning. And when I was alive, I preferred the city. Concrete, stone, glass—you can trust a thing that's already dead. It won't judge you. And it won't change on you . . .

The colors were muted in the deep shade. But a flash of shiny crimson caught my eye—hard to miss that color amid all these earth tones.

"Probably just a piece of trash, maybe a candy wrapper . . ."

Don't assume it till you've seen it.

A few more steps and I was staring at a glossy piece of "dead wood" stuck to a pine branch. Jack was right. This was no candy wrapper. It was a torn section from the dust jacket of *Shades of Leather*—the red couch edition. The slick paper was dry, too. Not rain-soaked like everything else around us.

"Emma's book thief must have come through here after the storm—"

Just then, I heard something moving. Not something small like a squirrel or raccoon, something much larger. I glanced around the spooky grove. "Do you think our suspect could still be lurking nearby?"

Who knows what shadows lurk in the hearts of trees. Keep your peepers peeled, honey.

Jack's close presence always chilled the air. Now I shivered for another reason. I could sense someone in the woods with me, and moving closer. But I couldn't tell from what direction.

"Jack, which way should I go?"

The ghost didn't answer. I listened harder. A cold raindrop slipped from a swaying branch and slithered down my neck. High above, a black-billed raven cawed a warning. Unseen birds fluttered and flew away.

"Jack? Are you there?"

Heavy footsteps came up behind me. Before I could turn, a strong hand clamped my shoulder, and a deep voice barked in my ear—

"What are you doing here?"

I spun out of the strong grip and found myself staring at a starched blue uniform shirt with a great big badge pinned to it.

"Eddie?"

Deputy Chief Eddie Franzetti frowned down at me.

"Answer me, Pen. Are you out here alone?"

"Yes, I'm alone."

"I heard you talking to someone."

Yeah, copper, that would be me!

The ghost was back. *Jack, where did you go?!*

I never left.

Well, you better keep quiet now. Don't distract me.

Impossible, sweetheart. The ghost's deep voice laughed flirtatiously. *You know I always distract you.*

I'm not kidding, Jack. This "copper" doesn't hear ghosts. If he thinks I do, the next time we "dialogue" will be in a hospital psych ward.

CHAPTER 10

Out of the Woods

I had reached the point when I could not see anything
clearly ahead. I needed help, and I got it.

—Ross Macdonald

"PENELOPE? PEN? DID you hear me?"

"What?! What is it?"

"I asked if you were feeling okay?"

"I'm fine, Eddie, just fine."

*Stop humoring him. He's Chief Ciders' flunky, isn't he?
Tell him to blow.*

I certainly would not. I'd known Deputy Chief Eddie
Franzetti since grade school. Once upon a time, I even had
a not-so-secret crush on him. The reason wasn't much of a
mystery. Eddie was kind, handsome, easy to talk to, and my
late older brother's best friend. He was also Pete's fellow
drag racer and took his senseless death in a road race as
hard as I did; harder, actually, because Eddie blamed himself for egging my brother on.

After Pete's fatal accident, Eddie stopped racing. He
sold his vintage Mustang and parlayed the money into his
education. With a degree in hand, he left the part-time job

at his family's pizza shop for a full-time career in law enforcement.

Now married with children, he was next in line for the top spot on the Quindicott police force—though it was beginning to feel like he'd been waiting for Ciders to retire longer than Prince Charles waited to ascend the throne.

"You shouldn't be out here, Pen." Decades younger than the chief, Eddie already had the intimidating "Ciders glower" down pat.

"Why shouldn't I be out here?" I shot back. "What are *you* doing out here?"

"Chief Ciders notified me about the suicide and asked me to locate the deceased's car. I did. Now I'm looking for a shortcut up to the house. Okay? Now it's *your* turn."

"I've been following the path a suspect took after leaving Emma Hudson's apartment."

"A suspect? In what?"

"Emma Hudson's death. We aren't convinced it was a suicide."

"We? Who is we? It can't be the chief. I already know what he thinks."

Then you don't know much, do ya?

Quiet, Jack!

"Did you hear me, Pen? Who is WE?"

I fluttered my hands, thinking fast. "It's just a figure of speech! The Queen's English, you know, the royal we . . . ?" I then recounted for Eddie my dealings with Emma Hudson—from her bizarre reaction to the pilfered book to the near wreck with Wanda and the strange scene inside the apartment.

Eddie tipped back his hat and scratched his head. "Did you actually see this person leave the house?"

"No. But I heard footsteps on the stairs. Then I came around the corner of the house, and the person had vanished. That's why I'm out here. I'm tracing the suspect's steps." I pointed to the glossy piece of torn book jacket stuck to the pine branch. "See? Evidence!"

Eddie's highly dubious expression told me three things:

(1) He didn't think much of my "evidence."

(2) He was seriously concerned about my stability. (No surprise, since he'd found me standing alone in the woods, talking to myself.) And . . .

(3) He was still on the same page as his boss, and that page read suicide, not homicide.

"Listen, Eddie, I admit I don't have hard evidence of foul play. It's all circumstantial, but you and Chief Ciders shouldn't jump to easy conclusions."

Eddie folded his arms. "Give me a little credit, Pen."

"Okay. But give me a little, too."

"I'll keep an open mind."

"Good. Now where does this path lead?"

Eddie put his arm on my shoulder. "Come with me."

CHAPTER 11

Auto Focus

In one way cops are all the same. They all blame the wrong things. If a guy loses his pay check at a crap table, stop gambling. If he gets drunk, stop liquor. If he kills somebody in a car crash, stop making automobiles.

—Raymond Chandler, *The Long Goodbye*, 1953

EDDIE AND I emerged from the woods onto cracked concrete. We'd found the narrow street behind the old Victorian house. There were only two vehicles in sight, Eddie's police car and a steel blue Ford Fusion with temporary plates.

The Ford was parked at an awkward angle, as if the driver were in a hurry, or too distracted to care about alignment.

Even if Eddie hadn't confirmed it, I would have known the Ford belonged to Emma Hudson. Back at the bookstore, Wanda Clark had rattled off the vehicle's make, model, color—pretty much everything except the mileage and Blue Book value. (Clearly, the minutiae of her husband's used-car business was primary conversation in their house.)

Let's see if Chief Blowhard is right and your pilfered potboiler is in that car.

Peering through the rain-beaded windshield, I saw an

empty coffee cup from Cooper Family Bakery tucked into the holder, but there was nothing on the car's seats or the dashboard, where Wanda said she'd spied that copy of *Shades of Leather.*

Just as I figured, Jack said. *The book isn't there.*

But I see something else.

On the floor mat, beside several balls of used tissue, was a small spiral-bound notebook. There was handwriting on the lined white paper, but it was too far away to read.

I was dying to get my hands on it, but I couldn't very well break into the car with a cop watching from two feet away.

Outwit him, baby.

How?

When I was still breathing air, the coppers I knew didn't play chess. Checkers was their speed. One move at a time. Get ahead of this flunky, and you can trick him into doing the crime for you.

Trick him how?

Jack whispered his idea, and I put it into motion.

"Hey, Eddie, did you know Chief Ciders was looking for a suicide note? See in there? You might have found one."

Eddie bent low and peered through the glass.

"Right," he said. "I'll open it up."

From his police car, he fetched an odd device that looked like several irregular metal rods attached to a door hinge. "It's an auto pick and decoder," he told me as he tested the lock. "This tool works with most Fords, so—"

With a chirp, the car unlocked. Then Eddie donned white cotton gloves and retrieved the notebook. I looked over his shoulder as he studied the pages. I snapped a few phone photos, too.

"This is just a mileage log, Pen. Mrs. Hudson was recording her car's miles per gallon on gas-hybrid versus pure electric battery usage. She was a stickler for saving the planet, I guess."

"Since the car's unlocked, would you mind looking for the book I told you about?"

Eddie checked under the front and back seats. Then he opened the trunk. He searched everywhere.

"Sorry, Pen, no suicide note and no book."

"Then it had to be taken—the book, I mean. And there was no note because I doubt very much this was suicide."

"My boss disagrees. But the autopsy should tell us more. Don't worry, Pen, we'll do this by the book."

"If that's true, then it's that missing bestseller you should be looking for, Eddie, and the person who took it. At least go back into the pines and collect the torn book jacket I showed you. You might even lift a fingerprint or two, just in case this *does* turn out to be murder."

"Fine, I'll do it."

I glanced toward the decaying Victorian house, standing beyond the neglected pine grove. "Do you know how long Emma lived at this address?"

"I'll have to talk to the landlord, or you can ask your nosy pal Seymour Tarnish. The mailman ought to know."

"And what about Emma's ex-husband? Are you going to speak with him?"

"She had an ex-husband?" Eddie adjusted his hat. "You're ahead of me on that one. But I'm sure the chief will ask me to look into it."

"If you do, I'd like to talk to Mr. Hudson, too—"

He was about to object when I quickly added, "There are some highly valuable books inside that apartment. If Mr. Hudson stands to inherit them from his ex, I would like the chance to make him an offer for the entire collection. Aunt Sadie and I might get lucky and snag them at a steal."

Eddie smiled and nodded. "If Mr. Hudson agrees to talk to you, I'll give you his contact information."

I was grateful but not surprised. Eddie was the son of a restaurateur. He understood the nature of a shop owner trying to survive.

Even in the shadow of death, we had to get on with the business of living.

CHAPTER 12

Two Visitors and a Funeral

Raising children is an uncertain thing; success is
reached only after a life of battle and worry.

—Democritus, b. 460 BC–d. 370 BC

I STRODE THROUGH Buy the Book's front door at five
o'clock sharp, eager to share the details of my experience
with Aunt Sadie. But it was my eleven-year-old son who
rushed to greet me.

"Hey, Mom, where were you?"

"Spencer!"

Sadie swiftly pulled me aside. "I'm glad your back." Her
lips were tight, her eyebrows drawn together. "I wasn't sure
what you'd want me to do."

"What's wrong? Why is Spencer here? Is he all right?"

"He's perfectly fine. Bonnie and I will take care of the
customers. But you better talk to your son. He'll tell you the
story."

"What story?"

Sadie didn't answer. Instead, she turned and headed back
to our busy selling floor, tousling Spence's copper mop on
the way. "You're on, pal!"

I stared down my son, and his lightly freckled cheeks

reddened, just like my late brother's. The older Spencer got, the more he reminded me of Peter: his handsome features; his bright vitality; and, lately, his proclivity for getting into trouble.

"Start talking. You weren't due back from your computer seminar for a few more days. How did you get here from Boston?"

"I'm sorry, Mrs. McClure, but this is my fault."

A girl about my son's age, maybe a year older, stepped up to stand beside him. In contrast to Spencer's favorite old blue jeans and sneakers, she wore her Sunday best dress along with a contrite expression. Her young face was framed by a cascade of curly brown hair. Behind her glasses, her eyes looked red, as if she'd been crying.

"I'm the one who talked Spencer into leaving—"

"You didn't talk me into anything, Amy!" Shoving back his bangs, my son transformed his guilt into protective defiance. "I wanted to help! That's what friends do—"

"Slow down," I said. "Help with what?"

"Attending her father's funeral," an adult voice informed me.

I turned to find a familiar face—one I hadn't seen much of lately.

Like Seymour, I'd known J. Brainert Parker since childhood. A distant relative of renowned author H. P. Lovecraft, he shared his cousin's fondness for macabre tales, along with the author's signature features. He had the same narrow frame, angular face, and mousy brown hair, which he tended to wear in a retro 1920s haircut—now surprisingly trendy.

On this day, however, Brainert seemed more forlorn than even Lovecraft in his most sullen, misanthropic portrait. Dark circles cradled his eyes, and his body appeared adrift in his midnight black suit. That suit had been tailored to fit, yet it now appeared a half size too large on his slender form.

Was his work taking a toll? Possibly—since he now had two occupations. Already a full professor at nearby St.

Francis University, Brainert recently joined the ranks of Quindicott's small business owners by sinking his savings into restoring our Main Street's condemned Movie Town Theater.

Surpassed only by his passion for books, my old friend's love of classic films ("where literature goes on the weekends") had inspired him to find a partner and donor investors. With tireless effort, he spearheaded the transformation of the building holding our single silver screen into its original movie-palace glory. One day, he hoped to secure it landmark status.

Fulfilling his vision had cost my friend time and money, but this was the first I'd seen any effect on his health. To the contrary, Brainert's work was typically the fuel on which his manic spirit ran.

So why the weight loss and look of weary worry?

Whatever the reason, it would have to wait until I got to the bottom of things with my son—and his little friend.

"This young lady is Amy Ridgeway," Brainert informed me.

The girl extended her hand. "It's very nice to meet you, Mrs. McClure."

Keen intelligence shone in the girl's bright brown eyes, and her bearing displayed admirable maturity. I was about to begin grilling her, but as I shook her hand, I noticed several curious customers glancing our way.

"Let's discuss this in private," I said and pointed to the dark doorway across the main floor.

Feeling a chilly mist follow me, I silently acknowledged the one observer in this place we couldn't possibly hide from.

Don't get your panties in a twist, Jack cracked. *You're the only one who can hear me. So who am I gonna tell?*

CHAPTER 13

Driven to the Grave

Girls . . . They can drive you crazy. They really can.

—J. D. Salinger, *The Catcher in the Rye*

INSIDE OUR SHADOWY Community Events space, I hung up my coat and flipped on the lights.

The large room felt drafty, and the ghost was no help, given his penchant for lowering temperatures. Even without his paranormal activity, it seemed a cold place to discuss family business.

You're standing in a family business, sister. Why not discuss it here?

Stay out of this, Jack. I mean it.

I pointed to the circle of chairs set up for Monday's Quibblers meeting, but Brainert waved me off, preferring to stand. The kids followed his lead.

"All right," I commanded. "Start from the beginning."

"Amy showed up at Dr. Ridgeway's graveside ceremony," Brainert began. "She was obviously alone, and after the service, I approached her. When I asked how she managed to get herself all the way to Quindicott from Boston, Amy pointed to your son, who was lurking among the gravestones like some romantic lead in a Gothic novel."

I frowned at Spencer and his eyes dropped.

Once again, Amy came to his defense. "It really is my fault, Mrs. McClure. I wouldn't want Spencer to get into trouble on my account."

"It's okay," Spencer told her. "My mom has a right to feel upset."

The maturity of my son's statement floored me. Was it Amy's influence? The idea unsettled me—though I couldn't think why.

Really? Jack guffawed. *I can!*

I told you to stay out of this.

I'm in it, sweetheart, whether you like it or not. I've got a front row seat to your little family drama, and I say give the little nipper a break. Your boy wouldn't be the first gullible guy to get tangled in a femme fatale's web.

Oh, Jack, you don't understand! This is about truancy, disobedience, taking unnecessary risks—and this little girl is hardly a femme fatale!

Amy spoke up. "Spencer thought it was dangerous for me to travel from Boston alone. That's the reason he came along. Please don't punish him because of something I did."

Listen to Shirley Temple. Why should a guy who gave a dame some assist end up in hot water for it? It just ain't right.

What Spencer did was risky and stupid. He should have called me first.

Why? So you could say no? In case you haven't noticed, doll, the kid's way out of the cradle. Five will get you ten he would have done it anyway.

Then he would have been in double trouble!

See what I mean? Jack replied. *You just don't get it.*

Get what?

Your boy did the right thing. He put himself in hot water to help out a friend. Most of these corny novels you hawk would cast your kid as the hero, not the heavy.

This back-and-forth was getting me nowhere. I couldn't argue with Jack and my son at the same time!

"Mom? Are you okay?" Spencer touched my arm.

I blinked to find my son, Amy, and Brainert all staring at me.

"You zoned out on us."

I cleared my throat. "We'll talk about your behavior later. Right now, I want you to take Amy upstairs. She can spend the night with us. Get her something to drink. There are cookies in the jar, but don't eat too many. I'll make dinner after I speak with Dr. Parker—"

"Yes!" Spencer whooped with excitement and faced the girl. "Since you're staying with us, you can try my all-time favorite multiplayer game. And you can meet Bookmark. She's a really cool cat. Last week she caught a mouse right here in the store!"

I cringed. This was not something I wanted my customers to know. Bonnie Franzetti, our cashier (and Eddie's younger sister), was the sole witness to the rodenticide, and I could trust her to keep a secret. I'd have to advise Spencer to do the same!

Meanwhile, Amy's eyes went wide. "You have a cat! What kind? My mother won't allow pets, but I love cats, Persians and Siamese, and—"

"Ah, Bookmark is just a regular little marmalade-striped cat, but she's a real badass—"

"Spencer! What did I tell you about using that language?"

"Sorry, Mom."

The kid's right. That killer kitty really is a bad—

Don't say it! I warned.

"It's okay, Mom, I won't," Spencer promised.

Did I say that out loud?

Spencer didn't appear to care. After he and his curly-haired VIP guest raced upstairs, I faced Brainert. "I assume you know what's behind all this?"

"Yes." He sighed. "A bad marriage."

With that, his energy appeared to flag. He wandered over to the circle of chairs and sat down. As I joined him, he told me that Dr. Kevin Ridgeway, his colleague and friend, had died in a traffic accident less than a week ago. This I knew because the local paper covered the accident. What I didn't know was that a former Mrs. Ridgeway existed, along with an only child, Amy.

When Ridgeway was killed, Amy was already studying at the same computer seminar as Spencer. Unless she had adult supervision, she wasn't permitted to leave the Boston University campus.

"Not even for her father's funeral? That doesn't add up."

"It does if you factor in her mother. The woman is honeymooning in Europe with her new husband. She heard about Kevin's death, but she told Amy to stay put, and she informed the seminar's administrators to keep her on campus."

"Let me get this straight. Amy's mother didn't want her attending her own father's funeral?"

Brainert shrugged. "Some people don't want their children exposed to death—the reality of it, even the idea of it."

"Clearly, Amy felt differently."

"That's correct. Spencer told me she was determined to be with her father as he went to his final resting place. When your son heard that, he said there was no way he was going to let his friend go alone."

I considered my son's own loss of his father and realized what he must have felt when he saw Amy's devastation at losing hers. I was beginning to feel a little more forgiving of Spencer's motivation.

"Apparently, they slipped away from their dorm and off campus early this morning, hours before their first class."

"How in the world did they get here from Boston?"

"Amy hacked her mother's Uber account and hired a car. They arrived too late for the eulogy at the funeral home, so the two proceeded directly to Quindicott Cemetery. That's where I saw them."

"And how did they plan on getting back from the cemetery? Another outrageously expensive car hack?"

"Spencer said if the hack didn't work again, he'd just call the police and, I quote: 'turn myself in, even if it means going up the river.'" Brainert shook his head. "Where did he learn such vernacular?"

I shrugged. "*Shield of Justice* reruns on the Intrigue Channel, along with *Dragnet* and *The Untouchables*."

Hey, don't forget Naked City!

Jack, your enthusiasm surprises me. Didn't you call those old crime shows overblown and unrealistic?

Sure, I did. No gumshoe worth his salt would do half the crazy things those lamebrain actors do. But as entertainment, it ain't so bad.

"Poor little Amy," Brainert said. "Kevin was a fine teacher. And a good father—from what she told me after the funeral. What happened on that highway was a senseless tragedy."

"What did happen? Did he skid and hit a tree? That road is notorious after the rain."

"According to the local constabulary, Dr. Ridgeway got out of his car on the highway close to midnight. At that point, they surmise a vehicle swerved into the shoulder and struck him down. Kevin died instantly, and the driver fled. There aren't any witnesses—at least none they can find."

"How did they know the time was close to midnight?"

"The impact shattered Kevin's watch, stopping it."

"Did his car break down?"

"No—and the circumstances are bewildering. Except for one broken taillight, the car had no mechanical problems or flat tires. Chief Ciders said Kevin's vehicle was in perfect working condition. The engine was still idling when they found it. Why he left his car on a dark highway, no one can say."

I shivered. "Why didn't the driver who hit him stop?"

"Frightened, perhaps. Chief Ciders suggested the driver wasn't aware they'd hit anything but a deer or raccoon. The lights are sparse on that stretch of highway, and there was fog."

Brainert pulled a slip of paper out of his lapel pocket. "In any case, Amy gave me a number for the resort in Sardinia where her mother can be reached, if you'd like to phone her. Or I will if that's—"

"I'll do it. I'm going to have to call the school anyway.

According to their rules, truancy is grounds for expulsion from the program, which means I'll have to talk them into letting Spencer and Amy back in. And I swear the cost of the international call to Amy's mother is coming out of his allowance."

Why not put him on bread and water, too?

"Oh, shut up!"

My friend blinked. "Excuse me?"

"Sorry, Brainert, I wasn't talking to you."

"It's all right. I know you're upset about your son. But, listen, I brought you something else besides Spencer and his little precocious friend."

"You did?"

I waited for Brainert to reach into his pocket and reveal his surprise, but what he brought me was far too large for that.

"It's in the back," he said, rising. "Follow me . . ."

CHAPTER 14

Pandora's Box of Books

A box without hinges, key, or lid, yet golden treasure
inside is hid.

—J. R. R. Tolkien, *The Hobbit*

BRAINERT LED ME across the Community Events space
to the store's office. Sadie and I kept a shared desk here,
along with a second computer and promotional materials
for our shop. A wall of metal filing cabinets, older than the
pyramids, stood back here, too—and they contained much
more than the store's purchasing history.

Not long ago, I agreed to take on a special project: the
archiving and digitizing of papers once owned by a New
York private investigator murdered on these premises. Jack
Shepard's files were an absolute mess, but I didn't mind. I
found reading his case notes, in his very own handwriting,
downright thrilling.

At the moment, however, Jack's files were not our focus.

Using the tip of his polished oxford, Brainert nudged a
large, open cardboard box on the floor.

"It's Dr. Ridgeway's reading library, or what's left of it.
His landlady handed it over to me this morning before the
funeral."

"A single box? That's not much of a library."

"A grad student from the Poli-Sci Department removed all pertinent papers and books in Kevin's discipline. This is what's left."

"What about his daughter? Will she want them?"

"Not these. Kevin already left all his money and some personal items to Amy. His academic books he left to the university. The rest—his leisure reading—he willed to me. I'll use any proceeds from the sale to support my restored theater. Kevin would have liked that."

"How did you even know Ridgeway? You mentioned Poli-Sci. That's Political Science, and you're in the English Department."

"We became friends through the Faculty Affairs Committee. Kevin supported my vision for expanding classrooms into the community. He even prepared a lecture for my new comparative film series: 'Cold Truths about the Cold War' with a double-feature screening of *Fail-Safe* and *Dr. Strangelove*."

Brainert sighed. "I'll have to ask one of his grad students to give the lecture in his place. As for the books—" He nudged the box again. "I leave the estimate of value to you and Sadie."

"I'm surprised he never came to our store."

"Most weekends he spent in Boston—to visit with Amy. He was actually born here in Quindicott, before his parents moved to Massachusetts. They're both deceased now, and Kevin is buried right next to them in the family plot."

"If he liked Boston so much, and his daughter was there, why did he move back to Quindicott?"

"It wasn't his original plan. When he took the position at St. Francis, he thought he could commute, but the long drives proved too taxing, so he relocated last summer."

"Is that when he divorced Amy's mother?"

"She divorced him. Anyway, in answer to your question of why you never saw him, he had a favorite bookstore in Boston. Old habits die hard."

You said it, fella.

Quiet, Jack.

I placed the box on the desk. "You didn't want to keep anything in here?"

Brainert shrugged. "I only glanced at it. Kevin's taste ran to military novels and political thrillers. Not my cup of cocoa . . ."

A statement like that from a professor of American literature was no surprise to me. But I knew it wasn't meant as a put-down, either, because my friend was far from a literary snob. In fact, Dr. J. Brainert Parker's personal enthusiasms for such writers as Poe, Conan Doyle, Ambrose Bierce, even his distant relative H. P. Lovecraft were frowned upon by some members of his own department.

Childhood affections die hard, too, however, and once upon a time, "the Brain" along with me and upperclassman Seymour Tarnish were complete genre geeks, devouring paperbacks when we should have been doing homework.

We'd spend summer afternoons roaming Prescott Woods in search of hobbits and elves and phantoms. In the evenings, we'd tell one another spooky stories in the dark. Never once did we consider the dog-eared paperbacks that we pored over were "beneath" the assigned reading by our teachers.

We loved books. We loved stories. Period.

Then I grew up, went to college, and received my degree in correct opinions. For a time, I even played the "my taste is better than yours" game, an argument older than Dumas versus Balzac (or maybe Cain and Abel).

Now that I was a bookseller, working alongside a woman with decades in the trade, I no longer dealt in theory but with the world of active readers. While some customers still loudly played the literary status game, the vast majority quietly prowled our stacks, making their selections and opening new books with the same innocent joy and excitement that I once did.

I had come full circle. In our little shop, we loved books. We loved stories. And we loved our customers. As Sadie put it: "We're here to serve them, not judge them."

Academia, on the other hand, was rooted in judgment.

Despite our shared devotion to books, professors and booksellers would always inhabit different planes. Of course, we sometimes came together to achieve the same goal.

That's why Brainert's sudden scowl surprised me. He directed it toward a stack of flyers advertising an appearance by Bentley Prize winner Dr. Roger Leeds.

"I'm disappointed Leeds failed to attend Ridgeway's funeral. We were all on the Faculty Affairs Committee, and he knew the man as well as I did."

Brainert tapped the flyers with his index finger. It wasn't a gentle tap, more of an angry woodpecker assaulting a utility pole.

"I suppose he's too busy with his newfound fame. It's not every day that one wins the Bentley Prize for Literary Criticism—as he'll incessantly remind you over cocktails at the faculty lounge."

I raised an eyebrow at that. Roger Leeds never struck me as a braggart. A long-toiling professor in Brainert's English Department, Leeds became an overnight sensation when the *Guardian*, *Paris Match*, the *Oxford Review of Books*, and the *New York Times* collectively raved about his study of colonialism's impact on Western literature.

Soon after the Bentley Prize nomination, Buy the Book hosted Dr. Leeds for a talk and signing. The event was standing room only, and we sold every book in stock. Now that he'd been awarded the honor, we scheduled a second event—much to Brainert's chagrin, apparently. His envy was barely disguised as he told me about the man's appearances on NPR and *60 Minutes*.

Enough! Jack suddenly thundered. *Will ya throw Puppy Dog Face a bone already?*

Excuse me?

Change the subject!

Oh. Yes. Good idea.

I pointed to the box on the desk. "Brainert, why don't we see what's inside?"

I said throw him a bone, not more dusty tomes!

Like it or not, Jack, this is the business I'm in—and unless you zip it, I'll send you back to your dusty tomb!

"Pen?" Brainert touched my shoulder.

"Yes?"

"The box?"

"Oh, yes . . ." I pushed aside the layer of brown packaging paper and almost immediately struck gold!

The second book down, in one of two neat stacks, was a rare autographed copy of *The Hunt for Red October*—a 1984 Naval Institute Press first edition. The holy grail of Tom Clancy collectables, copies of this hardcover have sold for over one thousand dollars. This one was in pristine condition.

I pulled out the next book on the stack, a signed 1974 edition of *Tinker, Tailor, Soldier, Spy* by John le Carré, also highly prized by collectors. Under that was a copy of Ralph Peters's *Red Army*.

Another rarity turned up next: a first edition of Stephen Coonts's debut novel, *Flight of the Intruder*. Though only in fair condition, it was also autographed, which upped the value. Underneath that was an out-of-print Daniel P. Maddox hardcover with a grim black cover, *Arms and Armor of the Middle Ages*, and a few more thrillers of much lesser resale value. However, at the very bottom of the first stack, I found a signed Donald I. Fine first printing of Dale Brown's *Flight of the Old Dog*.

I was flying myself, jazzed by this treasure trove of discoveries. Sadie would be even more thrilled. Her online customers included book collectors with editions like these on their wish lists.

What I turned up in the second stack, however, gave me another kind of shock, one that pulled me right back to the carnage at 1919 Pine Tree Avenue.

"Why in the world would Dr. Ridgeway have this?"

Brainert tensed. "Excuse me?"

I held up the red couch edition of *Shades of Leather*. "Dr. Ridgeway's reading was more diverse than you led me to believe."

Diverse? Jack cracked. *Yeah, that's* one *word for it.*

CHAPTER 15

A Shade Too Many

No matter what you do, somebody always imputes meaning into your books.

—Ted Geisel (aka Dr. Seuss)

UNLIKE MOST OF the collectibles in the box, *Shades of Leather* was unsigned. But its condition was pristine. Checking the copyright page, I gasped at the sight of the little 1.

"Brainert, this is a *first* printing!"

My friend shuffled uneasily. I assumed the discovery of the racy potboiler among his friend's collection had surprised or embarrassed him.

Well, he wouldn't be embarrassed when he got the money for its resale. "Dr. Ridgeway must have bought this the week it was released."

"Why do you say that?"

"Because the book is presently in its seventh printing. There are at least a quarter million copies out there now. But the first print run was small. Maybe five thousand copies of this first edition exist in the world. Most people weren't even aware of the book until it became a viral topic in social media and began climbing bestseller lists, weeks after its initial release."

From the way the hardcover handled, I could tell this copy had never been cracked. "I don't understand it. Dr. Ridgeway didn't even bother to read the book—"

"Unless he read the other copy," Brainert said.

"What other copy?"

"The one still in the box."

"What in the world?"

I found a second copy of *Shades of Leather*, the black couch edition this time. At that point I was not at all surprised to find the blue suede edition under that. I quickly went through the rest of the box and found three more copies of *Shades of Leather*.

What kind of a collector was Kevin Ridgeway? I wondered.

The kind who collects books men read with only one hand.

Behave, Jack.

I stared down Brainert. "There are six copies of *Shades of Leather* here, and they're all first printings. Do you have a clue why Ridgeway had these?"

Brainert simultaneously shrugged and shook his head. "Perhaps he was speculating."

"But this book is way out of his taste range. And there was absolutely no hint it would become a bestseller, let alone a collectible. It's a first novel published with a modest promotional campaign. *Shades of Leather* was just as likely to end up on a remaindered pile as on half the country's nightstands."

"There's no mystery here," Brainert insisted. "They're probably review copies. Keven wrote the occasional critique—"

"Publishers are on tight budgets these days. A publicity department wouldn't send six copies of the same book. A reviewer only needs one—"

As I lifted one of the bestsellers, a slip of paper fluttered to the floor. Brainert and I nearly conked heads diving for it. I was quicker and snapped up the flimsy sheet.

"Twenty-four copies of *Shades of Leather*, sent directly from the publisher's warehouse in Bethlehem, Pennsylvania. Brainert, this is a packing slip!"

"Whose name is on it?"

"There is no name, and no address, either. But it says there were twenty-four copies. Where are the other eighteen copies? Do you have a guess?"

Brainert's response was a blank stare, so I filled in the blanks for him.

"Since your friend made a hobby of collecting signed first editions, it appears he intended to have the author *sign* these, perhaps to resell the autographed copies—but again, it's a puzzle. At the first printing, he could not have known the book would be a hit, so why buy an entire case? He must have had some personal connection with the author. Is that it? Did he know Jessica Swindell?"

"Not that I'm aware of—"

"How about a woman named Emma Hudson? Did Ridgeway know her? Did he have any friends on Pine Tree Avenue?"

"Pine Tree Avenue? That area is rather on the wrong side of the tracks. I doubt Kevin knew anyone there. Why do you ask?"

I related the ugly details of our elegant customer's final hours. Brainert was appalled by the story, but he insisted the woman must have been unbalanced, and Kevin's death—and possession of six copies of Jessica Swindell's first printing—was merely a happenstance.

Nix to that! Jack cried in my head. *Happenstance doesn't just happen when it comes to two bizarre deaths in one small town, both with unexplainable links to the same potboiler. Show your friend the mug shot.*

I handed Brainert a copy of *Shades of Leather*. "Look at the author portrait, and tell me if you recognize that woman."

Brainert barely glanced at the photo before dropping the book on the desk. "I don't recognize her."

"You hardly looked at it." I forced the hardcover back into his hands. "Come on, apply your memory. Did you ever see anyone like her with Kevin Ridgeway? Could she be a grad student at St. Francis? Maybe a junior member of the faculty? The wife or daughter of a faculty member?"

"No, no, and no! You're making something out of nothing, Pen!"

"How can you say that? Emma Hudson's death is not nothing!"

"That's not what I meant—"

"Listen to me, even before Emma's death, I had questions about this book."

"What do you mean? What sort of questions?"

I tapped the publisher's logo, emblazoned on the spine. "I've dealt with Salient House many times, for signings, sales campaigns, publicity events."

"And?"

"I formally asked if Jessica Swindell would consider a signing with us. I promised we'd advertise in Newport, Providence, and Boston, that we'd move hundreds of copies. The reply was one sentence: 'Thank you for your inquiry, but Ms. Swindell does not do signings or public appearances.'"

"So? Historically, plenty of authors have shunned the spotlight. You've never heard of J. D. Salinger?"

"Salinger may have been a famous recluse, but we knew plenty about him—he was born in Manhattan; served in the army during the Second World War; published short stories in *Collier's* and the *New Yorker*, one of which he drew on to create Holden Caulfield." I turned to the dust jacket's back flap. "Read it—"

Jessica Swindell is an American author.
This is her first novel.

"So?" Brainert shrugged. "Ms. Swindell wishes to remain mysterious. I never thought I'd say this, but—" The academic in him shuddered. "Have you checked with Wikipedia?"

"I did—"

You did? Jack interrupted. *I never noticed you grilling some shady character named Wicked Pete.*

Ignoring the ghost, I told Brainert what I found in the *online encyclopedia (got that, Jack?)*. Under Jessica Swindell, there was no more than a stub, repeating the same book jacket bio.

"Then Jessica Swindell is *obviously* a pseudonym." Brainert practically rolled his eyes. "You know very well all sorts of authors write under pen names, for all sorts of reasons, including privacy."

"Privacy? Are you kidding? This author published a seminude photo of herself on her book's back cover!"

Brainert shrugged. "The picture is probably a surrogate."

"Now we're getting somewhere. If Jessica Swindell is a pseudonym for another author and the photo is bogus, then it very well *could* be an old picture of Emma Hudson!"

"Pen, seriously. Why do you care?"

"Why is it you don't? You usually love a literary mystery. Remember the Poe Code? We broke that together. The brow here may be lower, but the mystery is just as puzzling."

Brainert shook his head. "Leave it alone, *please*? It's not worth your time. *Shades of Leather* is no more than flash-in-the-pan fiction, written for a quick buck. You know very well this is not the type of book that backlists. It will be forgotten when next year's sexy new thriller bats its eyes at the reading public."

"That's not the point—" I tried to tell him, but he wouldn't hear it.

Suddenly, his smartphone belted out a few bars from a Bernard Herrmann score. As he read the text, a pained expression crossed his narrow face.

"Problems at Movie Town. I must summon Larry Eaton to clear the drains in the restrooms. If his power flusher fails, tomorrow's kickoff for our comparative film lecture series is bound for disaster!"

"Not *Pride and Prejudice* and *Austenland*? I was looking forward to that double feature—"

"That's next Sunday." Brainert bolted for the door almost as fast as Emma Hudson did. "Tomorrow is Professor Shirley Anthor, our top local authority on medieval history, comparing the Arthurian tropes in *Excalibur* with *Monty Python and the Holy Grail*!"

"Wait! Are you coming to the Quibblers meeting Monday night?"

"I'll be late," he called over his shoulder. "There's a Faculty Affairs meeting. We're voting on a suitable replacement for Dr. Ridgeway."

CHAPTER 16

Night Caller

Once upon a midnight dreary, while I pondered, weak and weary.

—Edgar Allan Poe

IT WAS HALF past eleven when I finally crawled between the sheets and set my eyeglasses on the night table, right next to the store's reading copy of Jessica Swindell's *Shades of Leather*.

Weeks ago, Sadie had devoured the book cover to cover and filled me in on the story. Because it wasn't my "cup of cocoa," to quote Professor Parker, I read only the first eighty pages, which gave me the premise and the lay of its literary landscape (*lay* being the operative word). With its blockbuster status and so many customers asking for it, the book didn't need much hand-selling from me, so I switched to a stack of other new titles.

After this trying day, I would have preferred a Sally Snoops adventure, my favorite comfort read from childhood. But I felt compelled to complete Swindell's bestseller for another reason: to discover any possible connection to the death of Emma Hudson. And (could it be?) Professor Kevin Ridgeway.

I cracked the book, where I'd left off, and began to read, aware my bedroom felt warmer than usual.

No ghost, not tonight.

Jack had skipped out on me around dinnertime. He did that on occasion—not unlike a living man, his energies and interest seemed to wax and wane.

Of course, I'd been crazy busy all evening, helping Sadie with the store, getting a meal on the table for Spencer and his little friend. Amy seemed a nice enough girl, though her visit presented complications.

When my mobile phone vibrated, I snatched it up, hoping it was the girl's mother *finally* calling me back. Hours ago, I'd tried to get through to the woman, with no luck.

The phone number Brainert gave me rang a resort's front desk on an island in the Mediterranean. A young man with a thick Italian accent took my message for Amy's mom but warned they were a "digital detox" resort. Mobile phones were collected upon check-in—so as not to disturb the retreat's "tranquility." Consequently, guests were only permitted to place calls in a special area, twice a day.

Unfortunately, the call coming now wasn't one of them. Seymour Tarnish, my intrepid postman, was texting me:

PARROT UPDATE!

Call me if UR not in dreamland.

I did call. But before the birdman launched into his fine-feathered report, I asked a favor.

"What kind of favor?" Seymour asked skeptically.

"You're the fastest reader I know. And you have a photographic memory—"

"True and true."

"—which is why I want you to come by the shop to pick up a novel. I want you to read it and give me your expert opinion."

"Hey, sure! Anything for a free book. What is it?"

"*Shades of Leather.* It's a new thriller that—"

"Already have it, Pen. Your aunt sold it to me last week. I couldn't help myself. Not after all the attention the thing got on TV."

"TV? I thought it was viral social media that made it big."

"Yeah, but the kickoff really began on *The Chat*. Then *Tina Talks* did a call-in about the book with a text-a-palooza scroll. The social media multiplied the exposure, and every late-night show in La-La Land made a joke about it."

"I'm still surprised you're reading it."

"I do, on occasion, peruse more than Shadow and Doc Savage reprints. So what is it you need to know about this trendy, tumescent thriller?"

"Everything. But first you have to hear me out . . ."

I finally revealed to Seymour what Emma Hudson alleged in our shop—that her picture was on the book jacket, labeled as Jessica Swindell's author photo.

"So Ciders was right? The woman was unbalanced after all?"

"Maybe."

"What do you mean maybe? You really didn't tell me much at the house today."

"How could I with Ciders bellowing down at us?"

"Well, tell me now!"

"In my opinion"—not to mention Jack's—"the suicide scene looked staged."

"You think someone croaked her?"

"Like I said, maybe."

"And why do you want me to read the book?"

"To look for any local connection you can find. Brainert's professor friend Kevin Ridgeway was run down on the shoulder of a road this past week. I found evidence that he bought an entire case of books for the author to sign. I suspect he might have known Jessica Swindell. I think she could be living right here in Rhode Island, or maybe Boston. That's where he used to live."

"Pen, that's an 'I suspect' and an 'I think.'"

"What I *know* is that something bogus is going on with

that bestseller. A dozen mysteries are swirling around it—including the fact that J. Brainert Parker wants nothing to do with solving any of them. He even tried to talk me *out* of investigating."

"Busybody Brainert? The Sally Snoops of American lit? That sure doesn't sound like him."

"He knows more than he's letting on. I'm certain of it. A close read of the book might give us some clues, and I don't have the time. I've got my hands full with the shop, and my son, and—"

"What's wrong with Spencer?"

"He ditched classes without permission and brought home a house guest."

"*Wruh-oh!* Thirty lashes! Are you putting him on bread and water?"

"Oh, please. You sound like Jack!"

"Who?"

"Uh, nobody—Jack and the Beanstalk. He rationalized bad behavior, too. Can you finish the book before the Quibblers meeting Monday night?"

"Heck, yeah. The font is easy on the eyes. And the type is young-adult-saga size. I'll power-read through the climax—and I'll bet there's more than one, if you get my drift!"

"Thanks, Seymour, I knew I could count on you."

"Hey, I came through for that poor bird, too."

"The bird, that's right! How is Emma's parrot? Did Ciders give you custody?"

"Yeah, and custody is expensive. Waldo is spending the night at Dr. Rudkin's Animal Hospital on Quincy Road, to the tune of three hundred smackers."

"Nothing serious, I hope?"

"Observation, mostly. The doc's afraid he might have gotten a chill from the door being open. Plus, there's that nasty molting issue. But if all goes well, I'll be picking up Waldo tomorrow. Soon enough he'll be good as new. I'm just glad I didn't have to take the dog, too."

"*Dog?* What dog?"

"Emma Hudson's dog."

"She had a dog? What kind of dog?"

"Search me. I never actually saw it. The first time I had
her sign for a letter, Mrs. Hudson had to lock the pooch in
the bathroom when she heard me climbing the stairs. It
sounded like one of those little yapping lap-dogs. I could
always hear it snarling behind the door when I dropped by.
I'm pretty sure it wasn't personal. That canine hated all of
humanity."

"But I saw no evidence there was a dog, and I was all
over that apartment before the chief arrived. Do you think
it got out and ran off?"

"No. And neither does Ciders—because all evidence of
the dog was gone, too. No bowl. No leash. No flea collars.
But I know what I know because, Pen, canine awareness is
a vital facet of mail delivery."

This was an unpleasant new wrinkle.

Did Emma Hudson give her dog away in anticipation of
suicide? If she did, why didn't she find a home for her poor
parrot, too? And if she was murdered, why steal her dog—
and all evidence that the pet even existed?

Just then, I heard an electronic beep.

"My Hot Pockets are ready!" Seymour declared.

"Midnight snack?"

"It's Saturday night, Pen. I'm livin' large."

CHAPTER 17

The Big Sleep

This was the best time of day, when I could lie in the
vague twilight, drifting off to sleep, making up dreams
inside my head . . .

— Sylvia Plath, "Superman and Paula Brown's New Snowsuit"

I COLLAPSED BACK against my pillows. By now the time
was close to midnight. Tomorrow would be a busy day, and
I needed to get some rest. Yet sleep didn't come.

In the blurry darkness, the ticking alarm clock seemed
to sync with my heartbeat, its steady throb pulling me back
to when I shared my bed with a living, breathing husband
and father, someone to discuss my worries with.

In all honesty, things were never easy with Calvin. We
wedded too young and too soon, each of us believing we'd
pledged ourselves to someone different. Most days we were
both unhappy. But at least he was with me, a proximal partner. And tonight, in the solitude of this empty bedroom,
listening to the ticking away of my minutes on earth, I felt
a tug of longing for my married days.

It was then I felt him. The temperature in my bedroom
plunged, sending a shiver from the back of my neck to the
tips of my blanket-tucked toes.

Finally, the ghost spoke.

So now you're sleeping on the job?

I smiled. "Tell me, Jack, what should I be doing?"

Workin' the case.

"I am. I spoke to Seymour, and he's reading—"

That's not what I mean. When I was a cop, most murders I saw were plain old street crimes. Straight, ugly violence. Solving them was basic. Two plus two. As a PI, I was hired because things didn't add up. And, honey, forget about straight—some of these cases twisted me like a pretzel.

"I know. I've been reading your case files."

Then you should also know: Whether I found 'em on the street or among the elite, when a corpse went cold, the first question I asked was always the same. What was the motive?

"That's my problem. I don't know the motive. All I have are two dead bodies, both with a strange link to a big bestseller; a mystery author; a sick parrot; and a kidnapped dog."

Funny thing—

"Funny? What's funny about homicide?"

You're right. Jack chuckled, and a cool breeze seemed to caress my cheek. *Murder's not usually a giggle party. But the details of your case remind me of two I worked when my ticker still tocked—a pair of capers that started with a kidnapped mutt and ended with solving a mystery around a missing author.*

"You'll have to help me find the file downstairs, so I can read about it."

Oh, I can do better than that . . .

I was going to ask what he meant, but I yawned instead. My limbs grew heavy and my awareness sluggish, as if an anchor were dragging me down, farther and farther into a drowsy sea. Finally, my eyelids closed, and—

I heard a sharp noise, like a car horn in traffic.

"Wake up, doll. We're here."

I opened my eyes. *What in the world?* I thought. Or more like *what* world? Because it wasn't one I recognized . . .

* * *

I WAS NO longer lying in a darkened bedroom. I was sitting in a splash of noonday sun in the back of an antique yellow taxi, complete with a boxy meter and an old-style flag switch. There were no seat belts on the hard leather cushion, and the safety glass between me and the driver was missing.

Outside the cab's window, the bustling crowd on the bright Manhattan sidewalk was costumed like extras in an RKO feature. Men wore suits with ties; women wore skirts, hats, and little white gloves. Not a sneaker or T-shirt in sight.

Then there were the cars—if you could call them that. They looked more like long, bulky boats on wheels, edged in chrome, each emblazoned with heirloom names like Packard, Hudson, DeSoto, and Studebaker.

Though my surroundings resembled the hard-boiled B movies I'd watched growing up, there was one significant difference between the world of the silver screen and the one I currently inhabited. Instead of film noir's gentle play of light and shadow, everything here was drenched in brilliant Technicolor.

I was snapped back to—well, let's call it *reality*—when the big man beside me thumb-flipped the cabbie a fifty-cent piece.

"Four bits, kid. Keep the change."

The gravelly voice was Jack Shepard's. But it was no longer in my head. I could actually *hear* it. The deep rumbling seemed as real as the noise of the bulky traffic around me; as real as the stench of unleaded gasoline and unfiltered cigarettes; as real as the soft feel of cotton gloves on my hands.

The white gloves, as it turned out, were the only part of my wardrobe that supplied any comfort. My feet were imprisoned in stacked pumps with heels higher than I ever wore. Constricting lingerie pinched my flesh. A too-tight skirt swathed my legs like a mummy's bandages. And the belted jacket that matched the skirt felt about as supple as furniture upholstery.

"Where are we, Jack?"

"Fifth Avenue. We're here to see a man about a dog—"

"Dog? What about the missing author?"

"We'll get to it. Be patient. That's what good detectives have, doll, patience."

He exited the cab. Then he turned to take my white-gloved hand in his, and I stared into steel gray eyes. The color practically matched his fedora. He'd tipped it back enough to show some of his short sandy hair.

Despite his softness toward me, Jack Shepard was an intimidating presence, the kind of man no sensible person would trifle with. The hard line of his square jaw was barely blunted by a Barbasol-scented shave, a nicety that made the dagger-shaped scar branding his anvil chin seem even more dangerous.

His double-breasted suit, cut for shoulders as broad as Fifth Avenue, tapered to a trim waist, and I knew there'd be a snub-nosed .38 tucked into the shoulder holster beneath his lapels. With long legs spread wide, his presence was so masculine, so alive and vital that I nearly gasped—

I yelped instead.

Stepping out of the taxi, I felt my head jutting back. Bobby pins rained down as I realized something attached to my cranium struck the roof of the cab. I managed to catch the offending object before it tumbled onto the sidewalk.

"A hat? Really, Jack! When have you ever seen me wear anything on my head when the temperature wasn't below zero?"

"When you're with me, sweetheart, you gotta blend in—and that's one stylish cake-topper I put on you. Real velvet, and pricey, too. It's from Saks Fifth Avenue."

An undone lock of hair drooped in front of my eyes.

"I'll need to fix myself up before you take me any-where."

With a nod, Jack tucked my arm under his, and we

crossed the sidewalk to a posh office building. "I know the door jockey here. He and I lose scratch at the same bookie."

Jack greeted the uniformed doorman, slipping him a tip. The man grinned wide, winked amicably at me, and pulled open the ornate door. We entered a mirror-lined lobby with a ceiling so high that the faintest sound echoed.

"Okay," Jack whispered. "Hurry it up and get your head on straight."

As Jack chatted with the doorman, I regarded my outlandish appearance in the curve-hugging red suit and a pink blouse with a neck bow bigger than a Christmas wreath.

Expelling a resigned sigh, I set to work on my appearance.

My undone hair had been coiled like a copper snake, and it took a bit of effort to re-form that swirl. When I finished, I topped my tresses with the ridiculously high hat in the shape of a cork from an old wine bottle. Once crowned, I did a little touch-up on my face with the vintage cosmetics I found in my purse.

As I powdered the shine off my nose, I couldn't help overhearing a conversation between an older man and his female secretary.

"Are you listening?" the man snapped as they moved across the lobby. "Mr. and Mrs. Stuart Emory will be in to sign those documents this afternoon. I know everyone is curious about the new Mrs. Emory, but I do not want our law firm to turn into a three-ring circus when they arrive."

"You can't blame the secretarial pool for being curious," the woman replied. "Sabrina Emory is suddenly one of the richest women in Manhattan. Her name is all over the society pages. Yet no one knows what she looks like."

"That's the way Mr. Emory wants it, and that is how it will be—"

As the pair entered the elevator, I noticed Jack in the mirror.

"Ready?" his deep voice rumbled in my ear.

"All finished," I said and turned to face him. "What do you think?"

His gray eyes registered pleasure as he swept me up and down. "You look swell, baby. Just swell. How do you feel?"

"Like a hood ornament."

"Good." Jack laughed. "You should fit right in."

"Where are we going? A used-car lot?"

"Nah." He took my arm and hooked it around his. "On the other hand, the place I'm taking you sure does make a mint on refurbishing older models."

CHAPTER 18

Hearts and Flowers

Sincerity. If you can fake that, you've got it made.

—George Burns

LA TRÉS JOLIE Casa de Beauty, on the corner of Forty-ninth and Lexington Avenue, was just a fox-trot away from the Waldorf Astoria.

Despite the stupefying mash-up of its name, Jack described the beauty parlor as "a swanky affair."

The decor was Streamline Moderne with a distaff twist, pink the dominant shade, and an overarching theme of hearts and flowers. Fresh flowers were everywhere, so many that the perfumed atmosphere was downright cloying, though not cloying enough to mask the acrid chemical odors from their costly "beauty treatments."

Then there were the hearts. For a moment, I thought we were entering the office of a cardiologist. The heart-shaped door opened to a waiting area with heart-shaped mirrors and love seats with heart-shaped backs.

Even the wall clock displayed little pink hearts to mark the hours and a pair of Cupid's arrows to do the pointing. But the biggest impression on the clientele was the coronary-themed fountain that pumped "genuine French champagne" (a little heart-shaped sign informed me of this).

After watching the gaggle of stylish society women circling the bubbly, I leaned close to Jack. "They're here for more than beauty treatments. The champagne pick-me-up seems to be the biggest draw."

"From the way these dames are tippling, it's more like a pick-me-up-off-the-floor."

Moving safari-like through the thick pile of pink rug, my gaze drifted to the only other male on the premises—a beefy gentleman sausaged into a tux and collar.

"Something's hinky with that palooka," Jack said. "He's dressed smooth as Dick Powell, but he's got a head like William Bendix."

"I doubt he's part of the swanky decor."

"He's muscle."

"I don't understand. Why would a house of beauty need muscle?"

"Because behind this bubbly curtain of beauty, they're hiding a bushel of ugly."

Jack and I approached the shop's counter. We waited a full minute, watching the pretty, young, pink-clad receptionist studiously ignore us. My loud "ahem" finally got her attention.

Despite the woman's tender years and innocent, (dare I say?) heart-shaped face, she immediately displayed a condescending grin.

Jack nudged me. On the way over, he'd briefed me on our little play. Forcing a smile of sincerity, I announced—

"I'd like a personal beauty consultation with Mr. Leroi."

The haughty young woman glanced down at her pink leather appointment book. Without opening it, she looked up again, her smirk morphing into a fake frown.

"I'm so sorry. Mr. Leroi is busy for the entire afternoon, the entire *week*, actually."

"Hold on, lady," Jack said as he reached into his lapel.

The instant my partner made his move, William Bendix

in Dick Powell's tux thrust a hand into his own jacket—and the muscle wasn't reaching for a bona fide PI license, either.

I laid my hand on Jack's strong arm and stepped in front of him. Leaning one elbow on the counter, I forced a wider smile. And this time when I spoke, my tone mimicked the imperious entitlement of our most obnoxious tourist season customers (always rich, usually from Newport).

"What my overzealous bodyguard is trying to say is that I *require* an appointment with Mr. Leroi, and I require it *immediately*. I know my name isn't in that cute little book of yours, but I'm *sure* you've heard of *Mrs. Sabrina Emory*."

The cackling around the magic fountain ceased. While the women spilled their champagne trying not to stare, William Bendix relaxed, his beady eyes returning to glazed indifference.

"So," I said. "Will Mr. Leroi see me?"

"Oh, of course, Mrs. Emory, of course!" the receptionist babbled. "But at the moment, Henri is in Boudoir 101, administering a Hangover Heaven to Mrs. Stanford of the Park Avenue Stanfords—"

"Which way?" I demanded.

"Through that door. But you can't—"

"Yes, I can. I don't need an escort. I'll find Mr. Leroi myself."

I gripped Jack's arm and dragged him through the curtained doorway.

"Nice job, partner," he rumbled in my ear.

"I passed your test, didn't I?" I whispered.

"With flying colors." He winked. "I didn't take you into that posh office building for nothin'. Always keep your antennae up for gossip. It can open more doors and twist arms better than the biggest palooka-for-hire. Now listen good, partner, because I'm privy to some gossip myself—the celebrity kind."

"I'm all ears."

"Hedda Hopper's column pegged Thelma Stanford as a well-heeled Hollywood lush who's been holed up at the

Waldorf since her Reno divorce. I checked on Henri Leroi's background, and that's just the sort of coin-heavy dame he likes to seduce."

"So?"

"So, we're going to expose this phony Frenchie, and give him a moment to savor thoughts of blackmail. Now, button those pretty lips. It's my turn to do the talking."

Then Jack started walking—and this was no stroll. He moved so fast that I had to scurry to catch up, no mean feat in these retro stilts.

"Jack, slow down—"

His wall of muscle halted so abruptly I stumbled into it. Once again, bobby pins flew.

With a shake of his head, Jack steadied me, but the damage was done. My tall tower of a hat was now leaning like Pisa's, and my soufflé of a hairdo was deflating fast.

Ignoring my renewed dishevelment, Jack cracked the door to 101, and together we peeked inside. I counted three cone-shaped hair dryers along the wall, all with domes large enough to double as ballistic missiles and connected to the ceiling by tubes of shimmering stainless steel. The empty reclining chairs under them were elaborate enough for zero gravity, but the fanciest seat in the house was in the center of the room.

A cross between a dentist chair and a medieval rack, the seat was occupied by Henri's sole customer—a slim woman of indeterminate age, swathed in a white smock and little else. I say "indeterminate age" because her face was obscured by tiny glass cubes filled with crushed ice and attached by suction cups to her skin.

"Oh, Henri," she moaned. "More ice to relieve my agony!"

Wearing a white lab coat, Henri Leroi bent over a wheeled cart stacked with more glass cubes, and a wild assortment of decanters and vials filled with colored liquids, jellies, and powders.

"I hear Dr. Frankenstein's supplying Henri's beauty products," Jack whispered.

Continental charm must count for a lot in this era, because Henri Leroi was far from an ideal man. Slightly paunchy with thinning dark hair, he sported the wormy mustache of a Three Stooges villain. When he spoke, his creaky accent was more faux than French, and his words were just as deceitful.

"My dearest Thelma, *ma jolie*," he cooed. "I wish to do so much more than relieve your pain, if only you would permit me."

"Don't speak of *amour*, Henri," the woman replied, her voice muffled by enough frozen water to re-sink the *Titanic*.

"Oh, *ma belle femme*, my blood runs so hot for you! I cannot contain my passion—"

"Don't speak of passion, Henri. Not yet." The woman waved her hand. "Why, the ink is hardly dry on my divorce, and I'm still terribly hungover from last night's soiree."

Henri swiped at a mock tear and patted the woman's hand.

"It pains me to see you suffer so. What more can I do for you, *mon amour*? Some of my tonic, perhaps?"

"No, no. Your touch is soothing enough."

Encouraged by her words, Henri's touch got a lot more soothing. Before we witnessed more than we bargained for, Jack coughed loudly.

Henri looked up with the expression of a man who'd got caught stealing from St. Patrick's poor box. He quickly regained his composure and squeezed Thelma Stanford's hand.

"*Pardonnez-moi, ma chérie.* Duty calls, but I shall return *tout de suite.*"

Henri hurriedly crossed to the door and closed it behind him.

"What is zee meaning of this!" he demanded.

"It's an emergency," Jack informed him. "I need to talk to you about a dog."

Henri's gaze shifted my way, and he smirked knowingly.

"*Oui*, I see! Zis is an emergency beauty consultation, no?" Placing his thumb on his chin, he eyed me appraisingly. With his free hand, he ruffled my clothes. "Ze Santa Claus suit is all wrong! Ze color clashes with the red of her hair. Zis pink bow is ridiculous, and ze preposterous hat makes her look like a bottle of Chianti—a *stale* bottle of *cheap* Chianti. *Oui, oui*, you are correct, *mon ami*. This woman's style is for the dogs—"

"I'm talking about your *wife's* dog, Henri. Or should I call you Henry . . . Henry Lembeck?"

The man's right hand groped for an electric button mounted on the wall. I alerted Jack to the threat. With a scowl, he ripped the button, and a long length of black electric cord, right out of the wall.

"This is a private meeting, Lembeck. No muscle, get it?"

"Monsieur, I protest! You mistake me for another."

"Can the vaudeville act. I know all about you, Lembeck. I checked with my old friends on the force. You have an arrest record as long as a gorilla's arm, and you're wanted in Louisville for freezing a dame's freckles off with carbon dioxide, along with half her face—"

"Zis, zis is not me—"

Jack lurched forward, his fists bunched, and the faux-Frenchman leaped backward so fast that his spine slammed into a heart-shaped mirror. It cracked right down the middle.

"You can stow the accent, too. The closest you ever got to France was Baton Rouge, where you did six months on a chain gang for passing bad checks. Need I say more?"

"All right, just keep your voice down," Henry Lembeck said, his Gallic accent suddenly gone, along with his bluster.

"The Pekingese, Lembeck. Or I waltz into Boudoir 101 and tell rich Hollywood divorcée Mrs. Stanford all about your record—*and* your ex-wife."

"Okay, okay. I sold the pooch to a Beverly Hills couple."

"Details, Lembeck."

At Jack's none-too-gentle prodding, Lembeck spilled the beans. He even turned over the uncashed check for the pooch.

"They're catching the *Super Chief* to the West Coast at

three thirty," Lembeck finished. "If you leave now, you can just make it."

Jack nodded once and jerked his thumb at the mirror.

"I'd get that fixed if I were you. It's seven years' bad luck, and you've broken too many hearts already."

I SHIVERED AS a frigid mist swirled around me. Opening my eyes, I found myself back in my bedroom, squinting at the face of my windup alarm clock, which read 4:05 A.M. I'd kicked off my blankets during the strange dream. Now I dragged them over me again.

"Jack, are you still there?" I yawned.

I'm still here, the ghost whispered. *Close those pretty peepers again and you'll see . . .*

The ticking of the clock lulled me back to the past once more, until the ticktock was replaced by the frenzied barking of a little dog. My nose was tickled by diesel fumes, mingled with a cool salt wind off the ocean.

Opening my eyes, I found myself standing outside a bustling terminal complex, next to a painted metal sign:

51ST STREET PIER

RMS *QUEEN MARY*

PASSENGER EMBARKATION

Around me, a horde of well-dressed, well-heeled ladies and gents streamed into the terminal's cavernous interior. Nearby, chauffeurs and taxi drivers unloaded heaps of luggage from vintage cars.

The dog yapped again, and I followed the sound to a gleaming Packard limousine, its whitewall tires scraping the curb. The doors were open, and in the back seat, a middle-aged matron was alternately cooing and shedding tears of joy. A feisty, tail-wagging red and gold Pekingese pawed at her fox stole while its busy pink tongue lapped her laughing face.

Surrounded by more suitcases than a graveyard had head-stones, the Packard was being unloaded by a hard-faced chauffeur with a gray mustache. As he struggled with a huge steamer, I finally saw Jack.

His broad shoulders were lending some muscle to the chauffeur, and together they wrestled the heavy case to the pavement.

As stevedores collected the suitcases, the chauffeur pumped Jack's hand. "Thank you, Mr. Shepard. Bennie the Bookie always said you were a straight shooter."

"Yeah, well, all that means is I pay off bum bets."

"It means more than that, Mr. Shepard. Mrs. Armitage is a good woman. She's always been generous with me and my wife. Her husband's death in the war was a raw deal. Losing Arianna, after being took by that despicable con artist, well, it nearly broke her in two, but you fixed things up for her. You did a good thing."

The chauffeur passed an envelope to the PI.

"It's double what you asked for. Mrs. Armitage insisted. She's a generous woman, like I said, and she's grateful to you." He leaned closer. "I also got a hot tip for you on the fifth race at Belmont. A fast filly with real potential. You'll find the details folded in with the dough—along with a lead on another job."

After a quick inspection, Jack tucked the envelope into his lapel pocket. Then he touched the brim of his fedora and offered his hand.

"Wish Mrs. Armitage and her pooch a bon voyage for me, and thanks for the tip on the pony. You're all right by me."

"Sweet ending to the story, I'll admit," I told Jack when he rejoined me. "But unless your client was the secret scribe of *Lassie Come-Home*, I don't see that mysterious author you mentioned."

Jack lifted an eyebrow. "What you saw was a conniving ex-husband who did his ex-wife wrong. Keep that in mind." Then he winked. "Anyway, you haven't heard about the lead on the other job. If I hadn't found the pooch, I wouldn't have gotten myself mixed up with a murder in the pulp trade, complete with blood on a manuscript, and a missing author."

"Really? That sounds intriguing. I'm game. Where do we go from here?"

"Sorry, baby, our next chapter will have to wait."

"Why?"

Jack lifted his sleeve and showed me the large face of his windup wristwatch. "I've run out of time."

"Oh no. Don't say that . . ."

Looking down at me, his hard face softened. Then he stepped close, and my heart beat faster. With his rough hand, he tipped my chin north. But as he lowered his head, lips poised to brush mine, the steamship's horn let out an ear-shattering blast, and Jack's solid form began to fade.

"Jack, wait! Don't leave me!"

One blink and I was back in my lonely Rhode Island bedroom, the clock on my nightstand ringing like crazy. With more force than necessary, my hand reached out and slammed off the alarm.

CHAPTER 19

Breakfast for One

I wake up every morning . . . and look at the obituary page. If my name is not on it, I get up.

—Benjamin Franklin (attributed)

IT WAS EIGHT A.M., and after the dreamy night with Jack, I was reluctant to roll out of bed. But, as they say, life goes on. At least, for me.

Come to think of it, it went on for the ghost, too—if you count his afterlife.

On my way to the kitchen to feed an insistent Bookmark her second breakfast, I passed through the living room. Spencer and Amy were already up, and so deep into their *Avenging Angel* video game world that they didn't notice me.

In the kitchen, I plied our "badass" marmalade-striped, mouse-killing kitty with kibbles, brewed a strong pot of Irish tea, and felt Jack's absence.

"Do you guys want some breakfast?" I called.

"No, thank you, Mrs. McClure," Amy replied. "We've already eaten."

"Yeah, Aunt Sadie made us oatmeal with walnuts and maple syrup. There's more on the stove."

"Where is Aunt Sadie?" I asked, and wasn't surprised by the answer.

"Mr. Napp picked her up in his van," Spencer called. "She's having breakfast with him at the bakery. Then they're meeting us at church—hey, what are you doing?!"

"I'm making tea!"

"Not you, Mom! I was talking to Amy."

Her precocious voice replied: "You can see very well what I'm doing, Spencer."

"I can see you used up all of your spirits," my son shot back. "What are you going to do if you get in trouble again?"

"I won't," Amy said with great confidence. "The gangsters think I'm dead, so they can't see me anymore."

"I guess that'll work," Spence said doubtfully, "but you better hit the next speakeasy to pump up your spirit strength, because you're going to need it later . . ."

Though I would have preferred my son and his friend making better use of their time than playing a game for hours on end, they were having so much fun together that I hated to interrupt.

If the ghost were here now, I know what he'd say: everyone deserves vacation time. In my estimation, that would include Jack Shepard. He often disappeared after we shared a dream. Creating it appeared to drain his energies.

I'd like to think he was hitting a cosmic speakeasy for some "spirit strength," too.

Suddenly, Amy screamed. I peeked into the living room just as Spencer was shaking his head.

"I warned you not to use all your spirit strength," he said. "Now the gangsters know you're alive, and they're going to come for you, big-time."

As the kids laughed together, I returned my attention to breakfast. Checking the covered pot on the stove, I found the oatmeal that Sadie had saved for me.

With a sigh, I dished out the single portion and sat down at the table, alone.

* * *

A SHORT TIME later, Sunday service was over and I stepped out of the church to find a brisk but sunny morning. While Bud Napp drove Sadie home, the kids and I walked back via Cranberry Street.

"Fresh air will do you good," I told the kids, and they didn't argue, especially since I promised we'd stop by Cooper Family Bakery.

As we strolled across the wide, grassy commons, my mobile phone vibrated. Once again, I hoped it was Amy's mother returning my call. But it was Eddie Franzetti on the line.

"I have the contact information I promised you for Emma Hudson's ex-husband. The man came into the station on his own about an hour ago."

"How did your interview go?"

"Mr. Hudson was friendly enough, as the Newport set goes."

"Wait. Philip Hudson is one of the *Newport* Hudsons?"

"I thought you knew."

"I should have, considering the quality of that book collection."

"Which I brought up right after I discussed the circumstances surrounding his ex-wife's death. I told Mr. Hudson that your shop was interested in acquiring the collection of books in his ex-wife's apartment, and he said he's willing to take your call—"

"Great."

"But in my opinion, you might want to hold off on contacting him for a few days."

"Because?"

"He seemed pretty broken up, Pen, and he's going to be busy making arrangements for Mrs. Hudson's funeral."

"Emma has no other family? Didn't she and Mr. Hudson have children?"

"Uh, that would be a definite no," Eddie replied in an odd, almost ironic way.

"Are you trying to tell me something?"

"No, nothing, Pen. It's not my business to judge."

Confused by that statement, I tried a more pointed question. "Does Mr. Hudson have an alibi?"

"Why would he need an alibi for an apparent suicide?"

"Because it's not so apparent to me."

That's when Eddie told me where Philip Hudson was at the time of his ex-wife's death—New York City. "He said he drove back late last night, Pen, arriving in Millstone long after Emma's body was found."

I asked who could verify that statement, but Eddie was done answering my questions. He suggested I get the rest of the news from the Sunday paper.

I *thought* he was being cute, so after I scribbled down Mr. Hudson's contact info, I thanked him and ended the call—just in time to buy Amy Ridgeway her first taste of Quindicott's famous Cooper Family doughnuts.

CHAPTER 20

All the News That Fits We Print

> Journalism consists largely in saying "Lord James is dead" to people who never knew Lord James was alive.
>
> —G. K. Chesterton

BACK HOME, I settled the kids upstairs and swapped my church clothes for comfortable slacks and a sweater.

We opened late on Sunday, and it was nearly that time, but I still needed a few minutes of privacy with Sadie to update her on the Emma Hudson saga. Unfortunately, when I arrived downstairs in our sunny shop, she already had company—

"That crazy old woman could have been a star on *Hoarders*," Vinny Nardini proclaimed.

I'd known Vinny since junior high. In his brown Dependable Delivery Service uniform, the big man with his bark-colored beard reminded me of an Ent, those walking trees in Tolkien's *Lord of the Rings*. The comparison was fitting since he carried nearly every book shipped to us from all the major publishers. With deliveries seven days a week, that added up to a lot of trees moving around in their literary afterlife.

"Hi-yoooo, Penelope!" Big Vinny's megaphone voice filled the shop. "This young lady and I were discussing the latest local scuttlebutt—"

Vinny always referred to Sadie as "young lady," even though she was twice his age. (Sadie never minded.)

"What do you think, Pen?"

"About what?"

"That hoarder on the other side of town," Sadie replied.

"Hoarder?"

"Died in a horrible accident," Vinny said solemnly.

My aunt displayed the front page of today's *Quindicott Bulletin*.

HOARDER DIES IN FATAL BUILDING MISHAP

Vinny's finger tapped the headline. "Teddy Brenner at the drugstore thinks the old building was compromised by the weight of all that junk the woman collected."

Sadie nodded. "In his editorial, Elmer Crabtree called on the city council to hire more building inspectors." She closed the newspaper. "The poor woman was probably squirreling away old trash and magazines, knickknacks, broken appliances, and goodness knows what else."

"Hiring new inspectors is a solid idea," Vinny said. "My friend Joe Walker, a volunteer firefighter, says lots of buildings on that road are one camel-back straw away from collapse."

I scratched my head. "I know what 'collapse' means, but what exactly is a 'building mishap'?"

"The article was vague, but it sounds like the hoarder fell when her balcony gave way under the weight of her junk."

"Whoa, hold on, Vinny. You said the victim fell off a balcony? What's the name of this hoarder?"

"Withheld by the Quindicott Police Department," Sadie said.

"When and where did this 'mishap' occur?"

"Yesterday afternoon on the west side," Vinny said. "That big, rundown Victorian on Pine Tree—"

"Pine Tree Avenue?" I cried.

"That's right."

"Let me see that!"

Sadie handed me the paper. I scanned the article and clutched my head.

"Only in the fevered imagination of Elmer Crabtree does owning a valuable collection of rare first editions constitute *hoarding*! And who is this anonymous source Elmer keeps quoting?"

Vinny shrugged. "They're anonymous."

"As usual!"

Half the town knew Elmer's "anonymous sources" came from messages left on his answering machine. Either that or City Councilwoman Marjorie Binder-Smith, especially when the subject of the article involved a pet project she was pushing or a scheme to tax local businesses, usually both. *And* as usual—

"Elmer didn't get one single fact straight!"

I really shouldn't have been surprised. Elmer Crabtree, the eighty-something editor in chief of the *Quindicott Bulletin*, was not known for his high journalistic standards.

Elmer wasn't even a journalist by profession. He was an entrepreneur who created the paper to supplement his coupon-printing business. The way he figured it, he could peddle ad space to the same local merchants for whom he printed coupons and circulars. Of course, that meant he had to *sell* the paper. So, every few days, Elmer would publish a sensational story more in the tradition of the *National Enquirer* than the *Boston Globe*.

Vinny rubbed his beard. "So what really happened, Pen? It sure sounds like you know something Elmer doesn't."

I knew Vinny wanted me to dish. The smaller the town, the less that went on, and the more folks gossiped about what did. But I was unwilling to feed that mill any further. Declaring the store was about to open, I focused on our delivery instead.

Stacked on his dolly were four boxes of books for the Leeds signing. A fifth box replenished our supply of *Shades of Leather*—now in its *eighth* printing. Four more boxes held a variety of steady selling backlist books.

After Vinny said good-bye, Sadie and I finally had some privacy, and I told her what I knew about Emma Hudson, the tragedy of her death, and the treasure trove of first editions in her possession. I finished by proposing my idea.

"If I can get her ex-husband to have dinner with me, would you come along?"

"Sure. I'll bring Bud, too. That should make Mr. Hudson more comfortable—having another older gentleman at the table. It will feel more sociable, as well."

"Good idea."

"Emma's death is a terrible tragedy, I must admit."

"Eddie thinks we should wait to contact Philip Hudson. He said the man was pretty broken up, and he may not be ready to speak with us."

"That's up to Mr. Hudson, Pen, don't you think?"

"I suppose."

She gave me a wise smile. "You know I'm no stranger to estate sales. I admit death is a delicate subject, and one must be respectful, but life goes on—and in this business, the early bookworm gets the book."

"You're right. That collection is valuable. We shouldn't wait."

"From your description, we'd have to take out a second mortgage to buy it outright."

"How about a consignment deal?"

Sadie nodded. "That would be best for us. Do you think he'd go for it?"

"I can certainly try to charm him into it."

The word *charm* brought back an unsettling image—that smarmy Henri Leroi, the duplicitous ex-husband from Jack's past.

I did plan to question Mr. Hudson about the death of his ex-wife. But I honestly didn't suspect him of being anything like that crazy character in Jack's dream. At this point, I found it hard to suspect him of foul play, either.

After all, Eddie said Mr. Hudson was in New York at the

time. And he mentioned how upset the man was over the news of his ex's death. The poor old guy.

Well, like Sadie said, it was up to him to decline our invitation to dinner. So, while Sadie opened the store to waiting customers, I went to our back office and called Mr. Philip Gordon Hudson of the Newport, Rhode Island, Hudsons.

He answered on the first ring.

I was ready with a string of apologies for bothering a grieving man, but there was no need. His enthusiastic response disarmed me.

"Mrs. McClure! Deputy Chief Franzetti said you might call. I'm so glad you did."

His voice sounded cultured and warm—and surprisingly upbeat. Still, I felt bad about calling so soon. "I'm sorry to trouble you at this painful and difficult time—"

"Never mind that. I understand you're interested in acquiring my late father's book collection?"

"Yes, but I thought—"

"You thought it belonged to Emma? Technically it *was* Emma's, but the collection was gathered by my father . . . I'm afraid it's all quite complicated."

"If the situation is in limbo, we can speak another time."

"No time like the present! But I prefer to meet face-to-face."

"How about dinner?"

"Perfect. Are you free tonight? Say eight o'clock? My friends tell me there's a delightful restaurant in your town."

"Yes, Chez Finch."

"Then I'll make reservations for us."

"My aunt and co-owner, Sadie Thornton, would also be involved in any purchase."

"Bring her, then. The more the merrier! And feel free to invite your significant other."

Oh, I'll be there, buddy. Make book on it!

It was Jack, speaking up for the first time since I crawled out of bed this morning. I couldn't stop my smile. *Hello, Jack.*

Good morning, sweetheart. Miss me?

"I won't have an escort for dinner," I informed Mr. Hudson, "but I'll be accompanied by Ms. Thornton and her friend, Mr. Budd Napp, a local businessman."

"Delightful. Eight o'clock. And dinner is on me." Without a good-bye, Philip Hudson ended the call.

I exhaled. "That was easy."

Too easy, Jack said. *And I didn't hear any "Hearts and Flowers" playing. He wasn't even acting the grieving widower, never mind actually grieving.*

"Well, they were *ex*-spouses. I suspect he's gotten over the pain of their breakup."

So, you're assuming their divorce was a civilized affair with a shake of a hand and a fond farewell? Not in my experience.

"Your experience was as a PI. Your files are filled with jobs catching Cheating Charlies."

Don't forget the Bamboozling Bettys!

"According to Eddie, Hudson has an alibi for the time of his ex-wife's death. And why would he want to murder her, anyway? The woman was already out of his life."

Your husband's dead and buried. Is he out of your life?

"Point taken. But last night, you talked about motive and opportunity. Eddie would argue that Mr. Hudson didn't have opportunity. He was in New York. And what about motive?"

That would depend on the divorce settlement. If the ex–Mrs. Hudson ended up with a few pricey books, and Mr. Hudson is already rollin' in lettuce, there'd be no reason to push the button on her. But if she walked away with the deed to Mr. Hudson's farm, it's a whole different ball game.

"Mr. Hudson did say the situation was complicated."

Then you're going to have to un-complicate it by prying all the juicy details out of the old-timer.

"Easier said than done. The last thing he may want to do is talk about his dead ex-wife. How do I get him to open up?"

Turn on the charm. Remember, he's a lonely old geezer with money. You're young, carefree, and quite the looker. So give him something to look at.

CHAPTER 21

Chez Mate

She was lovely, this woman. Tonight she had dressed
up for me . . .

—Mickey Spillane, *My Gun Is Quick*

THE EVENING STARTED predictably enough. Bonnie
agreed to extend her hours into some evening babysitting.
She was now ensconced in the living room with Spencer,
Amy, a fresh bowl of popcorn, and the *Avenging Angel*
game.

Bud Napp showed up a few minutes later. A lean, ener-
getic man just touching seventy, Bud looked dapper in an
off-the-rack pin-striped suit, silk tie—and "Napp Hardware" ball cap.

"You're taking that off right now!" Sadie insisted as she
fussed in front of the mirror with the bow on her silk
blouse, beneath her best embroidered sweater.

With a shake of his head, Bud removed the crimson cap
and helped Sadie with her coat. "We'd better get cracking.
It's nearly eight."

To Budd's chagrin, I had to run upstairs one last time.

When I'd changed for the evening, including fresh
underthings, I'd left something important behind.

You can say that again!

Sorry, Jack . . .

I found the tiny silk purse on my dresser and pinned it carefully next to my heart. Inside the soft pocket was an old United States Mint–issued Buffalo nickel. Some time ago, it had fallen out of the files downstairs—Jack Shepard's files.

When I'd first found the nickel, I'd kept it for luck, and quickly discovered Jack's past contact with it allowed the coin to work as some kind of transmitter. After decades of imprisonment within the fieldstone walls of our shop—the location, as he put it, of his "lead poisoning"—Jack was finally able to travel, as long as I remembered to take his lucky nickel along!

I'm with you, sweetheart. Let's hit the road.

WE DID HIT it, with Bud at the wheel, and not in his hardware store's battered old van, either. Tonight, Sadie and I were being squired in the man's big, shiny Chrysler sedan.

We traveled down Cranberry Street, past the commons and toward Quindicott Pond, our local name for a pretty Atlantic inlet (a real draw around our region for fishing and scenic boating).

Moving through a pair of wide-open antique iron gates, we followed the long drive that led to the Finch Inn. The early-fall evening was temperate, and I rolled down my window to enjoy the night air. An icy salt breeze stirred the tall oaks on either side of the road. Their rippling leaves and swaying branches reminded me of the nearby ocean. Like Jack, I couldn't see its body, but I could feel the effects of its tempestuous changes.

Farther out, the moan of a ship's horn drifted down from the treetops like the lonely call of a night bird looking for its mate.

Finally, the historic home showed itself. Lit by a golden glow from within and tasteful landscape lighting from without, the beautifully kept turn-of-the-last-century Queen

Anne looked like a colorful gingerbread house. Now a popular bed-and-breakfast, the Finch Inn featured three floors of luxury rooms, a widow's walk, and working fireplaces in all the suites.

Visitors found it hard to believe this cheerful, welcoming Victorian confection had a dark history, but then nearly everything in New England did. Once upon a time, this estate belonged to an insane relative of the McClure family—the very clan I'd married into (but that was another story).

Following the winding drive, we reached the part of the pond where the lapping of the inlet's tidal waters mingled with the sounds of laughter and the clatter of dinner plates. The inn's new glass-walled restaurant, Chez Finch, had been built close enough to the pond for its glow to be reflected off the whispering waves.

Innkeeper, owner, and hostess Fiona Finch greeted us in the entryway. Though diminutive, she was easy to spot in an evening dress the color of blue finch feathers, accessorized by a scarlet brooch depicting two macaws on the wing—one of her favorites among the hundreds of bird pins she'd acquired, "because," she said, "like Barney and me, macaws mate for life."

"You should have let me know you were coming!" Fiona cried. "We're busy, though I might be able to squeeze you in."

"Actually, we're meeting someone who's already made reservations."

Fiona's eyes lit with interest when I dropped the name of Emma Hudson's ex-husband, Philip.

She looked me up and down. "You've dressed to impress," she said with an approving nod.

I confess I made an effort tonight. Given Emma Hudson's posh wardrobe, I didn't want Mr. Hudson looking down his nose at me, thinking I was a country bumpkin who couldn't be trusted with a valuable consignment of first editions. I had to look the part of a successful business owner, and I did.

Digging through my old Manhattan wardrobe, I found a chic black cashmere sweater. I paired it with a pearl necklace and earrings, ebony tights, and a tailored skirt that I was amazed I could still squeeze into.

Fiona's interest in my appearance was a puzzle, however, until she led us to the restored oak and brass bar that once graced a luxury Pullman car, and introduced me to our host.

Flashing an easy smile, Philip Gordon Hudson set a gin and tonic aside and slipped off the barstool to greet us. My eyes widened in mild shock at the sight of him.

Who's the Alvin? Jack cracked.

It came as no surprise that a man with Newport ties would be impeccably dressed—and getting a head start with cocktails. What surprised me was that the tall, tanned, athletic man with the thick swath of blond hair appeared to be in his mid-forties. Emma Hudson had been at least twenty years older than her spouse.

"Good evening, Mr. Hudson," I managed to squeak out. "Nice to meet you . . ."

Hudson was the kind of golden-haired guy you'd expect to see in preppy clothes, lounging on a yacht with a martini. That said, he wasn't aloof or condescending. His manner was warm and welcoming, and his blue eyes sparkled in the candlelight as he pushed his sun-burnished bangs back with a strong hand.

Emma Hudson must have had something to land a pretty, blond daisy like this one, Jack said.

Well, she was certainly an attractive older woman—

Clear your ears, Penny. I said Emma Hudson must have had something. Like stacks and stacks of dough-re-mi.

You're saying he's a gold digger? That's crazy, Jack. The Hudson family is old money. Everyone in Newport knows the name. I'm sure Philip Gordon Hudson never wanted for cash. And believe it or not, there are May-December relationships that don't involve money, so you might consider the possibility that they really did fall in love.

I might, for the blink of a fly's eye.

Well, he's charming enough. I can see why Emma was seduced.

Seduced? Interesting choice of word . . .

"Delighted to meet you at last," Philip Hudson said, taking my hand in his. "Believe it or not, Mrs. McClure, my family's ties with yours go back a long way."

"Really?"

"The McClures and the Hudsons were among the first to settle this region. As a young man, I was a guest at Windswept many times, and I attended boarding school with Percy McClure, one of your cousins—"

"By marriage."

"Of course. I asked around and was told about the unfortunate circumstances of your husband's passing. You have my condolences."

"Thank you."

"At the same time, I heard many very impressive things about you, personally."

"Really?" Sadie interjected. "Curious me! Tell us what they're saying about our Penelope!"

"For one thing, I learned that while I was living a life of leisure in California, Mrs. McClure was cheerleading a successful revitalization of this town's business community. From what I've seen of the new Quindicott, I must say—I'm quite impressed. We could use Mrs. McClure's energy and vision in Millstone.

"And . . ." He locked his blue gaze on my green eyes. "I'm surprised no one mentioned that Mrs. McClure was so very . . . *attractive.*"

I was flattered—I couldn't deny it.

Jack could.

If this guy shovels on any more manure, I'm sending him to the garden to fertilize the flowers.

My aunt had the opposite reaction. While Jack continued complaining in my head, Sadie beamed like an honor student's mother.

"We're all very proud of our Penelope!"

The grin on her face and elbow to Bud's ribs also told me that my aunt's previously dormant proclivities for matchmaking me to "promising" bachelors were suddenly reigniting. Fortunately, before she could say anything else, Fiona informed us our table was ready.

To Sadie's unbridled delight, Philip Hudson gallantly offered me his arm. With a polite nod, I took it, and he escorted me through the dining room.

The glass-walled restaurant glowed with a golden warmth. Candles cast flickering light on the perfectly set tables. Logs crackled in the stone fireplace, but the dominant sounds were talking and laughter, punctuated by the pleasant popping of newly tapped champagne. Aromas of roasted garlic, *herbes de Provence*, and savory wine sauces tickled my nose as Fiona's staff scurried about with trays of tantalizing dishes.

I hadn't eaten since my morning oatmeal, and I was ravenous.

Your dining partner looks hungry, too, Jack warned. *But his appetite has got nothing to do with grub.*

Don't be silly, I scolded.

CHAPTER 22

Hot Pants, Cold Lap

Your job isn't to guard me—it's to see that there's plenty of excitement.

—Paul Cain, "Gundown," 1933

"WAITER! ANOTHER ROUND for everyone. And make mine a double."

The newly bereaved forty-something ex-husband with the golden tan, charming smile, and oh-so-perfect pearly whites stretched his long legs under the dinner table. When they brushed mine, he caught my eye and smiled—a gesture instantly followed by Sadie's jab to Bud's ribs for the second time that night.

Bud rubbed his side, cast Sadie a long-suffering look, and offered me a resigned shrug. The older couple had noticed what I already knew. The late Emma Hudson's ex was making a play for me; and given the man's inheritance of a small fortune in first editions, my matchmaking aunt appeared to be more than okay with it.

You better mind your Ps and Qs, doll, Jack warned me again. *Blondie has been eyeing your gams all night.*

Just then, I felt Philip Hudson's lower leg stroke my stockinged calf.

All right, Jack, I admit it. You were right about Hudson's intentions. As for my "gams," he's doing more than eyeing them!

A sudden blast of frigid air set the candle flames dancing and knocked over Philip Hudson's drink, right into his lap.

That ought to cool off Mr. Hot Pants!

Hudson leaped out of his chair, cursing the restaurant's "drafty" dining room. His easy, warm manner instantly iced over as he arrogantly bullied the waitstaff, who came to his aid with napkins and apologies, even though it wasn't their fault. The arrival of the second round—on the house—calmed the man's temper and warmed him back up.

I took a breath and warned Jack to back off. *Please let me handle him.*

You expect me to do nothing while this cluck handles you?!

Yes, if need be! Your personal feelings are clouding your professional judgment. This man's ex-wife is dead, and we both suspect she was murdered. Do you really want to frighten Hudson away before we get some answers? Besides, I'm perfectly capable of taking care of myself!

That's debatable.

I swear, if you don't behave, I'm leaving your Buffalo nickel as a tip for the waiter!

I don't buy your bluff, sweetheart, and I'm not backing off. If Mr. Hot Pants turns into Mr. Hot Hands, nickel or not, he's getting a knuckle sandwich.

BY TEN P.M., Hudson had regaled us with tales of surfing at Big Sur, bungee jumping in New Zealand, and white-water rafting in Chile. At the moment, he was wrapping up an adventure he'd shared with an American coffee hunter he met in Bolivia.

"I was mountain biking with a group when I met Matteo in a La Paz watering hole, and I ended up joining him for a drive along the notorious North Yungas Road—El Camino de la Muerte. We passed more fatal accidents than New Jersey has tolls, and we had to watch out for road pirates."

"Holy cats!" Bud said, impressed. "Did you run into any?"

"We did, and a motley bunch they were. Most were armed with machetes, though one gentleman had a rusty old rifle that looked more like a movie prop than a gun. Matteo bribed them off with a case of Jim Beam."

Philip Hudson laughed. "I really should pay Matt Allegro a visit, but I haven't been to New York City in ages."

Jack, did you hear that? According to Eddie, Hudson claimed he was in New York at the time of Emma's death!

Good work, doll. Hudson's been drinkin', so he's not thinkin'—and he just blew his alibi sky-high.

Well, you did teach me the value of gossip. Now what?

Tomorrow, you tell your friend with the badge what you found out tonight.

You think there's more?

Where there's smoke, there's a stogie burnin'. Let the man keep bumping gums, and who knows—you might hear a confession to murder.

Philip paused for a satisfying sip of his fifth Tanqueray with Meyer lemon and Stirrings tonic.

On the other hand, Jack warned. *This guy has a hollow leg—and he might be pulling yours.*

He can't be lying to both me and Eddie. One of his stories is false.

True, Jack said. *And, you have to admit, he's been floatin' more air tonight than the* Hindenburg. *Maybe that whole coffee pal pirate yarn is hooey.*

I exhaled in frustration.

Listen, baby, gossip is golden. But all that glitters ain't the truth. No matter what he tells you, you'll still need hard evidence to back it, and you won't find it sittin' in this fussy food aquarium.

But I can keep him talking, right?

Sure, why not. In gin veritas, and this cluck's been suckin' down hooch all night.

He was also talking all night, and I had to admit, his stories were riveting. Bud was entertained, and Sadie was completely charmed. She was so charmed, in fact, that she leaned over to whisper in my ear.

"Bud and I are going to leave early, so you and Philip can get better acquainted."

I objected. Strenuously. To my surprise, the ghost didn't.

Alone with you, and a couple more injections of juniper berries, and he's likely to get maudlin. That's when you jump in with the whole "I'm sorry for your pain" routine, followed by "I've been in your shoes." He's already got the hots for you. Lend a sympathetic ear, and he'll spill like a broken vase.

When Philip Hudson called for a sixth round of cocktails, I got the chance to test Jack's theory.

"I'm sorry, but I'm afraid Bud and I will have to go," Sadie said. "Bud has an early job, and I'm opening the store first thing in the morning."

"But we haven't talked about the book collection," Philip pointed out. "I'm sure we can agree on a fair price."

Sadie shot me a wink. "I have an idea. Why don't the two of you talk business, and Pen can brief me tomorrow."

"Or, perhaps we should call it a night," I said. "We can pick this conversation up again by conference call in the morning. After all, Mr. Hudson has a long drive back to Millstone."

Philip shook his head. "Not to worry, Mrs. McClure. I've taken a room at the bed-and-breakfast."

"Then it's settled, Pen," Sadie asserted. "Ask Fiona or Barney to call a cab to take you home when you're ready. I'll leave the light on for you."

As Bud and Sadie departed, Philip slid his chair closer to mine. His formerly bleary eyes were suddenly twinkling.

"I propose we talk business late into the night, and share breakfast in the morning."

Jack grunted. *He's not coy, is he?*

What do I do?

Play him. String him along and stall. With all the booze he's tippled, he's sure to pass out soon. Grill him before he's too pickled to do more than blubber.

"Well," I said to Philip, "if we're staying, let's take another look at that dessert menu, shall we?"

I ordered an apple tart with pastry cream, and French-pressed coffee. Philip opted for a sixth gin and tonic. While I savored the fruity-creamy pastry, Philip downed half his drink without tasting it.

Looks like Mr. Hot Pants is on the brink. You better crank up the questioning before he's completely embalmed.

I set my fork aside and took a deep breath. Then I reached over and touched my host's hand.

"Mr. Hudson . . . Philip . . . If I didn't say it before, I want to tell you that I'm sorry for your loss. I know you and your wife were divorced, but—"

I blathered platitudes until he wrapped my hand in both of his. Then, just as Jack predicted, he finally opened the floodgates, and the strange story of Philip and his late ex-wife poured out.

CHAPTER 23

California Dreaming

Sleeping with a man half your age can be exhausting, but if it's too much for him you can always find a younger man.

—Barbara Taylor Bradford, *Playing the Game*

"EMMA AND I met ten years ago, at a specialty food store on Sunset Boulevard. I was shopping for homesick foods, and this place had a great selection—crab cakes and chowder from Newport, New England lobster in season, and two brands of coffee syrup. That's what Emma was buying."

"Your wife was from Rhode Island, too?"

Philip laughed. "Emma Royce was a California girl, through and through. She was raised by a wealthy family in Pacific Heights, and only left San Francisco to start her own New Age spiritual center in Venice Beach. When we met, she was buying coffee syrup for a couple from Providence staying at her ashram."

Did he just mention an ashtray?

Ashram, Jack. It's like a school for spiritual thought and deep contemplation.

Deep contemplation? You mean like playing the ponies? Because I contemplated those racing forms every single day.

Quiet, Jack, I don't want to miss this story!

I gently detached my hand from Philip's. "How fascinating that Emma was so—otherworldly. Was she psychic? Did she have visions?"

Or was she just straitjacket crazy?

"Oh, she was nothing like that. Emma was very practical, for someone who grew up in the Age of Aquarius."

"What did she teach at her ashram?"

"Meditation. Relaxation techniques. Yoga. The *Kama Sutra*. Tantric sex—"

"Excuse me?" I said.

"You're not prudish, are you, Penelope?" Philip asked with a smirk. "Tantric sex is an ancient Hindu practice, a transcendent experience that's been around for at least five thousand years. Emma had the equivalent of a black belt in it." He gulped the rest of his cocktail. "I was almost thirty when we met, and I'd been around the block a few times. But Emma showed me a thing or two, I'll tell you."

File that under things I didn't need to know, I told Jack with a shudder.

Just keep him yammering.

Philip signaled the waiter for drink number seven—but who's counting? He certainly wasn't.

"So why wasn't Emma in Venice Beach, teaching at her ashram? What was she doing here, in an apartment full of rare books?"

"Things went south after a few years," Philip admitted. "People stopped coming to Emma's retreat. Some of them gave up all that loony tunes stuff entirely. The rest moved on to the next New Age trend. She tried, but poor Emma couldn't keep up."

"Your 'loony tunes' reference tells me you must have thought of the ashram thing as silly."

"I didn't practice any of it, except for the tantric sex. But the people who stayed there were nice enough, I suppose, if naive."

"Still, it's an odd choice of professions. Did you ever see

Emma behave strangely, or irrationally? Was she ever depressed? Do you think she was capable of suicide?"

"Absolutely not. I told Deputy Franzetti as much. What happened to her was an accident—one waiting to happen. There were structural issues with that old house. I even read it in your local paper. I've already hired a storage company to empty the apartment, first thing tomorrow morning, before the whole place collapses."

"Are you going to take the parrot as well as the dog?"

"Her pets were her business. They'll have to go to shelters."

"What kind of dog did she have?"

"A Yorkie, I believe."

"And you don't have her dog?"

"Me? Heavens, no! Frankly, I never saw a reason to take on the trouble and expense of an animal, unless you're some kind of breeder or a farmer who's going to earn something from it. One of the many things we fought about when we were married—she got those pets after we separated."

"Why *did* you separate?"

"Why does anyone? We made each other miserable. Emma was smart as a whip and twice as cutting, and she wasn't satisfied with the divorce settlement, either, even after I turned my late father's book collection over to her."

"She wasn't a book person, then?"

Philip shook his head. "She liked bestsellers, but she could never keep the authors or titles straight. My father's valuable collection held no value to Emma beyond what the books could earn at auction, which I thought was her plan."

Philip snorted. "Instead, she set up shop here in Quindicott, no doubt so she could be close to the money."

"What money?"

Suddenly, Philip set his cocktail aside and rubbed his bleary eyes.

"I'm sorry, Penelope, but I'm feeling a little woozy . . ."

Just when things were getting interesting, the pretty daisy swoons.

Don't worry, Jack, I'm not finished with him yet.

I tugged the man to his feet with one hand, while flagging the waiter with the other.

"Come on, Philip. Let's get you back to your room."

Suddenly, he grinned. "I like the sound of that!"

CHAPTER 24

Swinging with Mr. Happy

The fact that three-fifths of an octopus' neurons are not in their brain, but in their arms, suggests that each arm has a mind of its own.

—Sy Montgomery, *The Soul of an Octopus*

THIS, I DIDN'T count on.

The bracing night air—and/or the thought of me accompanying him back to his room—revitalized the man faster than a thirty-two-ounce energy drink. Still tipsy, he draped one arm over my shoulder and whistled while we walked.

On the lighted path from the restaurant to the Finch Inn, I pressed him again, asking what he meant when he said Emma was sticking "close to the money."

"As you may know, my father died last year—long before our divorce was finalized. Which means—"

"That Emma legally inherits half of what you do."

"Of course, I won't see a cent for months," Philip said with a resigned shrug. "Most of father's investments were in real estate, and the properties must be divested before funds can be distributed. I'm the youngest of five siblings, so my piece of pie will be small, no more than a few million."

The ghost groaned. *Only a few million? The shame! How can this Alvin ever set foot in Newport again?*

"I confess, my resources have been limited in recent years. But . . ." He sucked in the salty ocean breeze. "Just yesterday I managed to turn everything around. I secured a bridge loan from a Federal Hill moneyman. Enough to kick-start several renovation projects, with a commitment for much more funding in the future."

"Federal Hill?" I echoed. "You mean the neighborhood in Providence? You were there yesterday?"

"Yes." He smirked. "Didn't I just say that?"

Jack, did you hear?!

I got it, doll. Phil scores a big-time loan on the day his ex joins the angels? Interesting timing.

His timing is the least of it. He told the police that he was in New York City. But Providence is only a short drive away!

A guy only lies to the coppers when he has something to hide.

And Hudson has plenty to hide, I told the ghost. *This deal he's describing isn't with a bank, but a "Federal Hill money-man." Organized crime is still around in New England. He might have made another deal while he was at it, one that involved the murder of his ex-wife—*

Don't jump the gun. In my day, moneymen weren't the same as button men. I'm sure it's the same in your day, too. If Philip wanted the button pushed on his wife, he was talking to the wrong kind of mobster.

I shivered. *What if he wasn't?*

Haven't you been listening? Hudson may have picked up your tab tonight, but he's cheaper than Scrooge before his Christmas scare. He's worried about losing a dime over a pooch and a parrot; why would he drop a bundle for a job he could do himself for nothing? Are you getting my drift, baby? Take it as a warning. If Hudson was in Providence, he was close enough to do Emma's murder neat.

Neat?

All by his lonesome. That explains why there was no

forced entry at Emma's digs, no sign of a struggle. It may even explain that nice meal still simmering in its pot.

You're right—

Which brings me back to my warning. Right now, you're strolling alone in the dark with a possible murderer.

As if I wasn't already spooked enough (pardon the pun), Philip Hudson chose that moment to drop his gym-toned arm from my shoulder to my waist.

"I saw your shiver," he said through a toothy smile. "You feel it, too, don't you? The chemistry?"

I'll give him something to feel. Just say the word!

"Too fast for me, Philip." I squirmed away from his touch.

"I apologize," Hudson quickly countered. "A little too much imbibing. Don't be put off, Penelope. I was serious about talking business until dawn. Just talk, I promise. We have a lot to discuss."

"I really don't think it will take that long to agree on consignment for a book collection. I assure you that you'll get the highest possible bids. My aunt Sadie has decades of experience in the trade with a vast base of customers who collect—"

"Forget the books! I have a more important proposition. One you really *must* consider."

We'd arrived at the bed-and-breakfast. It was after midnight, and the exterior lights were off. The ornate wraparound porch was illuminated only by the glow shining through the sitting room windows.

As we crested the stairs, Philip suddenly grabbed my hand and pulled me toward a wicker love seat swing, hanging from the porch ceiling.

"Please, sit with me and talk."

"No. It's late and I should—"

"Just *listen*. My father's property holdings are in Millstone, amounting to over half the town. With the deal I've made, what I don't inherit, I can buy up at fire-sale prices from my father's estate. In a few years, those old, distressed properties can be transformed into profitable holdings."

"That's very commendable. I'm sure you can—"

"I don't want to do it alone. I want *your* help."

"Mine?"

"I want you to fix Millstone the way you transformed Quindicott."

"But, I didn't do that by myself!"

"Of course you did! Those hayseeds aren't any more imaginative than the dimwits who skulk the streets of Millstone. They needed guidance. Someone with vision, someone smart, sophisticated—someone like you—to show them the way."

Our legs bumped the hanging love seat.

"You did it once, Penelope, and you can do it again. Work your magic on Millstone, and we can both make millions."

"But I already have a business—"

"Your aunt's bookshop? You think too small for someone with the McClure name. You're lovely and talented and—" He leaned close. "And our relationship doesn't need to be all business . . ."

He moved closer, and his hands started groping.

"Slow down, Philip!"

As I struggled once again to get free of him, I could feel the cold fury of Jack's ire. The icy mist around us was building and building—

Stay calm, Jack. I can handle this guy!

Detaching myself from Philip's grip, I stepped backward.

Meanwhile, over his shoulder, I saw the cold mist blow the love seat backward until the gravity-defying wicker swing nearly bumped the porch roof.

Before I could stop him, Philip attempted to sit where the seat had been—and tumbled right to the floor.

"Philip, are you hurt?" I asked.

"Only my pride," he said, embarrassed. But not embarrassed enough to restrain his wandering hands as I helped him off the hardwood. In that short time, he managed to cop more feels than a TSA agent.

When he was on his feet again, he wrapped his arms around my waist, so he could "steady himself."

Then he pulled me tight against him and put his lips to my ear. "Think about it," he whispered hotly. "A union of a Hudson and a McClure will make the society columns. We can work side by side, twenty-four seven, our full attention devoted to the restoration of Millstone—"

"It's too much to ask, Philip. I have a son to raise—"

Not to mention an octopus to wrestle!

"We can send your boy to a top boarding school. This is no place to raise a McClure, anyway. And with the child gone, you'll feel free with me, free to let loose with cries of tantric joy—"

Egad, this man is repulsive! I thought, shuddering when his hands moved south faster than Sherman's army.

Okay, partner, I've had about enough. If you don't deal with this cluck, I will!

No, Jack! I've got this!

With a hard shove, I broke free and took two steps backward. "Sorry, Philip," I said firmly, "but I'm going home."

Once again, Philip's warm facade iced over. His lips curled into a sneer. "Don't be stupid, Penelope. Think about what I'm offering. A chance to do more than be a shopkeeper at some small-time store. To earn millions instead of thousands." His eyes had turned cold, his hands balling into fists. "Come with me upstairs. By morning, you'll see things my way. I won't take no for an answer—"

Was this how Emma felt? I wondered. *Did he push her to the edge of the balcony—and beyond?*

He began to lunge toward me, and that's when the ghost released his supernatural grip on that hanging love seat. Down it came, slamming right into Philip Hudson.

I leaped clear as he stumbled forward. With a girlish squeal, he plunged headfirst into a wicker chair. It promptly flipped over, sending Philip tumbling across the porch like a bowling ball.

After crashing into a planter, the man lay still.

"Philip!" I ran up to his limp body. "Are you alive?"

He moaned.

Suddenly, the porch lights went on, and Barney Finch appeared at the front door.

"Tarnation! What's all the racket?" He reached into his sport jacket and slipped his glasses over his nose. "Is that you, Pen?"

"Yes, and I'm afraid one of your guests has had too much to drink."

Barney's eyes went wide. "Mr. Hudson! Let me help you up."

Stumbling to his feet with Barney's assistance, a dazed Philip caught my eye, put a "phone hand" to his ear, and mimed the words "call me." Then he winked.

"I'll get Mr. Happy settled in his room," Barney said. "Use the phone in the parlor to call Sandy at the cab company. She'll make sure you get home safe."

CHAPTER 25

Irish Tea and No Tales

Today's gossip is tomorrow's headline.

—Walter Winchell

EARLY THE NEXT morning, I dragged myself into the kitchen. Collapsing at the table, I rubbed my bleary eyes and wondered how two glasses of sparkling water could give a girl a hangover worthy of New Year's Eve.

Sadie, meanwhile—who'd shared an entire bottle of wine with Bud—was humming a happy tune.

"Good morning, dear!" With eyes bright as the clear September sky, my aunt poured me a steaming cup of Irish tea.

I groped for the milk, splashed it into my cup, and gulped the strong brew, praying it would revive me.

"Late night?" she asked. Her smile held the wrong idea.

"It's not what you think."

"That's all right. You don't have to kiss and tell."

"I promise you, there was no kissing, and there's nothing to tell."

Of course, that wasn't true. There was plenty to tell . . .

Philip Gordon Hudson was a sloppy drunk. I had no idea if the man was a murderer, but I wasn't surprised by his octopus hands. In my experience, which included my late husband, boys who grew up with a great deal of wealth tended to get what they wanted, when they wanted it. If trouble came, rich and powerful relatives often shielded them from the consequences of their actions, to protect their own reputations as much as their kin's.

There were pitfalls to this type of upbringing, including extended adolescence, a grown man or woman with a hollow core and disappointingly weak character.

Whatever made Philip Hudson the man he was, however, did not overly concern me. Last night, I'd simply seen enough to know that, even if he *wasn't* guilty of murdering his ex-wife, I didn't want him in my life, my son's life—or even the life of the business I shared with my aunt.

That said, I had to be careful.

Sadie believed Hudson to be an upstanding man and "promising" prospect to lure me out of single-mom widowhood. If I spilled all my worries and speculations to her over morning tea, Vinny Nardini would likely hear it by lunchtime, and before you could say "megaphone" the entire town would get an earful about Philip Hudson.

Jack advised me to listen to gossip, not spread it.

I didn't disagree. In general, I believed in the law and due process. Societies that embraced slander for solutions ran the risk of looking more like our ancestors of nearby Salem than the enlightened members of *Star Trek*'s bridge.

In private, however, I was dying (forgive the pun) to tell my resident spirit everything that I was thinking and feeling, but he was AWOL again. Those supernatural antics at the Finch Inn had sapped his strength. They'd certainly sapped mine. No wonder I had slept like the dead. There wasn't even a new dream, which was just as well. The one Jack had shared still haunted me.

That creepy "Continental" con man, Henri Leroi, masked a criminal heart with a slick veneer. The ex-husband in Jack's case had some things in common with Hudson, a man who hid his own brand of creepiness behind a facade of superficial charm and Newport sophistication.

What also concerned me about Hudson, in addition to

his shaky alibi, was what sounded like a focus on enriching himself without a thought of endangering the citizens of Millstone by letting a "Federal Hill moneyman" gain a foothold in that sleepy community.

Was my assumption right about the moneyman being shady? Or was there another explanation? Did Philip lie to the police about being in New York on the day of his wife's death? Or did he lie to me? And was that the extent of his wrongdoing? Or was he a murderer, too?

"You have a lot on your plate today," Sadie pointed out as she set a bowl of goodness down in front of me—warm oatmeal, Maine blueberries, and a drizzle of local honey.

I dug in, thanking her in a grateful garble of chewing. ". . . and you're right about my plate. It runneth over."

I had two truant children to deal with all morning; a busy bookshop to run on an afternoon shift; and a Quibblers meeting this evening.

Before it all began, however, I had something more to do: absolve myself of this awful feeling that I had key information to catch a killer—one who walked among us. I shivered, and not because the haunting spirit was near. Jack was still flirting with eternal rest.

Ironic as it was, the ghost didn't scare me. What fueled my fears was raising a child near anyone who thought he could get away with murder.

"SPENCER! AMY!" I called an hour later. "Shut off your game and get ready to go. I'm driving you back to Boston. But first we're walking over to Cooper Family Bakery."

Spencer whooped. "Amy! You've got to try their black-and-white donut. They only have them on Mondays and Tuesdays, and they sell out super quick."

"I like donuts. Sometimes my au pair makes us beignets."

"What's a *ben-yay*?"

"It's a French donut. The shape is square with a powdered sugar topping. You'd like it."

"These donuts are the regular round kind, with holes in

the middle, but they are *the best* for miles around. Everyone says so." Spencer faced me. "Can I have two?"

"You can have one now, and maybe one for later, during the drive to Boston. I'm going to get you and Amy back into your seminar."

At least I hoped I could; that's what I'd told Amy's mother when she interrupted my sleep of the dead.

It was close to four in the morning when the woman finally returned my call—at least, I think it was. All I know is, outside my window, the Rhode Island sky was still black as a tomb when my mobile phone vibrated . . .

THE FORMER MRS. Ridgeway—now the brand-new Mrs. Bergen—was not at all apologetic about calling two days after I'd initially tried to contact her (she and her new husband were detoxing from all devices, she zealously explained). She wasn't sorry for waking me out of a deathlike sleep (in Sardinia it was a glorious, sunny morning), never mind feeling the least bit of remorse for missing her ex-husband's funeral.

Mostly, she was unhappy because her daughter felt it necessary to "jeopardize a golden educational opportunity, to pay respects to a corpse."

Her tone chilled me as much as her words, and I felt sorry for Amy, who had to grow up with such an unfeeling parent.

"Perhaps this is a good thing," Mrs. Bergen reasoned. "With Kevin gone, Amy will have to get used to the fact that Gustav is now her father."

I attempted to convey how broken up Amy was about her biological father's death.

"There is no need for you to tell me about my own daughter. I spoke with her last evening on the phone while *you* were enjoying yourself at dinner. I'll arrange for therapy when I get back. We can't have feelings getting in the way of her academic progress, but I really can't understand why she's so emotional—unless it's your son's influence. In the last year since our divorce, I've done my best to keep Kevin's involvement to a minimum. Except for the trust fund he's left her, which was a shock, I can tell you, the man was useless . . ."

I let the woman rattle on and imply the moon. As my dear old dad used to say, *Don't waste good energy trying to convince a donkey it's a jackass.* There was, however, one piece of information worthy of my attention.

"Excuse me, did you say Amy's father set up a trust?"

"Yes, and I can't imagine where Kevin got that kind of money. While I was married to the man, he only taught college part-time while trying—and pathetically failing—to succeed as a novelist."

Mrs. Bergen said she was relieved when I told her of my plan to drive Amy up to Boston with Spencer and attempt to talk the administrators into letting them both back into the program.

"Do your best!" she exclaimed. "And keep me informed."

Without so much as a thank-you, she hung up.

HONESTLY, I WASN'T all that surprised by the woman's rudeness. I'd encountered enough of the attitude in my late husband's family.

Whether they were accomplished, busy professionals moving in a kind of whirlwind of self-importance; spouses of the same; or dowagers like Calvin McClure's imperious mother, they often had to be reminded not to treat "common" people with the same blunt directives they gave to their employees, service providers, and domestic staff.

"Mom, can I have a mug of the Coopers' hot cocoa, too?" Spencer asked after shutting down his game. "It's wicked good chocolate!"

"Get ready quick, and I'll consider it . . ."

At the moment, I had more to wrestle with than my son's sugar consumption. I had a lawman to look up.

Last night, while Philip Hudson pulled me into a thicket of conflicting statements, Jack advised me to track down a badge and tell him my story. So, while Amy and Spence were grabbing their coats, I put in a call to an old friend, one I could always count on to lead me out of the woods.

"Hello, Eddie?"

CHAPTER 26

Civil Bakery Service

Smile! You're on Candid Camera!

—CBS TV, *Candid Camera*, 1959–1967

"I DON'T UNDERSTAND, Pen. Why *exactly* do you want me to tap into the sidewalk security system archive?"

"I'll explain everything when we meet."

"Okay. I can be at your bookshop in half an hour."

"No, Eddie, we have to meet at the Cooper Family Bakery." Suddenly, Deputy Chief Franzetti clammed up.

"Eddie? Are you there?"

"Yeah?"

"What's the matter?"

"Does it *have* to be the bakery?"

"Why? Are you on a diet or something? It's the *bakery's* security footage I want us to look at."

Eddie blew out a sigh. "All right. I'll be there in thirty."

That gave me just enough time to make the short walk down Cranberry Street, get Amy and Spence settled at a table with their doughnuts and cocoa, and bring the co-owners— Linda Cooper-Logan and her husband, Milner—up to speed.

Despite all my preparations, I was not ready for what happened when Eddie arrived.

"Well, if it isn't Deputy Chief Franzetti!" Linda bit out

with a distressing amount of venom. "Have you come to write me another prohibitively expensive ticket?!"

I asked Linda to explain what happened, and she did— *loudly*.

A few days before, a fifty-pound bag of flour burst on the street during a morning delivery to the bakery. The bakery was very busy, so it wasn't cleaned up until afternoon. The security camera caught the incident, and Eddie cited Linda and Milner for littering. The word *toxic* was added to the citation—as in "unlawful dispersal of a toxic biodegradable"—because the bleached white flour "posed a significant threat to the gluten intolerant."

"That's ridiculous!" Appalled, I turned to Eddie.

I could tell by the embarrassed look on his face that Eddie agreed with me. "What could I do? I didn't write the law. Councilwoman Marjorie Binder-Smith saw the incident, showed us the security footage, and demanded that Chief Ciders issue the citation. Since Ciders likes his morning coffee and doughnuts, he passed the buck to me."

I held my head. These idiotic citations were just another brick in the wall of the business community's divide with the city council—and the subject of our Quibblers meeting this very evening.

The whole thing had started with the installation of the Usher Security sidewalk cameras on the facades and back entrances of all the Cranberry Street businesses.

Just like Linda, Brainert, Bud, and every other business owner on Cranberry Street, Sadie and I had to pony up cash to install these 24/7 cameras in order to remain "compliant" with this new local "safe community" ordinance.

Super, everyone thought, *we all want safe streets and sidewalks*.

Shortly after the cameras went live, however, we business owners began discovering surprises on our doorsteps: littering tickets for loose trash and leaves that had blown in front of our store entrances overnight. Fines were issued daily for other minor (and sometimes idiotic) "infractions," and some shops were getting hit two times a week.

"If you ladies want to blame anyone," Eddie told us, "blame the city council."

A short strand of platinum hair escaped Linda's hairnet, and she shoved it back under. "That's not who your dad blames, is it?"

Eddie folded his arms. "That's hitting below the belt, don't you think?"

According to town gossip, the elderly owner of Franzetti's Pizza had been fined when squirrels scattered garbage in the back of his pizza parlor. He was so angry, he banned all Quindicott policemen (including his son Eddie) from his shop.

"One of my microwaves is on the fritz," Linda taunted. "Maybe you should ticket me for contributing to the possible leakage of radiation!"

I stepped between them. "Can't we all just get along? Please? For the next twenty minutes, anyway?"

"Fine," Linda said in a tone that indicated it wasn't fine at all.

But at least she stopped arguing with Eddie and focused instead on helping Milner wait on customers.

Relieved, Eddie slapped a digital notebook on an unoccupied table. Still standing, he tapped into the shop's Wi-Fi. "Okay, Pen, let's get this over quick before Linda comes at me for Round Two. What do you want to see?"

"Footage from Saturday morning, the day Emma died. From the moment the bakery opened until Linda ran out of cinnamon buns—"

"That would be five minutes after the football crowd rolled in," Linda reminded me from behind the counter.

Eddie blinked. "What *is* this, a marketing study?"

"No. Emma Hudson stopped at this bakery the day she died, and I suspect someone else did, too."

Eddie gave me a sidelong glance. "And who would that be?"

"Philip Hudson, Emma's ex." I lowered my voice to a whisper. "The man who just might have murdered her."

CHAPTER 27

I Spy with My Little Eye

"Probably," Nora said.
"It's a word you've got to use a lot in this business."

—Nick Charles replying to his wife, Nora, in *The Thin Man*

EDDIE OPENED HIS mouth to protest, but I cut him off.

"Before you go all 'Chief Ciders' on me, I want you to listen to what I have to say . . ."

I filled Eddie in on what I'd learned during my dinner with Philip Hudson—that his alibi about being in New York City on the day of his ex-wife's death might be a lie. "He told me he was in Providence . . ."

I informed Eddie about Hudson's financial woes, and the deal he claimed to have made with a "Federal Hill moneyman," which could lead to corruption in nearby Millstone, the kind of corruption that could creep into our own hometown next.

Eddie frowned over the duplicitous alibi, but he waved off my shady moneyman worries.

"Hudson wouldn't be the first member of the snob set to be involved with criminal activity: Ponzi schemes, money laundering, tax evasion, embezzlement, stockpiling narcotics with bogus prescriptions. Hell, most people believe mob-linked bootlegging enriched a Boston family that produced a president. Hudson may be dirtying his fingers in a dubious pie, but it doesn't make him a murderer."

"Here's what I think probably happened," I countered.

"'Probably' being the operative word." Eddie folded his arms.

"Keep an open mind!" I pleaded and cleared my throat. "So Emma is broke and waiting around for her share of Philip Hudson's inheritance, which Philip confirmed to me is legally owed to her. Philip makes up some reason to see Emma, and she invites him over for brunch. On the way to see his ex, Philip stops at this bakery and buys a box of cinnamon buns and a couple of baguettes—the items found in Emma's kitchen the day she died, items we know Emma didn't purchase herself because Linda remembered selling her a coffee and one bun—"

"How could she remember one customer?"

"Easy. Linda had clothes envy for Emma's lilac cashmere sweater—*and* Emma was one of the few people who filled out a church raffle ticket that morning."

"Fine. Go on with your theory."

I took a breath before the big finish. "When Philip arrives at Pine Tree Avenue, he finds an emotionally distraught Emma. Maybe he's been drinking. They argue. He might have lashed out and struck her, knocked her out. Panic sets in. She might call the cops on him when she comes around, maybe even sue. But if he tosses her off the balcony, flees the scene, and gets the heck out of Dodge to establish an alibi, he's certain it will look like she jumped or fell. His troublesome ex-wife would be out of his life for good, and he'd be a richer man."

"This is all pure speculation, Pen, and very tough to prove. I canvassed the building, and none of Mrs. Hudson's neighbors were at home at the time of her death. So we've got no witnesses to any kind of argument."

"Well, I was there. I heard footsteps leaving that apartment, and I think we can prove it was Hudson. Catch the man on that security tape with baguettes and cinnamon

buns in hand, and you'll not only prove he made a false
statement to the police about his alibi, you'll place him at
the crime scene. Pressure him with that one-two punch of
hard evidence, and he may just fold and confess."

Eddie still seemed doubtful, so I doubled down.

"Think of it another way. Wouldn't it be *great publicity*
for Usher Security if Chief Ciders could tout the fact that
the highly unpopular system actually provided evidence to
catch a *murderer* in our midst?"

"Okay, you sold me," Eddie said.

I tried to contain my self-satisfaction—and nearly asked
Jack Shepard what he thought of my success. Then I remembered: I'd left his Buffalo nickel in its special little
pillbox, which effectively kept Jack in the box of our bookstore.

After his antics last night, I thought we both needed a
break from each other. I mean, *really*, that crack about my
ability to take care of myself being "debatable"—it made
me steam.

Now, however, I regretted my decision, if only to prove
to the ghosted gumshoe that my PI skills were getting better. Or at least weren't as "hinky" as he believed them to be.

*I'm sorry you can't hear me, you big lug, but I think
you'd be proud.*

As I stood there, missing my ghost, Eddie cued the sidewalk footage to the moment Milner opened the shop. In fast
motion, we sped through the first half hour of images in
less than a minute and a half.

By nine A.M. on the digital clock, we'd seen Rita Kelso,
Wanda Clark, Sylvia Lodge, and Eddie's sister, Bonnie
Franzetti, carry baguettes away from the bakery.

"We're lucky—baguettes are easy to spot," Eddie said,
and within a few seconds, he was freezing an image. "That's
Mr. Brink."

"Where?"

He pointed out a heavy-set man in his seventies with a
neatly trimmed gray goatee.

"Whitman Brink. I know him. He's a lovely man, and a regular customer at our bookstore."

"Well, he's got a pair of baguettes, *and* a pastry box that might very well contain those cinnamon buns you saw in Emma's kitchen." Eddie checked the digital timer. "He purchased them at 8:55 A.M. Plenty of time to take them to Emma."

"Why would you assume that?"

"Because of his address. Mr. Brink resides at 1919 Pine Tree."

"What?"

"Emma Hudson's landlord provided me with the names of all seven of his tenants. Brink lives on the first floor."

I chewed my lip. This wasn't going the way I'd planned. "Mr. Brink's purchase might be a simple coincidence, Eddie. Please, let's keep looking for Emma's ex-husband."

But we didn't see Philip Hudson, not once.

When a parade of SUVs brought a rowdy army of teens into the shop, I knew my theory was shot to hades. Linda already advised us that she'd run out of cinnamon buns during the Saturday morning football stampede. Eddie shut down the security feed.

"Hudson isn't here, Pen."

"I don't understand. It all fit together perfectly. He has to be guilty. Hey! What about Emma's phone? Did you find any calls from her ex?"

"We haven't recovered her phone."

"But you've accessed Emma's account, right?"

"We can't find an account. We didn't even find a bill in her mail pile. She was probably using a prepaid disposable phone."

"Which vanished, along with the book she took from my store."

I pondered that for a moment. "You said no one was home when you canvassed the building, but don't you think it's possible someone living at 1919 Pine Tree stole the phone before I arrived? When I got there, the door was wide open."

"I already checked them out. That old building is home
to a criminal assault parolee and his common-law wife, two
methadone addicts, and a registered sex offender—along
with the late Mrs. Hudson and Mr. Brink, of course. But,
like I said, none were home that morning."

"They all had good alibis, I assume."

Eddie nodded. "The methadone heads were at the clinic
in Millstone, getting their fix. The parolee, his wife, and
the sex offender were all at their jobs."

"What about Mr. Brink?"

"When I spoke to the landlord, he told me Brink was
gone. Said he drove away in his old jalopy, looking for sub-
jects to paint. He did that every day."

"That's right," I confirmed. "Mr. Brink paints watercolors. He had some lovely work displayed in my Community
Events space during the Summer Art Show. He even sold a
few. I'm just surprised he lives at such a seedy address."
When Eddie shrugged, I acknowledged the obvious. "I
guess money troubles can come to anyone's door, can't
they? Even someone with artistic ability, a love of books,
and a sharp mind . . ."

Just then, I remembered that ridiculous "Fatal Building
Mishap" headline in the *Quindicott Bulletin*. "Do you think
Mr. Brink was the 'anonymous source' quoted in Elmer
Crabtree's article? The person who claimed Emma's death
was due to the balcony breaking?"

Eddie shook his head. "Believe it or not, Elmer confessed to me who his anonymous source was for that story:
Philip Hudson."

"Really? Why?"

"My guess is Hudson's running a scam, trying to set the
stage for an insurance claim or negligence suit. With those
newspaper quotes, he probably thinks he can sway a civil
court judge to let a lawsuit go forward, even if it has no
merit."

"A jury would never believe that claim!"

"Like a lot of these cases, Hudson doesn't need it to go
that far. If he can threaten a suit, the property owner might

be frightened enough of court costs and lawyers' fees to pay off Hudson, some modest settlement that lets him off the hook and makes Hudson and his case go away."

"Or Hudson is trying to use gossip to influence the public," I countered, "keep people in town from becoming suspicious of Emma's death. If that's the case, it points even more strongly to him as a murderer."

"Maybe, Pen, but your theory has absolutely no proof. Hudson didn't appear on the bakery security camera. And lying to me about an alibi—if he did—isn't something I'll be authorized to arrest the man for."

"At least question him again."

"Oh, I plan to, based on what you heard last night, but he may claim the lie was to *you*. Let's see if he can produce evidence that he was out of town. If he can, then—"

When Eddie stopped talking, I realized something had distracted him, something more immediate than Philip Hudson's duplicity. Eddie's outraged gaze was peering through the bakery window at his own police car.

"What the heck do those two think they're doing?!"

I was about to ask Eddie who "those two" were when I followed his gaze and saw Amy and my son, Spencer, sitting in the front seat of Eddie's cruiser, using police equipment, as if they were brand-new rookie recruits.

CHAPTER 28

Grand Theft Auto

To a father growing old, nothing is dearer than a daughter.

—Euripides, *Helen*, 412 BC

DEPUTY CHIEF FRANZETTI was through the bakery's front door in a flash, me on his heels.

As we crossed the sidewalk to his patrol car, I noticed Spencer nudge Amy. She quickly punched a button on the dashboard and folded her arms, the picture of innocence.

Meanwhile, Spence grabbed the steering wheel and pretended he was driving—complete with childish car noises—until Franzetti yanked the door open and ordered them both out.

"What were you two doing?" he demanded.

"I've never been inside a real police car," Spence answered sheepishly. "I thought it was cool, like my *Grand Theft Auto* game."

"You're lucky I don't charge you with *attempted* grand theft auto!"

Spencer spotted me behind the deputy chief, and his cheeks turned bright red. Then he lowered his eyes and rubbed the back of his neck in a peculiarly adult manner—once again, much like my late trouble-loving brother.

"We're really sorry, Officer, sir," Amy said, as her lower lip began to quiver. "We were just playing, that's all."

Eddie leaned through the open door to check the car's interior. He jiggled the emergency brake, examined the radio and the computer hooked to the dash by a metal rack.

When he rose and faced the children again, tears were welling in Amy's eyes.

"Look, no harm done, and no need to get upset, Amy." The ice in Eddie's tone thawed under the rain of the little girl's tears.

"Don't worry, Officer Franzetti," Spencer said. "It will never happen again."

"Good!" Eddie's tone hardened again as he turned his attention back on my son. "Because that was a really stupid move, Spencer. No more stunts like that, okay? I don't want to be arresting you a few years from now for something worse. We've got enough juvenile delinquents in Quindicott as it is."

I stepped around Eddie. "Okay. My turn. That baloney about *Grand Theft Auto* might have gotten you off the hook with Officer Franzetti, but not me. You two are far too bright to get yourself in trouble without a good reason. Tell me the truth. What were you really up to?"

Amy's eyes dried up fast as she exchanged guilty glances with Spencer.

I folded my arms. "We are not *budging* from this spot until you tell the truth. Explain the car. What did you want in there? How did you even get in?"

Amy pushed up her glasses. "Well, Mrs. McClure, when we came outside, I noticed the police car window was down. I peeked in and saw the computer was running, so I reached in and unlocked the door."

"Yeah," Spence said, jumping in. "The dash computer was still logged in to the mainframe at the station, so—"

"So I typed in my father's name. I wanted to see the police report on the auto accident that killed him."

"Why?"

"Nobody told me what really happened, Mrs. McClure. Nobody even *talked* to me about it!"

Eddie rubbed the back of his neck. "We didn't want to trouble you, Amy—"

"But I know things!" the girl insisted. "You should have come and talked to me. That's why Spencer helped me get into the police computer. I wanted to see if the police knew who killed my dad, and why."

Eddie sighed. "There's no why, Amy. It was just a tragic accident."

"I don't think so." Amy shook her brown curls. "On my first day at the university seminar, Dad texted me this . . ."

Amy showed us the message on her phone:

Honey, I'm sorry we couldn't be together while your mom is on vacation, but I'm proud of you for earning a spot at the seminar.

Things have been tough since your mom and I split, but there is good news. I've just finished a project that's paying so well we're going to take that trip to Disney World during spring break.

There will be more money, too, lots more. It's owed to me, and I still have to work out some details. Once I do, I'll be able to move back to Boston. I'll get to see you more often. For now, you can count on us being together for a whole week in the spring. I promise.

Do your best! I'll see you as soon as I straighten out this money situation.

Love, Dad

"Don't you see?!" Amy said, her tone almost pleading. "My dad was arguing with someone over money. That sounds serious!"

"You father didn't use the word *argue*," Eddie reasoned.

"He wrote 'straighten out this money situation'—that sounds like an argument to me!"

"Grown-ups often have discussions about money," Eddie countered. "That's not unusual, Amy."

"But you didn't even know about this, did you, Officer? Not until I showed you my dad's text."

Eddie's stiff expression told me this bright girl was right.

"And what about the footage from the university parking lot?" she went on.

"What footage?" I asked.

"In the police electronic file on my dad, I found this security camera footage of my dad arguing with someone." She held up her phone. The girl had taken a video of the police tape. "Who is that man? I can't see his face, and you came out and stopped us before I could—"

"That man is another teacher from the university," Eddie said, "and we've already spoken with him. His name is Professor Parker—"

Brainert? That surprised me. *He never mentioned having a fight with Kevin on the night the man died.*

"Dr. Parker already told me about their discussion," Eddie continued. "Your father wanted him to get a bite to eat, but Dr. Parker had to grade papers and couldn't join him. If you were to watch all the footage, you would see that your father and Professor Parker drove off in different directions. Dr. Parker went home—"

"And Dad got killed on the highway."

"Sometimes accidents happen," Eddie said.

Amy squeezed her eyes shut. Then she looked down, her long curls falling forward to cover her face. "My dad said we were going to be together. A whole week of fun. He promised . . ."

I knelt and gently pushed back Amy's curtain of hair. Her eyes were filled with tears again, big ones, real ones.

"Do you want to go somewhere and talk, honey? I know you enjoyed the church service on Sunday. Would you like to speak with Reverend Waterman again?"

Amy shook her head and wiped her eyes. "The reverend was nice enough to me, but if it's okay with you, I'd rather go to the cemetery and talk to my dad."

That I understood. "Sure, honey. I'll take you there."

CHAPTER 29

Something to Do with Death

Perhaps the mourners learn to look to the blue sky by
day, and to the stars by night, and to think that the
dead are there, and not in graves.

—Charles Dickens, *The Old Curiosity Shop*, 1841

QUINDICOTT CEMETERY, "OLD Q" to longtime resi-
dents, dated back to the founding of the town itself. Some
of the earliest tombstones, scattered among the twisted
trees of the ancient section, displayed dates from the early
1700s.

The early generations of the town's settlers like the Mc-
Clures, the Hudsons, the Lodges, and the Smiths were buried here—though the more recent dead from these families
were interred in splendid Newport mausoleums.

Less prominent inhabitants included Aunt Sadie's father;
my mother; my older brother, Pete; and my own dear dad.

The most recent arrival at this fateful address was
Amy's father, Dr. Kevin Ridgeway, his grave next to those
of his mother, father, and grandparents. Still just a grassless
mound, surrounded by a sea of lush green, the scent of
fresh-turned earth was strong. No tombstone yet marked

the man's final resting place. The ground was too soft to set it. Only a metal marker shined dully in the bright autumn sun.

Amy walked ahead and stood silently beside the grave. Though the day was clear, the birds were quiet, the only sound a rustling of alder leaves around us.

I wasn't sure what to do, but Spencer knew. He told me to leave them alone for a while, that he would come find me when they were done. Then he hurried forward to join his friend.

I watched from a distance as Amy and Spencer stood side by side, unspeaking. Then Spencer took her hand, and they began to talk.

I was touched by Spencer's tenderness toward his friend. I was proud of him, too. But as I moved away to give them privacy, a disquieting feeling rose up; not jealousy, exactly, but something like it.

My son was whispering secret things to a female that wasn't me. Spencer was still a child, of course, and would need his mother for years. But one day, he'd find her, the love of his life, a soul mate. And I would be left alone.

That dreadful, awful feeling of losing a life entwined with yours was far from new to me. Only a few rows beyond, my entire family was buried under another alder tree. I'd lost my mother when I was close to Spencer's age. Then I lost my older brother and finally my father. As I walked toward the site, I heard a strange sound—and then I saw a man, partially hidden behind the wide trunk of a century-old oak.

The man stood among the gravestones, in front of a painter's easel, his thick legs braced, his beefy arm slashing violently, intently splashing color onto canvas.

With a start, I realized I knew him. Whitman Brink, a regular customer at Buy the Book, and, according to Eddie, Emma Hudson's downstairs neighbor.

Mr. Brink was a large man, not as paunchy as Chief Ciders, but tall and thick around the middle. His skin had good color from painting outdoors every day, but the deep wrinkles in his fleshy face seemed to mark every one of his seventy-plus years.

"Hello there, Mr. Brink!"

"Mrs. McClure? What are you doing in this solemn place? Surely you're not delivering the new Dennis Lehane I ordered?"

"That's not coming out until next week. Actually, I came to visit my family. They're buried right over there." I pointed out the spot.

With a nod, he said, "My own family is interred here, too. Wife and daughter, side by side, with a plot waiting for me."

I followed his gaze to a pair of simple tombstones. "Your wife had a beautiful name . . . Lydia—"

"And my daughter was Lillian."

I read the dates. Mr. Brink's wife had died just seven years after his daughter. "Lillian was only thirteen?"

"She died of leukemia," he said with a curt nod.

I'd never looked closely at Mr. Brink's clothing before. When we spoke, my focus tended to be on his animated blue eyes or neatly trimmed gray goatee. With Eddie's revelation of his address, however, I noticed the fraying of the collar and cuffs on his rugby shirt, the worn state of his khaki pants, and the cracked and scuffed leather of his deck shoes.

"I've lost the light," Brink said. Glancing at the sky, he scanned the western horizon. "Guess I should pack it in and head home."

"And home is 1919 Pine Tree Avenue, right?"

"Not for much longer. I'll soon be moving from that distressed address to the Estates, the gated community on Larchmont Avenue. A long time ago, my wife and I had a home up there, and I so loved the hills."

"That's good news for you. You must have sold quite a few paintings to afford such an exclusive address."

He chuckled. "My paintings are good but far from fetching a small fortune. No, this windfall came from a publishing venture, Mrs. McClure. I can't say more now, but there will be an announcement soon."

"A publishing venture?" My curiosity was more than piqued. "You can't give me a hint? Is it a thriller or maybe a crime novel?"

"Sadly, though I attempted it at one time, I will never be the new Tom Clancy, or a neo-noir sensation like James Ellroy. But at my age, you take your literary success where you can find it."

"Will I be seeing the book soon?" I pressed. "Or is it published already? As a local author, Sadie and I would be happy to arrange a signing."

He put his index finger to his lips. "I can't say. Not yet."

I did my best to keep a calm face, but inside alarm bells were clanging. *Could Whitman Brink be the mysterious author I've been searching for?*

Brink began folding up his easel, and I helped gather his things.

My next line of questioning would be tricky, and I'd have to sound casual. "I heard there was a death at your address the other day—"

"God, yes. It was awful," Brink said, shaking his head. "Poor Emma."

"You knew her?"

"One of the fallen."

"Excuse me?"

"Emma had fallen on hard times, as I had. We met at the Laundromat across the street from the senior center and shared our tales of woe. I found her to be an interesting woman."

"Did you speak with her recently?"

"The day she died. I was supposed to have dinner with her that very evening, but when I got home late that afternoon, I learned the terrible news—"

"But you'd already delivered baked goods for the meal, hadn't you? Cinnamon buns and baguettes from Cooper Family Bakery, right?"

Mr. Brink's jovial expression clouded. "Are you psychic, Mrs. McClure? Or just nosy?"

"I'm sorry, but I was the one who found Emma. She'd visited my bookshop, and a certain book, a big bestseller, disturbed her terribly. I was concerned, so I drove to her apartment to check on her. That's when I found her body."

"She was disturbed?" Brink said, confused. "By a book, you say? How odd! Emma always seemed so rational. But she *did* commit suicide, so perhaps I didn't know her as well as I thought."

"So you don't think it was an accident?"

"You mean that baloney in the local paper? The house at Pine Tree may look like a dump, but it's not a hazard. I saw with my own eyes that Emma's balcony and railing are still intact."

We'd reached Brink's car—not the "jalopy" his landlord described, but a brand-new Lincoln Continental with a Stuckley Motors license plate frame. When he popped the trunk to load up the easel, I spied a catalog for the St. Francis University Adult Education Program.

"I see you attend St. Francis."

"Three courses in the Political Science Department last year, back when I still dreamed of writing a hit thriller." He chuckled again, but it sounded hollow. "Oh well. Life certainly can throw us curves. This semester I may have to take a course on money management."

Political Science at St. Francis University?

"I knew a Professor Kevin Ridgeway who taught in that department. Did you—?"

"Professor Ridgeway was a wonderful teacher. I thoroughly enjoyed his course examining the causes of the Cold War. The geopolitical tensions are still with us. In fact . . ."

Mr. Brink knew Professor Ridgeway! My heart beat faster with the revelation. *Jack, did you hear that? Jack?!*

I listened with anticipation for that gruff, cynical voice in my head, the one who helped me process facts and evidence, point me in the right direction, and come up with a plan of action.

But Jack wasn't with me. I'd left him behind.

"Hey, Mom!" Spencer called. "We're ready to go when you are. Mom?"

"Mrs. McClure? Your son and his young lady friend are here."

"Oh, yes," I said, blinking back my focus—in more ways than one. "It's been nice talking with you, Mr. Brink. Do drop by the store."

"I'll be there Wednesday. For Dr. Leeds's lecture."

"Right. See you then!"

CHAPTER 30

A Nickel for Your Thoughts

Find a place inside where there's joy, and the joy will burn out the pain.

—Joseph Campbell

OH, SO NOW you want my help?

Several hours later, Jack's tone was understandably peeved. When he finally awoke from his slumber, he found his Buffalo nickel on my dresser, and me vamoosed without it—and him.

You gonna tell me why?

"Why I left you behind?" I asked, pulling my car onto Cranberry Street.

I'm a gumshoe, sweetheart. I think I can guess that.

"Then you want to know why I came back for you?"

To be precise, after driving back from Boston, it was the Buffalo nickel I'd returned for, the same coin now cozily tucked in its little silk purse, and pinned once again to my underthings.

"It's because I missed you."

Of course you missed me! I know you by now, baby, better than you know yourself. My question is about our case.

*You remember? The dame who took a nosedive off her pet-
rified balcony? Where are you driving us?*

"1919 Pine Tree Avenue."

The scene of the crime.

"Close."

I need more than one piece of the puzzle, doll.

With Jack back on the case again, I took the length of
our drive to paint him the bigger picture . . .

A FEW HOURS ago, I'd made the trip up to Boston with
Spencer and Amy in the back seat. The traffic was light,
and the kids behaved. Unfortunately, that was where my
luck ran out.

No matter how much I argued, reasoned, and (as frustration set in) begged and pleaded with the seminar director,
he refused to allow Spencer and Amy to return to campus
for the remainder of the program.

"If it were up to me alone, Mrs. McClure, I'd acquiesce.
Amy is an especially brilliant student, and the loss of her
father is certainly a mitigating circumstance. But the rules
are in place for legal reasons. Truancy at their age is serious
business. If your son and Amy had gotten hurt or worse,
our program would have faced heavy liabilities. Sorry. My
hands are tied."

A student assistant supervised Amy and Spencer as they
packed up their belongings. Then, after a bite to eat at Spike's
Junkyard Dogs (Amy's idea since they were her dad's favorite), we piled back into my car.

By the time we were heading south to Quindicott, I realized I wasn't all that upset about the situation. There was
nothing more to be done, so why agonize over it? In the
end, I came around to Jack's way of thinking.

For weeks, Spencer had been looking forward to the
seminar. He'd given up a lot to stand by his friend, and I
knew why after overhearing some of the things he told her.
The loss of his own father was something that still pained

Spencer, and I realized that helping Amy through her grief was also helping my son.

I knew something about a child's grief, too, and it wasn't easily assuaged by grown-up rituals—formal prayers and services; carnations and flowers; verses of poetry and handfuls of dirt. A child's loss was more basic, and I hoped we were taking good enough care of Amy.

I thought about her day, visiting her dad's grave, laughing over memories of her father at Spike's Junkyard Dogs—not unlike a wake—and now relaxing and laughing with a trusted friend.

That seemed like pretty good grief therapy to me.

Still, I hoped to find some time to speak with the girl alone, about her loss.

That very loss—her father's tragic "accident" by the side of a road, with no car trouble and no witnesses—concerned me for another reason, and I planned to discuss it with Deputy Chief Franzetti when I got back to Quindicott.

As it turned out, I didn't have to wait that long.

During a bathroom break at a roadside McDonald's, I found a text from Eddie on my mobile:

Hudson's alibi solid.

Checked it out myself.

As the kids shared an order of fries (at Amy's special request) and played digital games on their phones, I stepped outside for privacy and quickly called my friend with the badge.

Eddie confirmed that Philip Hudson was in Providence at the time of his wife's death. The proof was produced by his lawyer, along with a statement apologizing to Eddie and the Quindicott PD. Hudson claimed his lie about being in New York City was a *protective* measure.

"My client wishes his business in Providence to remain private," the lawyer told Eddie. "If you need anything else from Mr. Hudson, you'll have to request it through me, thank you."

"And you believe all that?"

"When in doubt, verify," Eddie said. "So, I called the Providence Hilton, where Philip Hudson supposedly stayed. It's all confirmed, Pen, including security camera footage. Hudson spent the night and checked out around the time you called the chief to report his ex-wife's death. He couldn't have killed her."

"By now, Eddie, I'm not all that surprised."

"Why? You seemed so sure."

"Evidence is mounting against another suspect, as painful as it is for me to admit. I have someone else in mind."

"Anyone I know?" he asked warily.

"Whitman Brink."

"Whit? The nice old guy who sells watercolors at flea markets? Pen, please don't tell me you want me to charge him over a couple of baguettes and a box of cinnamon buns."

"Hear me out, please? I have good reasons to suspect Brink."

I told Eddie about my conversation with the man at the cemetery; his familiarity with Emma; and his appointment for dinner that night.

I *also* informed Eddie that Brink took courses taught by Kevin Ridgeway, who I now suspected was also involved in writing *Shades of Leather.*

"I think they collaborated on the book. It adds up with Mr. Brink's newfound wealth—and Professor Ridgeway's at the very same time. At the cemetery, I saw Mr. Brink's expensive new car. He told me he's moving to that luxury gated community on Larchmont. Where did that money come from?"

"Did he *say* where it came from?"

"A publishing venture."

"And you believe that venture is cowriting *Shades of Leather*?"

I quickly reminded Eddie what happened in my bookstore just hours before Emma's death. "She completely flipped out when she saw Jessica Swindell's author photo. She claimed it was a photo of herself. Eddie, what if it was? What if her downstairs neighbor, Whitman Brink, fell in love with that sexy vintage photo, thinking it was the perfect way to help sell Jessica Swindell to the public? What if he snatched it when she wasn't looking?"

Eddie took a breath. "You know what I'm going to ask next, right?"

"Right. How do we prove all this?"

"Exactly." At the other end of the line, I heard a police radio squawking about a jackknifed trailer on 95. "When you have that figured out, give me a call back."

CHAPTER 31

Ready, Player Three

We didn't lose the game; we just ran out of time.

—Vince Lombardi

THE REST OF the drive home, I pondered Eddie's question. I had no answers. And with no lucky nickel, I had no ghost to help me come up with any.

Back at the bookstore, I followed Spencer and Amy upstairs.

"Wow, look at that!"

As I moved to the bedroom to change into more comfortable shoes, I heard Spencer marveling at something in the living room.

"What's going on?" I asked.

He pointed at the TV. "My *Avenging Angel* game. I know I shut it down before we left."

"He did." Amy nodded vigorously. "I saw him, Mrs. McClure."

"But we found it this way—" Spencer pointed in awe.

"So it turned itself on?" I didn't see the big deal.

"It did more than that!" Amy adjusted her glasses and studied the screen. "*Avenging Angel* has ten levels. Spencer hasn't been able to get beyond Level Three. And I barely made Level Five. This game appears to have *played itself* up to Level Nine!"

Spencer scratched his head. "Do you think Aunt Sadie was playing while we were gone? That must be it. I never knew she liked video games—or she'd be so good at it!"

"Look!" Amy toggled the images on the screen. "There's another player's name entered, after Spencer's and mine."

Uh-oh, I thought. "What's the name of the third player?"

"P. Dick," Spencer read. "Who's that?!"

"Must be a joke!" I said, my voice reaching dog-whistle pitch. "You know Aunt Sadie. She enjoys those private detective stories! You kids get settled in. I'll be back shortly."

Downstairs, I brought Sadie up to date on our truancy situation. Spencer would need to go back to school tomorrow. And Amy would be here with us through Friday.

I'd already rung Amy's mom to inform her of the seminar's decision to deny Amy and Spencer's readmittance. (Miracle of miracles, the woman actually answered her phone when I called.) She was distraught when I explained the situation. But her stress changed to relief when I offered to take care of her daughter until the girl's au pair returned from France.

"So glad I won't have to trouble my parents," the woman said. "They're busy closing the summer house in Nova Scotia. Amy told me she likes being with you and your son, and Gustav and I won't be back in the States until the weekend—impossible to change plans, you understand."

She also informed me that she would now be able to keep in "closer touch" with Amy and me since she and her new husband were leaving the digital detox resort in Sardinia and heading to a private villa they'd rented in Costa Brava. Then she hung up.

I would quickly learn that "keeping in touch" meant texting lists of instructions on Amy's dietary guidelines and rules of behavior.

I'd no sooner explained as much to Sadie when a new text popped into my phone from Amy's mother: yet another list of restrictions for her daughter.

On top of no sugar, no gluten, and only organic produce (which she texted me on the drive back from Boston), she now added no video games.

When she sent that first set of rules (the dietary restrictions), I worriedly consulted Amy. The girl sighed with the maturity of a jaded grad student.

"Oh, Mrs. McClure, I'm so sorry you're being bothered by all that nonsense. I'm not diabetic or gluten intolerant, and I don't give a fig if my figs are organic! My au pair and I never follow those rules. Honestly, neither does my mother." She checked her watch and pursed her lips, calculating the time zone difference. "She's probably sucking down a plate of seafood pasta as I speak—with a giant helping of tiramisu for dessert. It's her favorite."

"I see . . ."

My conclusion? For the short time that the precocious Amy Ridgeway was under my supervision—and her mother was self-servingly out of the picture—my rules would be the ones she lived by.

Sadie agreed, and I added a decision about how she should spend her time with us.

"I don't feel comfortable sending Amy to school with Spencer. I don't know how she'll get along with the kids or the teachers, and she's still in a delicate state. I think we should keep an eye on the girl here."

"Good idea," Sadie said, and she had an even better one. For the rest of the week, Amy was going to attend "Bookshop School." "How many kids have the chance to learn how a business like ours works?"

"So we're going to put her to work?"

"And teach her a thing or two!" Sadie nodded. "That's how I learned the business from my father."

Of course! I smiled my agreement. Given Amy's smarts, I figured she'd be able to run the place solo after a few days, and by Friday our computers were sure to have open-source software upgrades.

Finally, I told Sadie that I needed to run an errand.

"It won't take long."

"Go," she said. "I'll cover part of your afternoon shift."

"Oh! One last thing. Don't fall for the kids' joke on you."

"What joke is that?"

"They're going to pretend you played their *Avenging Angel* game while we were out. You know kids—they enjoy little pranks."

"Sounds like a hoot," Sadie said with a wave. "I'll play along."

With a sigh of relief, I headed out to the car. This time, I left the kids and took Jack's Buffalo nickel.

"SO, WHAT DO you think?" I asked the ghost.

I think that fancy kiddie game is too easy. The thugs are all right, but there's no racetrack or proper gin mills—

"Not the video game! The Emma Hudson case! And what were you thinking playing the kids' game, anyway?"

Hey, a guy's gotta do something to occupy his afterlife.

"Well, now you have a murder case to challenge you. So tell me. What's our next move? How do we prove my theory about Mr. Brink?"

Simple, doll. That's kid stuff, too. Call back your copper friend. The two of you show up at the old guy's apartment, all innocent like. You pretend you're only there to find out more about the dead woman. While the copper distracts the geezer with questions, you look around his place—real casual like—for evidence.

"What evidence exactly?"

Didn't you tell your Brainiac friend that early copies of that potboiler were hard to come by?

"Jack, you're a genius! If I see a first printing copy—or better yet multiple copies like Ridgeway had—I can rattle him with questions!"

Now you're cookin', doll! Apply some pressure to squeeze out the truth. With the copper's help and a little luck, the old man will break down and confess.

* * *

"IT'S WORTH A try," Eddie said, after I pulled the car over to call him with "my" plan.

"Really?" I said with happy relief. "You're game?"

"Why not? I talked to the medical examiner's office earlier today. He's dragging his heels getting the autopsy report to us. Some kind of complication. So I might as well follow up on any lead I can get. Anyway, if Brink knew Emma that well, maybe he can provide more background for the file."

"Great. I'll meet you at the house on Pine Tree Avenue."

And when you go inside, doll, don't forget the nickel!

CHAPTER 32

Sally Snoops Among the Shelves

When you get older, keeping the private stuff private
seems less important.

—Lawrence Block

"MRS. MCCLURE? OFFICER Franzetti! To what do I owe
the pleasure?"

Despite his polite greeting, Whitman Brink appeared
anything but happy to find the law at his door. With a tense
smile, he pulled at the edges of his open flannel shirt, trying to hide the paint-spattered tee underneath. But the
frayed flannel was too tight around his middle to button, so
he tugged on his sweatpants in a fruitless attempt to hide
the holes in both knees.

Poor old guy, Jack muttered. *Looks like he's one step up
from skid row. I've seen bums go down that ladder too
many times.*

Well, pay attention, I told the gumshoe, *because Whitman Brink has reversed direction—and he might have
killed his upstairs neighbor to keep the gravy train on
track.*

"May we come in, Mr. Brink?" Eddie asked. "I'd like to
speak with you about Emma Hudson."

Reluctantly, Brink stepped aside.

Yowza! Jack cried. *Forget what I said about being one step above skid row. He's there. Even I'd commit murder to get out of this dump!*

"Sorry for the mess," Brink said. "I'm moving in a few weeks, and the place is in chaos."

True, there were boxes scattered about. But it was clear from his reddening cheeks the man was more embarrassed by the peeling wallpaper and stained carpeting. Even the furniture looked like it came from the estate of Miss Havisham.

"Let me move those," Brink said, shifting a stack of watercolor canvases from the couch to a threadbare throw rug.

"Please, sit. Can I get you anything? Coffee, perhaps?"

"Nothing, thanks." Eddie sank so deep into the sagging couch I feared he'd disappear.

I remained standing. While Eddie distracted Brink by peppering him with questions, I hunted for those first edition copies of *Shades of Leather*.

It was no easy task. Despite the shabby surroundings, Brink had a fine collection of books. It appeared he spent the bulk of any social security checks on reading matter. Hundreds of hardcovers, in mint condition, packed the shaky shelving in his cluttered living room.

As I scanned the titles, Eddie continued with his questions—

"You were supposed to have dinner with Emma the day she died."

"That's right. Emma and a friend."

"A friend? So, this wasn't a *romantic* dinner?"

Brink laughed. "Certainly not. Emma was an interesting woman, but we had little in common. Emma wished to introduce me to her friend because, like me, she was a booklover."

"But you never met this other woman?"

"I never even found out her name."

Unplug those ears, doll. The geezer just mentioned a mysterious dame.

*I heard, Jack, but I'm more interested in finding proof
that Brink is the mysterious dame named Jessica Swindell!*

I hit the third wall before I located a copy of *Shades of
Leather*. At last! I quickly pulled the bestseller down and
flipped to the copyright page. Holding my breath, I scanned
the tiny parade of numbers. When I saw the 6 at the end, my
hopes deflated.

This edition wasn't a first printing; it was a sixth. And
the bookmark inside, promoting Professor Leeds's upcoming appearance at our store, meant Mr. Brink bought it at
Buy the Book.

If Brink had free author's copies sent from the publisher,
he wouldn't have wasted money on purchasing one.

I released a frustrated sigh. So far, the only thing I discovered on this trip was what I already knew: Mr. Brink
was a loyal customer.

Meanwhile, Eddie continued his questioning. "Did you
ever meet Emma Hudson's ex-husband?"

"Once, in passing. Philip seemed like a decent chap."

A decent chap?! Jack boomed. *Sure, if you're partial to
a degenerate boozehound and Ollie the Octopus wrapped
up in one cuddly ball.*

Quiet, Jack, I'm listening.

"Did Mrs. Hudson feel that her ex-husband was a decent
chap?"

"She seemed fond of him. But she told me she'd grown
impatient with his overindulgence in alcohol and reckless
business ventures."

Eddie made a noise, like a low grunt, and I knew he was
considering my warning about Philp Hudson's possible involvement with the mob.

"What sort of business ventures did Mr. Hudson pursue?
Do you know?"

"Let me see . . ." Mr. Brink stroked his gray goatee.
"Emma mentioned he opened a surf shop when they lived
in Venice Beach. Then there was a mountain bike rental
company. After that he invested in a bungee jumping op-

eration and a water park start-up that never materialized due to California's drought."

"Not very lucky, was he?"

Mr. Brink shrugged. "From what Emma told me, these ventures were mostly financed by her money, and every one of them failed. In the end, she grew weary of Philip and suggested, when they moved east, that they go their separate ways . . ."

As Mr. Brink continued answering Eddie's questions, I froze solid, in complete shock. Housed here on these shaky old bookshelves was a pristine collection dedicated to the yellow-haired, big-glasses icon of my childhood, *Sally Snoops and Her Curious Kitty* by beloved author Patti Jo Penrod.

Before anyone had heard of *Goosebumps*, the "spooky, kooky *Sally Snoops*" completely dominated the children's book trade.

I started reading the series near the end of its run, as a little girl. I cherished each adventure, and bought or borrowed every one I could lay my hands on. But soon they just disappeared—the first loss of many I would experience as a child.

Even today, the *Sally Snoops* books were difficult to find. Neither Sadie nor I had ever come across a complete set. Now, here I stood, staring at an entire shelf packed with *multiple* copies of all seventy-six titles!

Stop gaping at the pretty paper and pay attention! Jack cried.

Okay, okay!

"Your landlord told me you were out painting when Mrs. Hudson died," Eddie was saying. "Is that correct?"

"Actually, no. I was with a Mr. Clark, over at Stuckley Motors, from about ten in the morning until late afternoon. I took my time at the lot. Over lunch, we discussed financing, but I decided to pay cash."

Eddie raised an eyebrow. "Cash? For a used car?"

"Cash for a brand-new car. I've come into some money, you see."

"From what, may I ask?"

Brink stiffened, his tone turning indignant. "I'm sorry, Officer, but I don't see how my finances are pertinent to your investigation. I'm happy to help you with what I know about Emma Hudson and her life, but the business of my own is none of yours."

Hey, dollface, Jack snapped. *You payin' attention? Mr. Brink is on the brink of tossing the copper out. You better step up your dance before this melody ends.*

Jack was right. I saw no other copies of *Shades of Leather*, not in this room, anyway. I would have to think fast, find a way to lead the man back to a friendlier frame of mind. Remembering our chat at the cemetery, I pointed to the *Sally Snoops* books.

"Excuse me for interrupting, Mr. Brink, but may I ask you about this wonderful collection?"

Still frowning, Mr. Brink dragged his angry blue gaze away from Eddie. "What do you wish to know?"

"Did these *Sally Snoops* books belong to your daughter?"

At the mention of his lost child, Mr. Brink's harsh expression softened. "In a way, Mrs. McClure, I wrote them to entertain my daughter during her long illness."

"You mean you *read* them to entertain her."

"No. I wrote them."

CHAPTER 33

Ghostwriter

An idea, like a ghost, must be spoken to a little before
it will explain itself.

—Charles Dickens

I WAS CERTAIN I'd misheard the man. Either that or my
elderly customer was delusional. So I tried again—

"Mr. Brink, surely you're not telling me that *you* are the
author of *Sally Snoops and Her Curious Kitty*?"

"All seventy-six titles, Mrs. McClure, plus two that were
never published."

"I always thought a woman wrote them."

"Of course you did. Everyone did. That was by design."

"You mean there isn't a real Patti Jo Penrod?" *The man
really must be delusional*, I told Jack. *I know very well
there was!*

"Miss Penrod was an elderly secretary at my series' publishing house. She posed as the author for personal appearances. I allowed that ruse because the royalties were high.
And my daughter required almost constant care, so there
was no way I could write the books and promote them, too."

As he spoke, he rose to retrieve two items, a framed
photo and a polished wooden plaque. The frame held a pic-

ture of Mr. Brink in a tux, sitting beside Miss Penrod at a formal ceremony. The plaque was a children's book award for one of my favorite *Sally Snoops* adventures: *The Disappearing Dinosaur Bones.*

"I'm very proud of this award. I consulted with paleontologist Bob Bakker to get the details right. Good man. He advised the artist, too."

Finally, I believed him.

Mr. Whitman Brink, one of my most unassuming customers, was the beloved creator of one of my favorite story characters from childhood. *Jack, I wish you were more than a ghost, so you could pick me up off the floor!*

With almost little-girl excitement, I clapped my hands. "Mr. Brink, I have to tell you how much I enjoyed the books you wrote. Sally was like a best friend to me. I absolutely loved her!"

"You and a million other little girls. But there was only one fan I cared about."

"Your daughter."

With a forlorn smile, he nodded. "Lilly was sick for five years. During that time, I wrote one novel every two months—cancer is expensive, you see, and I needed money. But she was enchanted by the stories, and that drove me, too. My Lilly was the first person to read every adventure, and she lived to see thirty of the *Sally Snoops* books published. After she was gone, I kept the series going in her honor. I suppose it was my way of coping with the loss." Mr. Brink paused and swallowed. "The books kept her alive for me a little longer . . ."

Seeing the pain in his expression, I offered my condolences. So did Eddie. "I'm a father, too, sir. I can't imagine going through what you did."

After a respectful pause, I couldn't help asking, "Why did you ever stop writing the books? Was the series canceled?"

Whitman Brink harrumphed. "It was never *canceled*, Mrs. McClure. The books were selling, but the publisher was poorly managed, and the company went bankrupt."

"You didn't try to publish the series elsewhere?"

"I had too many other problems. My wife's grief overwhelmed her. She began to drink and abuse her medications. I tried my best to save her, but she eventually perished from a fatal combination of barbiturates and whiskey."

Exhaling heavily, the big man's shoulders sank.

"The sad truth is I didn't have the rights to those books, or even the character I created. I was desperate for funds and signed a very bad contract. After the company went under, the rights were tied up with the bankruptcy. No one could legally publish *Sally Snoops* for decades, not until now."

"*That's* your publishing venture?"

I closed my eyes with relief. When I opened them again, I exchanged glances with Eddie. He simply shrugged.

"It took me twenty-five years, but now the rights to all the *Sally Snoops* belong to me. Academy Books, the big children's publisher, is reprinting the originals, along with the two unpublished works, and I'm writing new adventures starting next year."

Cri-ma-nee! Jack groused. *This burg is full of scribblers. How is it you can't finger the right one?*

Me? What about you? I challenged. *You're the professional!*

Try to remember that the next time you want to leave me at home playing kiddie games. You better make sure I tag along from now on, Penny, or you're liable to forget your own name.

"As I said before, Mrs. McClure, I'm far from the new Tom Clancy, but at my age I take literary fame where I find it." Brink put his index finger to his lips. "Please. Tell no one. Academy plans an official announcement very soon, and I don't wish to steal their thunder. That's why I was so reticent to speak about it at the cemetery."

There was an irony here that Jack appreciated. I arrived suspecting Whitman Brink of murder. Now I was offering the man my sincere congratulations, and gushing about his work like a complete fangirl.

Serves you right for suspecting this dignified old gent.

Really, Jack, now he's a "gent"? That's a far cry from your "geezer" ready for "skid row."

That's because I no longer suspect the man of tossing a dame off a balcony.

Well, I couldn't be happier to be wrong. Though now I'm out of suspects.

Jack laughed. *People are no good. You'll never run out of suspects.*

Before I said good-bye to Mr. Brink, I made a point of inviting him to appear at Buy the Book for a special talk and signing, whenever his new *Sally Snoops* books became available.

"Really, Mrs. McClure? You think people around here will show up to hear me speak—and sign kiddie books?"

"I absolutely do!"

"You know, I attend all your author events . . ." Emotion entered Mr. Brink's deep voice, and his bright blue eyes began to glisten. "For a time, your bookshop was about the only thing keeping this lonely old man from sitting at home and staring at walls."

"Sadie and I always appreciate seeing you at our store. And we'd be honored to host your appearance."

"Goodness, Mrs. McClure, you overwhelm me . . ." Pausing to look away, he deftly swiped a tear. "I assure you, the honor will be mine."

OUTSIDE AGAIN, IN the brisk, fresh air, I said good-bye to Officer Franzetti, apologizing the whole time.

"Don't worry about it," Eddie said, before driving off. "That's police work, lots of dead ends—and, hey, I did get some good background for the file."

I was about to start my own car when my phone vibrated. I tensed, fearing it was *another* text from Amy's mother, who managed to be both an absentee and a helicopter parent.

With relief, I saw this message was from Seymour Tarnish.

Congrats, Pen U were correct!

The author of *Shades of Leather* is a local, and I know who. Someone we both know.

For once I was ahead of Seymour—no mean feat, considering our postman was locally famous for being a past champion on *Jeopardy!*

Though Mr. Brink turned out to be a "dead end," as Eddie put it, the evidence still held up for Professor Ridgeway's involvement, given the first editions of *Shades* in his possession and the text message he'd sent to his daughter before his death. I only hoped Seymour found a way to prove it.

With a feeling of reassurance about this new development—and a literary one, at that—I headed back to my bookshop.

CHAPTER 34

Call to Order

Big Brother is watching . . . look busy.

—Brandon Boyd

THAT EVENING, BUD Napp banged the ball-peen hammer he used as a gavel, calling to order the official meeting of the Quindicott Business Owners Association.

I always thought of Bud as an even-tempered man, but tonight the lanky hardware store owner slammed the tool with enough force to threaten the collapse of the folding table Sadie had set up for the officers.

Beside him at the shaky dais, Fiona Finch primly stood and began reading the minutes of our last meeting. She didn't get far before Bud cut her off—

"Our first and only order of business is that confounded Big Brother security system that's bleeding us dry!"

Loud applause filled our Community Events space. Tonight's meeting was packed, much larger than our usual gathering. But the situation was dire, the stakes high. Bud himself characterized tonight's assembly as "a first step in the liberation of the town's business community from regulatory oppression!"

Of course, we were all aware that Bud was politicking—

part of his campaign to unseat Councilwoman Marjorie Binder-Smith—and he'd certainly chosen a popular cause.

Since the installation of the sidewalk security system, most of the merchants on Cranberry Street had been fined, for one infraction or another. Now the business owners took turns rising to voice complaints against Usher Security, the city council, and the local police.

In the middle of Dan Donovan's tale of a broken bottle that led to a costly citation for "a hazardous sidewalk condition," my ghost blew up.

Mother Machree! When are these clodhoppers going to stop jawboning around the cracker barrel? We need to address the serious business of murder!

The entire roomed shivered with Jack's frigid blast.

"Sadie, can you please turn up the heat?" someone called.

"It's a drafty room, and that's that," she shot back.

Bud winked at his girl. "We're New Englanders! We can take it!"

I gritted my teeth—to keep them from chattering. *Jack, will you please turn down the deep freeze? My lips are turning blue.*

Your pretty lips are the only reason I'm sticking around.

There's more reason than that, and you know it. I already told you, after this big meeting is over, a smaller group is staying behind to discuss the death of Emma Hudson . . .

Before the meeting, I'd sent out texts to the core Quibblers and asked them to stay late for a short session of literary detection. When I mentioned the subject was *Shades of Leather*, most responded with unprecedented enthusiasm. And Seymour was thrilled to learn he'd have a sizable audience for what he felt was a huge announcement.

Okay, the ghost grumbled. *But if I have to listen to these unwashed rubes and chawbacons much longer, I'm scaring this bunch out of this joint and onto Cornpone Street—*

"That's enough!" I said—out loud. *Whoops.*

Linda Cooper-Logan glanced at me strangely. Sheepishly, I displayed my smartphone as if I'd been using it, shook my head, and mouthed the word "kids."

She nodded knowingly.

Thirty minutes later, J. Brainert Parker arrived. Fresh from his Faculty Affairs Committee meeting, he was dressed in his usual preppy finery. Just as I'd noticed on Saturday, his tasteful, tailored clothes were hanging off his waning physique—and my worries about my old friend surfaced again.

From his spot many seats away, Seymour noticed the professor's arrival, but he didn't appear worried. The expression on his grinning face was pure excitement. He even shot me a double thumbs-up.

You still there, Jack? I asked, checking my watch a short time later.

Am I still awake—that's the question!

You better be. This business talk is almost over.

Good, said the ghost. *Then we can get down to the business of solving a murder.*

CHAPTER 35

Undercover Hostess

I'm not very good at eavesdropping . . .

—The claim of a witness in *I, the Jury* by Mickey Spillane

BY NINE P.M., the official Quindicott Business Owners Association meeting had broken up, and our unofficial Quibblers roundtable formed.

With another sharp bang of his hardware store hammer, Bud called our post-meeting meeting to order.

More than a dozen members of the larger group had remained behind, pulling up chairs for our literary investigation, including a few whose interest surprised me.

I stood and faced the circle of chairs.

"Some of you may have heard the news—or read a version of it in Elmer's paper—but there was a death on Pine Tree Avenue last Saturday. I'll tell you right now that Elmer got almost every fact wrong. Emma Hudson did not fall from a broken balcony, due to hoarding. The police believe her death was a suicide. But I think it could be murder."

The word *murder* got everyone's attention—everyone, that is, except burly, shaggy-haired Leo Rollins, no-nonsense owner of Rollins Electronics and a decorated veteran of the Iraq War.

"Hey, what gives? I thought this discussion was going to be about that steamy new bestseller *Shades of Leather*, not the Pine Tree Avenue version of *Sally Snoops and Her Curious Kitty*."

"What's wrong with *Sally Snoops*?" Linda Cooper-Logan demanded. "I loved those books."

"Yeah. When you were nine," Leo said. "I heard *Shades of Leather* is a real *adult* book. That's why I stuck around."

Linda blinked. "You haven't read it?"

Leo put his thick arms behind his head, thrust out his dark blond beard, and sat back in his chair. "I'm waiting for you folks to tell me all about it."

"Then you'll be glad to know this discussion is indeed about *Shades of Leather*," I informed Leo, "because Emma Hudson's death is connected to that book."

Milner Logan looked skeptical. "Now how can that be, Pen?"

"That's why I asked you all here, to help figure it out."

Once again, I shared Emma's story, from the moment she entered my bookshop until she died hours later. I told everyone about her chatty parrot, the vanished copy of *Shades of Leather*, and the missing Yorkie.

Leo shook his shaggy head. "I knew it. *Sally Snoops*."

Ignoring Leo, Fiona Finch's hand shot into the air—just as I hoped it would. Jack said to use gossip to open doors and reveal secrets, and no one was a better conduit of town gossip than the owner of the Finch Inn and its gourmet restaurant. As she rose to speak, Fiona twisted her flamboyant peacock brooch with nervous excitement.

"I heard about Mrs. Hudson the night *before* the story hit the papers!"

Aunt Sadie spoke up. "Joyce Cummins told you, didn't she? Chief Ciders' secretary must have you on speed dial!"

Fiona frowned. "Since they installed the security system, poor Joyce is doing double duty. She's been too busy to chat."

"Yeah, too busy spying on the rest of us," griped Leo Rollins.

"When *did* you find out about this dead woman?" Bud asked.

"On Saturday night, around seven o'clock. The first wave of weekend diners was just arriving when two men from the state police crime scene unit and a gentleman from the medical examiner's office arrived at Chez Finch, without reservations, of course. Fortunately, I was able to seat them at a table near my hostess station."

"Yeah," a smirking Seymour cracked. "That's the one with the microphone. All the other tables at Chez Finch have numbers, but that one's called the Watergate!"

Fiona scowled.

"How did you know who they were?" Bud pressed. "They weren't in lab coats or anything, were they?"

"I'm telling you, she bugged their table!" Seymour insisted. "When it comes to surveillance, the Finch-ster could teach the CIA a thing or two!"

"Don't be ridiculous!" Fiona lifted her chin indignantly. "The reason I *know* is because the man from the medical examiner's office used his departmental credit card to pay for the dinner."

"Oh, wonderful!" Seymour threw up his hands. "A government bureaucrat running wild with an expense account. But I'm sure they were careful, right? Just a quick dinner—with an aperitif. Lillet is nice, but oh, so pricey on your menu. Then there's that bottle of French wine to help choke down all those heavy sauces, followed by dessert and brandy, which goes down so much nicer when you know you're getting behind the wheel of an official government vehicle, instead of your own."

Fiona planted her hands on her hips. "What's your point, mailman?"

"I work for the government, too. Where the heck is *my* expense account?"

Brainert rolled his eyes. "For what? Dr. Scholl's foot powder?"

"Enough!" Bud cried. "Tell us what you heard, Fiona."

"Well, first they complained about being called in to work on a weekend. I heard the ME remark that Chief Ciders wasn't completely convinced the woman killed herself, though it looked that way."

What do you know, Jack? Maybe I got through to the old grouch.

Chief Clown-around acts like a real cop? Will wonders never cease?

"Later, during the main course, the men from the crime scene unit were in a lather over fingerprints."

That caught my interest. "They didn't get enough?"

"They collected *too* many, and from more than one individual. There were two sets, at least. And they found multiple sets in every room. Far too many prints for a casual visitor to leave. When I served their after-dinner drinks—"

"I knew it!" Seymour cried.

"—they wondered if Mrs. Hudson had a houseguest or roommate."

Or a dame-hungry honey-dipper, Jack quipped.

"How about the dog?" I asked. "Did they mention the dog?"

"Not once. I would have heard."

"Because you bugged their table," Seymour insisted.

I'm starting to wonder if those extra mitt prints belong to Phil the Masher, Jack said. *He and Emma wouldn't be the first ex-married couple to reignite the old torch between two hot-sheets.*

Could be, Jack. Philip seemed awfully enthusiastic about that whole tantric sex thing. Then again, Mr. Brink mentioned that Emma had a book-loving friend. He was supposed to meet her over dinner on the day Emma died.

"So," I spoke up, "we have a dead woman with a mysterious friend or roommate—"

Or a randy ex-husband with hot pants.

"—who vanished, just like the stolen copy of *Shades of Leather*, and Emma's dog."

Okay, Perry Mason. You've got the judge and jury all googly-eyed. Time to call your first witness.

Not yet, Jack. There's something else we have to cover before we bring on Seymour.

I opened a box in the corner and passed out copies of the eighth printing of *Shades of Leather*, delivered from the publisher yesterday.

"It was the author photograph on the back of the book that set Emma off," I said. "So, let's take a closer look at that picture."

CHAPTER 36

Every Picture Tells a Story

A photograph is usually looked at—seldom looked into.

—Ansel Adams

WE ALL STUDIED the photo of the lovely young woman with dark hair, a coyly cocked head, and a come-hither expression that appeared as if she couldn't decide whether to look innocently lascivious, or lasciviously innocent.

She appeared to have light-colored eyes under a veil of dark hair, though we all agreed there was no way to be sure, because the photoshopped image had been artfully drained of strong hues, rendering everything in a muted sepia tone.

"This is supposed to look like a vintage photo, but I don't know if it really is one," Leo Rollins said. "It's hip to put filters on photos or selfies. That kind of software is built into some phone apps."

"But what if it really is an old photo?" Seymour countered. "I mean, huge Margaret Keane eyes like that haven't been fashionable since the 1970s."

The woman in the photo wore nothing more than an opaque bedsheet and false eyelashes. Her full lips were painted to form a heart, and the eyebrows had been shaped to complete the wide-eyed "baby doll" look working overtime to convey both naiveté and sensuality.

"No," Fiona said after donning her reading glasses. "This *is* a vintage photograph. I see enough old magazines at flea markets to know. This looks like something out of a late-1960s issue of *Cosmopolitan*."

"It could have been made to give that impression," Linda pointed out.

I looked to Brainert for a comment, but he remained silent, arms folded, angular features locked in a grim expression.

Something was wrong here. This wasn't like Brainert. He always enjoyed giving his opinion, especially when it involved a mystery.

"Let's focus on the eyes," I suggested, trying to stay positive and keep the discussion going. "Camille Paglia once wrote that it doesn't matter whether a Hollywood movie is set in the past, the present, or even the future; you can usually pinpoint the decade it was filmed in by the women's eye makeup. I'm sure the same rule applies to photography."

"This girl's look is very Twiggy," Aunt Sadie said.

Joyce Koh, the teenage daughter of the Korean American man who owned Koh's market, made a face. "She's scrawny, but I wouldn't call her a twig, Ms. Thornton."

Sadie laughed. "No, no, dear. You're too young to remember. Twiggy was a *person*. A fashion model from the 1960s who was famously thin."

"You're right, Ms. Thornton, before my time!"

"Mine, too, thank you very much," Linda said. "But Milner and I did enjoy binge-watching *Mad Men*. It reminded us how cool those times were: the fight for civil rights, the British Invasion, Woodstock, free love—"

Free love? Jack snorted. *That's a giggle. Love never comes free. There's always a cost.*

"It was an ugly time, too," Bud said. "And I'm speaking from experience, not a television show. We had the draft.

The war in Vietnam. The assassinations of JFK, Martin Luther King, Bobby Kennedy."

"That's right." Sadie nodded. "There were riots, drugs everywhere, those Manson murders, chaos on college campuses—"

Best of times, worst of times? Jack quipped. *I think I've heard that one before. I mean, the start of the Great Depression wasn't so bad when you consider Gallant Fox winning the Triple Crown. Then there was the end of Prohibition, a real cackle—the rise of the Nazi Party, not so much.*

"Let's get back to the picture, shall we?" I said, pointing out that there was one more visual clue in the portrait—the odd diamond-shaped window that backlit the subject. I pulled up another photo and sent it to everyone.

"I found this Polaroid in Emma Hudson's apartment. It is so blurry I can't make out the woman's face, but that distinctive window behind her suggests it was taken in the same spot as that author photo. What do you all think?"

"Seems the same to me," Linda said, and Milner nodded.

Fiona loudly cleared her throat. "I probably have the most experience here with architectural integrity. You all know, Barney and I meticulously researched authentic high Victorian colors for our inn—"

"Of course we all know," Seymour muttered. "You've told us a thousand times."

"In my expert opinion, Penelope, it is the same window!"

"What about this date written on the back?" Bud asked. "Does that mean anything?"

"Excellent question!" Seymour stuck his nose in his phone. A moment later he looked up with a grave expression. "On that date in history, the Weather Underground detonated a bomb at the Pentagon in protest of the Vietnam War."

There you go! Jack cracked again. *Best of times, worst of times!*

I gritted my teeth and took a breath. "I think we can dismiss the Weather Underground from this investigation.

What I do know is that this Polaroid is a real vintage picture, and it was in Mrs. Hudson's possession."

Milner scratched his head. "I seem to recall Richard Avedon said his photographic portraits were more about him than they were about his subject. Maybe we should consider what the photographer was trying to say about himself through the author portrait. What was he trying to portray?"

Linda frowned at her husband. "Who said the shutterbug was a man?"

"She's right," Seymour said. "In my opinion, Bunny Yeager was the greatest glamour photographer of all time."

Suddenly, Fiona cried out. "I've got it!"

"What?" I leaned forward. "Do you see a breakthrough clue on the photo?"

"It's obvious, Pen!" She pointed to my copy of *Shades*. "There is always a photo credit on the back cover flap of hardcover books, right under the book designer's credit. Contact the photographer—whether it's a him or her—and you'll have your answers!"

Seymour rolled his eyes. "Oh, for the love of—"

"Excuse me, Tarnish," Fiona huffed. "You have a problem with my idea?"

"Not the idea. The photo credit. Look for yourself."

Seymour passed Fiona his copy of the book. She eagerly flipped to the back flap and frowned. I didn't need to look; I already knew.

"What's it say?" Bud asked.

"*Dead End*, that's what."

"The postman's right." Fiona sighed. Then, as primly as she read our weekly minutes, she shared the words aloud: "Photo by Jessica Swindell."

That news seemed to deflate the room.

"Tell you what," I said. "Let's forget about the photo and focus on the text. Seymour? If you please . . ."

CHAPTER 37

A Flap Over Copy

A good love story always keeps the pot boiling.

—James Patterson

SEYMOUR TARNISH ROSE and faced the group. He'd set his phone aside for a copy of *Shades of Leather*, plumed with multi-colored Post-it notes.

"Pen asked me to give this book a close read with an eye for unmasking the identity of its author. Could it be someone local? Did this person have ties to Emma Hudson—perhaps use an old photo without her permission? These are the questions I kept in mind as I turned page after page after page after—"

"Get on with it!" Bud griped.

You tell him, Gramps! Jack cheered in my head.

"So, you might ask, what is this book about?" Seymour opened to the flap copy. "Minus the publishing hyperbole—okay, maybe a *little* publishing hyperbole—*Shades of Leather* is the story of lovely and innocent Justine, who sells high-end furniture to a rich clientele in an exclusive Manhattan shop.

"Enter a handsome, mysterious, and wealthy customer seeking an Italian leather couch. The charismatic Lyon

Cage quickly ensnares young Justine in his quest for, and I quote, 'perfect leather and much, much more!'

"The enigmatic Mr. Cage purchases one leather couch after another, seducing Justine on each one in new and kinky ways. When each lovemaking session ends, Lyon has that couch hauled away. And Justine is called upon to provide a new one."

This all sounds very . . . uplifting, Jack said with a laugh.

"The final paragraph of the flap copy reads, 'During Justine's erotic journey, she is drawn into a mysterious underworld of crime and corruption. She witnesses puzzling events, encounters sinister and dangerous people, and uncovers a deadly secret that changes her world forever.'"

"Sounds like your standard pulp potboiler," Bud Napp remarked.

"Think so?" Seymour pulled one of the Post-its loose. "Here is what one reviewer had to say, and I quote: 'This novel is chock-full of highly charged eroticism and violence worthy of the Marquis de Sade.'"

"See, they hated it," Bud declared.

"Nope, they loved it. This is a starred review!"

Bud shook his head. "I guess I missed that course in school on appreciation of erotic violence."

"So," Seymour said, dropping the book (all six hundred pages of it) on an empty seat with an echoing thud, "who here has actually read *Shades of Leather*?"

There was a little bit of nervous tittering, and Brainert shifted uncomfortably. Finally, Dan Donavon raised his pink, pudgy hand.

"My wife read me the racy stuff. But I think she was just angling for a new couch."

"I read it," Fiona said. "A young couple stayed at my inn two weeks back. They left behind a well-used copy, and a couch with broken springs. Naturally, I was curious."

"Naturally," Seymour echoed and shot me a glance. "I hope old Barney's holding up better than that couch."

"I heard that," Fiona sniffed. "I'm sorry I mentioned it!"

"Aw, don't be," Milner Logan told her with a wink.

"Linda read it, and it gave her some great ideas. I didn't read it myself, you understand, but watching *Sports Night* on the couch is a whole lot more fun—ouch!"

Linda not so gently elbowed her husband into silence.

"I read one of the couch scenes to Bud," Sadie said with a sly smile. "He was so rattled he needed a second beer."

Ann Schram, the soft-spoken owner of the town's new flower shop, actually spoke up. "I didn't read it, but I will now."

I knew Joyce Koh had read it—she bought her copy at my store. But I understood her reluctance to mention it in front of her conservative father.

"We know Leo Rollins *didn't* read it," Seymour said. "Though it looks like he's reading it now."

"Huh? Were you talking to me?" Leo asked, tearing his eyes away from the open book.

"Of course, *Shades of Leather* isn't that original," Seymour said. "It's basically just a retelling of the French fairy tale 'Bluebeard.'"

"There are other versions of this story?" Linda asked.

"Why? You want to read those, too? I don't think our old couch can take it." Milner's offer was answered by another jab to the ribs.

"There's a German version by the Brothers Grimm," Seymour supplied. "It's called 'The Robber Bridegroom.'"

"That's also the title of a Eudora Welty story," Brainert *finally* offered, his academic instincts overriding his obvious reluctance to speak on this subject. "Welty's story is loosely based on Grimm, but it's set in Mississippi." The professor smiled for the first time that evening, satisfied he'd one-upped his frenemy. "I just thought since *Shades of Leather* is a novel, I would expect a *novelistic* inspiration—not an obscure fairy tale."

Joyce Koh spoke up. "I'm sorry, but I don't get how *Shades of Leather* is like a fairy tale. Can someone explain?"

"Sure, I will!" Seymour said, beating Brainert to the literary lecture. "You see, in 'Bluebeard' there's a magical key and a secret underground chamber filled with dead brides, whereas in *Shades* there's a secret combination to a

Stanley padlock and a backyard burial ground packed with burned-out couches."

Leo Rollins looked up from the book and stroked his beard. "So, this woman rewrote a fairy tale to make it dirty? 'Cause it's *real* dirty."

Seymour ahemmed. "I prefer the term *erotic*, or perhaps *suggestive*—except the writing actually describes what it suggests."

"I'll say." With that, Leo returned to the book.

"There's a little more to *Shades* than trashy salaciousness," Seymour continued. "There are subplots and side stories involving shady characters and weird events."

"You mean the boring plotty parts," Linda said.

"For instance, there's a cabal of international arms dealers and drug traffickers planning a coup in some unnamed Central American country. They throw elaborate Manhattan parties that attract young women like the heroine Justine. There's a jealous suitor who murders his romantic rival before Justine's eyes; not to mention a corrupt politician doing business over the phone with the New England mob while he's literally in bed with the heroine. I won't name names, but that mob character sounds an awful lot like a real-life, now-deceased Mafia don from the 1970s. And, of course, there's Lyon Cage, the enigmatic, couchseducing Bluebeard of the story."

"But all that stuff is kind of dull compared to the main story," Fiona said.

Seymour smirked. "Kind of dull compared to the kinky stuff, you mean?"

"Those sections do seem forced," Sadie agreed. "Almost as if they were part of a different novel. Some moralistic fable about old money, international crime, and political corruption."

"Harold Robbins meets *Fear of Flying*, right? Well, that is my point, which I'll get to in a moment." Seymour paused. "Does anyone remember a novel called *Naked Came the Stranger*?"

Only a grinning Sadie raised her hand.

CHAPTER 38

The Write Stuff

It ain't whatcha write, it's the way atcha write it.

—Jack Kerouac

"*NAKED CAME THE Stranger*? I'd like to read that book!" Joyce Koh cried, ignoring her father's disapproving scowl.

"Not to worry, Mr. Koh," Seymour responded. "Joyce's sentiments would have been right in line with much of the general public at the time. As literary hoaxes go, *Naked Came the Stranger* was bigger than Clifford Irving's faux biography of Howard Hughes, because *Naked* was actually *published*. It even spent thirteen weeks on the *New York Times* bestseller list before the truth was exposed."

Leo Rollins was impressed. "Who was the genius who wrote it?"

"The name on the cover was Penelope Ashe, and that cover was pretty scandalous for 1969. More *Playboy* than Publisher's Row."

"Sounds better and better," Joyce Koh gushed.

"*Naked* tells the tale of a married couple who host a chat show on New York radio. When the wife finds out her husband is having an affair, she goes wild. I mean she turns into a total cougar in heat!"

Fiona groaned. "Must you be so vulgar, Seymour?"

"*Descriptive*, Fiona. I'm being descriptive. Anyway, the jealous wife steps out with a bunch of guys, including a handyman and a mobbed-up crooner who sounds awfully familiar to Rat Pack fans."

Milner shrugged. "And we care because?"

"Because *Naked Came the Stranger* has the same sort of sexy vignettes as *Shades of Leather*, except there aren't any"—Seymour made air quotes—"*boring parts*. You know—subtext, character development, thematic elements—niggling nonsense like that."

Fiona harrumphed. "Someone must have liked the book if it was on the *New York Times* bestseller list."

"Right alongside novels considered classics." Seymour ticked off each title with his fingers: "Mario Puzo's *The Godfather*, *The Andromeda Strain* by Michael Crichton, *Portnoy's Complaint* by Philip Roth, Chaim Potok's *The Promise*—"

"We get it, Seymour." Linda ran her hand through her short platinum hair. "Who is this author again?"

"Penelope Ashe. She made her first public appearance on *The David Frost Show* in 1969. Following an introduction by Frost, the curtain parted and two dozen staffers from the Long Island *Newsday* walked onto the stage."

"There's no Penelope Ashe?" Joyce said, disappointed.

"The author was portrayed by the sister-in-law of one of the writers for meetings with the publisher, but the story was written in round-robin fashion by a bunch of *Newsday* reporters led by a guy named Mike McGrady. They went on Frost's show to confess that the hottest read of the year was an elaborate practical joke."

"Why go to all that trouble?" Joyce asked.

"Because they made lots of money, silly girl," her father barked.

"They did," Seymour agreed. "But they had another motive, too. The hoaxers were determined to write the most steamy and mindless book possible, and make it a rousing success. They were out to prove that America's literary taste was in the toilet."

"How did *they* make it a rousing success?" I asked.

Seymour shrugged. "They worked in media. Maybe they used the tricks dreamed up by talk show host Jean Shepherd for his 1950s literary hoax, *I, Libertine.*"

Hah, it figures at least one of my lowlife relatives would turn to larceny, the ghost cracked.

Jean Shepherd—not Shepard, I clarified for the ghost. *Coincidence, yes, but you're not related.*

Brainert tapped his chin. "Didn't Shepherd urge his radio listeners to go to bookstores and ask for his phony book?"

Sadie spoke up. "As I recall, the 1950s bestseller lists were compiled not only by sales, but also by the number of requests bookstores received for a certain title."

"That's right." Seymour nodded. "And so many people asked for *I, Libertine* that the *New York Times* listed it as a bestseller. It was deemed so salacious that it was banned in Boston—a hoot because it had yet to be written! Science fiction author Theodore Sturgeon was hired to churn it out, which he did in one marathon typing session."

"And so the first literary practical joke since Edgar Allan Poe's 'The Balloon-Hoax' was born," Brainert noted.

"There were others," Seymour countered. "*Coffee, Tea or Me?*—the 1967 bestseller supposedly penned by two randy airline stewardesses—was really written by a PR man for American Airlines."

"And Seymour already mentioned Clifford Irving," Sadie reminded them. "He actually went to prison for peddling that fake biography of Howard Hughes."

"So, are you saying *Shades of Leather* is nothing but a practical joke?" Fiona asked.

"No, Fiona," Seymour replied. "What I am saying is that *Shades of Leather* appears to be a group collaboration, just like *Naked Came the Stranger.*"

"How could you possibly deduce that?" Bud asked.

"You don't have to be a literary genius to spot the differences in style and vocabulary. From the erotic scenes I get a real Erica Jong or *Story of O* vibe—"

Seymour opened *Shades of Leather* to a bookmarked page.

"In most of the book, Justine, the tender-aged heroine, talks like a Valley girl on stupid pills. No kidding, one step above barks, chirps, and grunts. But on page 386, her diction inexplicably improves."

"'Unbeknownst to Lyon,'" Seymour read, "'I had acquired the first two numbers of the lock's combination. But what machinations would be required of me to gain those final digits?'"

Seymour pulled his nose out of the book.

"Beside the fact that this dialogue reeks of something out of a Wilkie Collins Victorian thriller, I question the use of words like *unbeknownst* and *machinations* by a character who, six pages earlier, refers to Almas caviar as 'kind of squishy.'"

"They are perfectly good English verbs that should be part of any high school graduate's vocabulary," Brainert insisted, almost defensively.

"Allow me to continue," Seymour sniffed. "The Victorian-era dialogue I just read simply does not compare to the lively, bawdy banter in the sex scenes. And neither resembled the didactic discussions about narcotics trafficking and post–Cold War tensions the diplomat character intermittently tortures Justine—and the reader—with."

"What are you saying?" Brainert demanded.

"My analysis is clear," Seymour replied. "*Shades of Leather* appears to be written by three different and distinct authors." He ticked off each with his fingers. "A woman of wit and humor, with a talent for the bawdy. An academic with a discipline in international affairs. And a stuffy, humorless professor of American literature whose ability to write compelling fiction has been marred by the stultifying influence of academic writing."

Brainert Parker jumped to his feet.

"You base this cockamamy theory on a character's use

of *vocabulary*? That's a flawed assessment, Seymour. Salient House has editors. I'm sure they have college degrees *and* use polysyllabic words—unlike those pulp hacks you read."

"You, of all people, should know that much of 'classic' literature started out as popular entertainment!" Seymour shot back. "Shakespeare, Dumas, Dickens, Mark Twain, H. G. Wells—they wrote for the masses. It was you and your fussy academic colleagues who turned a vital art into a pompous, esoteric snooze-fest."

"That's not the point!" Brainert yelled. "Your ill-conceived accusations sully the reputation of a fine academic. And with Kevin Ridgeway's daughter under this very roof! You have sunk to a new low, mailman."

A stunned silence followed.

Seymour smugly folded his arms. "Thank you for the confirmation, Professor."

"What are you talking about?"

"I didn't name any names. *You* did."

Brainert waved his hands. "Everyone knew who you were talking about."

Leo Rollins blinked. "I didn't."

"Me, either," Joyce Koh said.

Seymour's gaze locked on Brainert. "Time's up, Dr. Parker. Are you going to fess up?"

"To what?!" he sputtered. "I have nothing to confess! I'm not the one engaging in slander!"

"Knock it off. I know the truth. Why don't you just admit it?"

"Admit what?"

"The last time I saw the word *unbeknownst* on a printed page—and that's *a lot* of years of reading—was the one-word title of that horror story you wrote in ninth grade. Why, there were so many four- and five-syllable jawbreakers in that whopper you should have included a Merriam-Webster dictionary with the Xeroxes you handed out in Mrs. Meyer's English class."

"How dare you imply—"

"Oh, stop with the fevered outrage and confess already. You're one of the trio of authors of this pulp potboiler. I'll bet you and this Kevin Ridgeway concocted *Shades of Leather* together, like a couple of dirty old farts. You both knew you needed a woman's touch for the erotic scenes, so you hired one for a literary three-way."

"I've heard enough! I'm not listening to this character assassination one moment longer!"

Grabbing his coat, Brainert bolted for the exit. He moved so quickly that he nearly bowled over poor Bonnie Franzetti.

"Pardon me," Brainert said to Bonnie. "I wish to depart from this *madhouse*. Will you assist me and unlock the front door, posthaste?"

Bonnie looked confused. "You mean *now*?"

"Posthaste—immediately, NOW!"

A few moments later, we heard Bonnie jingle the keys and Brainert slam out.

"Good night, Professor Parker!" she called.

Cold silence followed.

CHAPTER 39

Sleepless in Rhode Island

To expect the unexpected shows a thoroughly modern
intellect.

—Oscar Wilde, *An Ideal Husband*

"WHAT A DISASTROUS revelation . . ."

I was in bed, staring at the ceiling. My alarm clock read
1:15 A.M., and I listened to its ticking with wide-open eyes.
When I felt that breath of cold air on my cheek, I welcomed it.

*So, the mailman pitched a mean curveball? Well, here's
a clue. In the detective game, you almost never get a clean
throw across the plate. There's usually something screwy
about every ball that comes your way.*

"What's with the baseball metaphors?"

*Maybe it's because half this town is batty, and your
Brainiac pal is king of the belfry.*

"We're all a little eccentric in this town. Yes, Brainert's
an enigma, but that's nothing new. He never had many
close relationships beyond Seymour and me. His partner at
the theater is pure business. Dean Wendell Pepper is a recently divorced—and thus newly freed—ladies' man."

And? No female entanglements for the egghead?

"The choice would be male, if he'd ever make one. And

I wish he would. I want Brainert to be happy—to have someone he can confide in. If I had to guess, I'd say he had a bit of a crush on Professor Ridgeway, and the man's death is hitting him hard because of his feelings. But it's only a guess. And that's the problem."

In case you hadn't noticed, baby, you have more than one of those.

"This one is personal, Jack. I'm hurt that Brainert lied to me. We've always been close friends, yet he refused to trust me with the truth about his involvement with *Shades of Leather.* I think Seymour was upset by it, too. I'm sure it's why his analysis was so biting. When your best friend cowrites an international bestseller and doesn't bother to mention it to you, well, you can see where Seymour felt hurt—and maybe a little jealous."

Just like Brainert. Wasn't he actin' jealous the other day?

"You mean when he saw our promotional material for Professor Leeds? Sure, maybe academic jealousy is one of the things that's been eating Brainert—or keeping him from eating, given what looks like stress weight loss. On the other hand, he could very well be stressed over being found out. Given the low first printing on *Shades of Leather,* Brainert probably thought the book would come and go with modest profits and little fanfare, just an anonymous small venture to make some extra money for his theater project. Now that the book is as big as it is, he's probably dreading the reaction of his academic community."

One man's Treasure Island *is another man's trashy read, am I right?*

"Exactly. If an accomplished colleague like Dr. Leeds learned that Brainert helped write what he would deem a tacky, commercial potboiler, Brainert could end up a laughingstock at best and lose his standing in the department, if not his entire teaching position. Not that Brainert *admitted* to being a cowriter of the work, but the similarities to that teenage story he wrote sound incriminating enough. And, of course, he blurted out Kevin's name, an inadvertent admission in itself."

You know your Brainiac friend has more to answer for than penning pulp fiction, don't you, doll?

"I can't bring myself to consider it."

Then I'll do it for you. Remember all those dusty volumes of American lit stacked up in the dead woman's apartment? Maybe she gave a call to your local egghead emporium, asking for some expert advice."

"It's possible. I can't deny that. With all those important first editions in her possession, Emma might have hoped for a sale of the collection to the university, for its archives. Brainert may have been sent to evaluate the books. He could have known her that way. If he did have contact, then he's a suspect in her death. That's a possibility I can hardly conceive of."

You're forgetting about the third party, baby.

"No, I'm not. I was getting to that. Seymour's literary analysis claims a woman was a part of this three-way erotic-thriller writing team: 'a woman of wit and humor, with a talent for the bawdy,' to quote the postman."

And Emma Hudson's female friend is still missing, ain't she?

"My thought exactly. Brainert must know who she is, but will he tell me?"

Rest those peepers, and I'll give you a few other things to concern yourself with—and remind you of something you probably forgot . . .

CHAPTER 40

Trouble in Hell's Kitchen

Fighting means you could lose. Bullying means you can't. A bully wants to beat somebody; he doesn't want to fight somebody.

—Andrew Vachss

I BARELY CLOSED my eyes before Jack returned me to the island of Manhattan. Once again, he turned the clock's hands to 1947, and I was strolling along a sidewalk beside the big private eye.

"It was nice what you did for that woman," I told him, "reuniting her with her dog, I mean."

"Nice and profitable," Jack said, adjusting his fedora. "Remind me to call Bennie the Bookie. I need to play William's tip."

"And lose what you've just earned?"

"Leave it to a dame to squeeze all the juice out of life."

"Didn't your client's chauffeur leave you something else in that envelope of cash?"

"Yeah, doll, a tip on another client—he's in the book business, just like you. Only he's on the scribbling and printing end."

"He's a book publisher?"

"Why you askin'? Didn't I just tell you? I used the pay phone at the terminal to call the man. I suggested we meet tomorrow at his office, but he's in too much of a hurry to hire me. Says we should talk over drinks, so I suggested a bar not far from here, where we can do just that—and he can pick up the tab. We're heading there now."

Away from the busy ship's terminal and its luxury passengers, the surrounding neighborhood was pretty seedy. Three- and four-story walk-up tenements crowded the block, with a gritty-looking set of toughs perched on every fourth or fifth stoop.

Jack moved closer to me, wrapped my slender arm around his iron bicep. "We're heading into a dicey area, sweetheart. It's got a bad reputation with a name to match. Stick to me like glue, okay?"

We passed a pair of young women walking boldly, sans white gloves or hats—the mark of feminine refinement in this era. One of them glanced in my direction, snapped her gum, and tossed her platinum blond hair.

"Well, ain't *she* a fancy so-and-so."

And if that wasn't enough, one of the bruisers on a nearby stoop pointed at me and wolf-whistled. Soon he was joined by others, winking and whistling at me.

"Jack, I don't like this."

He glanced at the grinning men and frowned. "What's the matter? You can't take a compliment?"

"In my time this would be called harassment."

"Why? Dames don't want to be admired in your time?"

"We call it objectification."

"You girls want to be called on *what* occasion?"

"No. Objectification! Women in my time prefer to be seen as whole people—not objects to be crudely judged on our body parts."

"Sorry, kid, this is my time. To men on the street—hell, to men everywhere—your body parts are going to be an object of interest on all occasions."

Our little talk was distracting, but only to us. The toughs kept whistling, and the street became grittier.

"Jack, this doesn't look safe."

"They don't call it Hell's Kitchen for nothing. But don't worry your pretty red head. If you ain't looking for trouble here, you probably won't find it."

Despite Jack's assurance, we walked right into it—trouble, that is, by way of a four-man street brawl.

To my distress, instead of moving on, Jack Shepard stopped.

Whether it was his PI curiosity, street cop hardness, or ex-GI captivation with the sight of a raw fight, he paused to observe three nautical-looking palookas pushing around a nicely attired gentleman.

Before I knew it, Jack shoved me into a newsstand kiosk.

"Stay put," he warned. "And stay out of this."

The dagger-shaped scar on Jack's chin flushed red, and I knew why. What we assumed was an argument was looking more like an assault on a helpless victim, a lean, middle-aged, affable-looking gentleman in a pin-striped suit and wide yellow tie.

The gent's tailored suit was of exceptional quality. I knew because the largest attacker used the suit's lapels to lift the man right off his feet!

"You'll stop askin' questions about Mickey Sizemore if ya know what's good fer ya," the big man growled through a rack of gold teeth.

A second bruiser hopped from foot to foot, in a feeble imitation of a real boxer. A third slugged the gentleman in the kidney, to punctuate the big guy's point. None of these thugs noticed Jack's approach, though he quickly became the center of attention.

"You call this a fair fight?" Jack's voice was surprisingly calm, like he was asking the time of day. "What a crew of mooks."

Gold Teeth released the gent, who tumbled to the curb in a heap. With a mouth like a Tiffany shark, the big man turned his vicious, glittering grin on Jack Shepard.

"What are you gonna do about it?"

Jack braced his legs. "For starters? Flatten you."

"You and what army?!"

"Just me," Jack assured him. "How many slugs to the kisser do you think it will take to bring a big ape like you down, anyway? Two? Three? The whole nine yards?"

Stunned to face a foe actually spoiling for a fight, instead of a typically cringing victim, Gold Teeth thrust his hand into his worn peacoat and pulled out his equalizer—a bright, shiny .38.

Though he had a pistol pointed at his midriff, Jack didn't flinch.

"You really don't believe in a fair fight, do ya, you big, dumb ox?"

Though Jack was fearless, I wasn't. At three to one odds, and a gun in the mix, I had to do something. So, I thrust my hand in my purse, dropped a coin on the counter, and grabbed a pack of chewing gum. The news dealer hardly noticed. Like everyone else on this block, he was gawking at the brewing brawl.

Eyes on the gunman, I unwrapped two sticks, folded them into my mouth, and gagged. "God, what is this?!" The brand was called Black Jack, and the gum literally was black. It tasted of aniseed, and I desperately wanted to spit it into the gutter, but I didn't.

Still chewing, I yanked off my cork-shaped hat and tossed it there instead. A bunch of bobby pins followed, and I shook my copper hair loose. Finally, I took a breath and walked right up to the bruiser with the gold dentures.

"Hey, handsome," I said, chewing furiously while tapping the big man on his meaty shoulder. "Can ya tell me where I can catch the Canarsie Line?" I snapped my gum and give him a wink. "This burg has got my silly head all turned around!"

My ruse was enough of a distraction for Jack to make his move.

As the gunman's eyes bugged in my direction, Jack grabbed the gun and twisted it in his hand. For a moment, the two tangoed. Then I heard an ugly snap, and Gold Teeth howled. When they separated, it was Jack waving the pistol.

Gold Teeth should have been scared; instead, he was outraged. With a roar, he charged Jack like a Pamplona bull.

Just like a good bullfighter, Jack stepped aside. Then he squeezed the trigger, firing a single shot that blew the sailor's cap off the big man's fat head.

Before the blast's echo faded, all three thugs were in full retreat.

"I bet they don't stop till they get to Coney Island." Jack slipped a wink my way. Then he helped the pin-striped gent to his feet.

"I appreciate your gallantry, sir!" the man said. "I was mighty useless, just now."

Jack tucked the revolver in his coat and slapped the gent's back.

"Don't beat yourself up, Rochester. As neighborhoods go, this one's not too friendly. I wouldn't be slumming myself if I didn't have a private eye license—and this dame— for protection."

The gent's gaze discovered me and brightened faster than a campfire on a moonless night. "And who is this delightful creature?"

"My lucky Penny. She comes in handy sometimes."

Jack scanned the street. "Your friends won't be coming back, but with all the stares, there's no reason to let our feet sink into this concrete. I say we grab a cab and get you home."

"But I can't leave," the gent protested. "The future of my business depends on finding a man who vanished in this neighborhood."

Jack's gray eyes narrowed. "This guy must owe you a bushel of cabbage to bring you down to Hades' Kitchen without muscle."

"He owes me far more than money, sir. Mickey Sizemore owes me a manuscript." The gent extended his hand. "My name is H. L. Macklin, editor in chief and owner of—"

"Hey, it's you! I didn't peg you for a guy in the scribbler

business. Do you publish scandal sheets? You know, rip-snorting pulps?"

"Books, Mister . . . ?"

"Shepard. I'm Jack Shepard."

"*You're* Jack Shepard?! The man I spoke to on the phone?"

"The very same. You already know Penny."

"To be honest," Macklin said, donning spectacles, "I haven't had much luck with private investigators, but perhaps our meeting signals a change of fortune. Instead of that bar you mentioned, how about we share those drinks back at my office?"

"Why not? I've got nothing else on my docket."

"Oh yes, you do, Mr. Shepard. Mickey Sizemore, that man I mentioned, is my top-selling author. He's gone missing. And I'm hiring you to find him."

CHAPTER 41

Mickey's No Mouse

HERMIT, *n*. A person whose vices and follies are not sociable.

—Ambrose Bierce, *The Devil's Dictionary*, 1911

SOON AFTER THE three of us reached H. L. Macklin's Madison Avenue office, I concluded that the founder of this budding publishing empire was a man who could charm the opposite sex.

I knew because half the young women in Macklin's employ watched with envy in their eyes as I walked beside their boss. When Macklin led us to his inner sanctum, his secretary—a mousy brunette young enough to be his daughter—openly glared as if we were romantic rivals.

"Now that we're alone, the lady and I should be formally introduced," Macklin told Jack, as if I weren't present. "Who is this lovely creation?"

"Penny McClure, my partner."

Macklin's eyes twinkled. "So, you have a fondness for secretaries, too." The little man faced me. "Miss McClure, I'm charmed—"

"Mrs.," Jack corrected. "War widow. And she ain't my secretary."

"Sure, sure, Mr. Shepard, whatever you say." Harry flashed white teeth as he took my hand and kissed it. "I find it a rare pleasure to meet someone so lovely, so poised, so fashionable, and so . . . unmarried."

"Uh, thank you, Mr. Macklin."

"Darling, please. It's Harry. Just Harry!"

"Harry-Just-Harry" poured on the compliments for another minute or five. The office door was open, and a pair of attractive young editors frowned when they saw their boss gushing over another woman. I was relieved when he finally closed the door.

Macklin's corner office was posh but absurdly chaotic. Manuscripts were stacked on every surface, including the wide cushions of his long leather couch. The man's massive carved walnut desk was covered in books, letters, and so many manuscripts that his phone was half buried, and his brass nameplate shoved off to make room. Its polished surface lay forgotten in the thick pile of his antique Persian rug.

In an age without central air-conditioning, the tall windows were wide open—despite the fact that we were twenty floors up. As the dull din of traffic wafted up from the street below, stiff breezes wildly stirred the brocade drapes and launched the occasional piece of stray paper from one end of the room to the other.

The only orderly area in the place was the well-stocked bar in the corner, which shouldn't have been a surprise, given the empty Jameson bottle on Macklin's desk. No doubt, cocktail hour came a few times a day for this busy publisher—and we'd arrived for one of them.

Macklin poured three whiskeys from a new bottle, we toasted, and he doubled us up with refills. Finally, the publisher sat behind his desk while Jack shoved aside enough manuscripts for us to get comfortable on the office couch.

"Jack, before you start looking for Mickey Sizemore, I want to be honest about something."

"Shoot, Harry."

"You aren't the first detective I hired to find Sizemore. Pinkerton tried, but came up empty."

Jack snorted.

"What? You don't like Pinkerton?"

"I got no beef with them. They knock on doors, beat a bush or two, ask polite questions that wouldn't intimidate a sawdust baker hoarding ration coupons. Then they write up a nice, pretty report, complete with a carbon copy, and deliver it to their client. Why, I'll bet they handed one to you, too, didn't they, Harry?"

"They did," Macklin said. "It was pretty flimsy. Not even a picture. Just a couple of contradictory descriptions from casual neighbors that sound like two or three different people."

"So, what gives with this guy?"

"Sizemore's a phantom. A hermit. A misanthrope. He doesn't gamble. He doesn't frequent bars, and he's got no family or gal pals. None that I know of."

"Don't authors have agents?"

"Not Mickey. His first manuscript came out of the slush pile, and I negotiated the buy through some two-bit Bowery lawyer who up and ran off to Hollywood! I'm telling you, Mickey Sizemore is a mystery, an enigma—"

"To the gumshoes at Pinkerton."

"Don't sell Pinkerton short, Jack. They did find out one important detail. After his lawyer took off, all I had on Sizemore was a Hell's Kitchen PO box. The detectives managed to find Mickey's real address, some dive in Brooklyn—"

"*After* your scribbler already skedaddled, right?"

"Unfortunately, yes." Macklin eyed Jack and saw the skepticism there. "Look, I didn't just hire anyone. I went with Pinkerton on the recommendation of my good friend Dash—that's Dashiell Hammett. Did you know he was once a Pinkerton detective before he was a writer?"

"Do tell," Jack replied. "And I'll give fair odds your pal is a better scribbler than he ever was a detective."

"You're probably right." Macklin threw back his shot, then shook his head. "I wish I'd published Dash, back in the day. He hasn't done much since the war, but I'd sure like to try for a reprint of previously published short stories. A nice edition, something he'd be proud to put on his shelf."

"Is Mickey Sizemore in the same league?" I asked. "As Dashiell Hammett, I mean?"

"Mickey's got a style all his own . . ." Maybe it was the booze, but the publisher went maudlin. When he spoke again, his gaze seemed miles away. "Sizemore spins the kind of yarn no one else has the guts to tell. The man's one of a kind. He writes with tears, blood, and sweat. Mickey is—"

"Missing," Jack said flatly. "And he's an author that earns?"

Macklin instantly snapped back to unsentimental reality. "His first two novels sold like hotcakes. No, they sold *better* than hotcakes—like GIs swapping nylons in Paris. Mickey is no mouse. As a writer, he's a straight flush. But that bastard owes me one more novel, and he's vanished—with the hefty advance I dropped on him, too."

Macklin removed his spectacles and leaned over his desk, blue eyes as big as a trapped animal's.

"Jack, I'll tell you a secret. My company's in the red. If that damn manuscript doesn't arrive this week, we can't go to press. If we can't go to press, my company's bankrupt. Then my options are limited to skipping the country, or . . ." He sighed, pointing to the billowing drapes. "Jumping out one of these windows."

"Don't worry, pal," Jack soothed. "I'll find out what happened to your author. I'll need that address Pinkerton gave you—just for a starting point, you understand."

"Sure, Jack. Anything you want."

Macklin used a buzzer to summon his secretary. The young, mousy brunette responded at once, waltzing in with a worshipful smile for her boss.

"Miss Moreland, would you please fetch me that Pinkerton report? It's filed with Mickey Sizemore's contract."

"Certainly, Mr. Macklin!"

As the girl departed, she shot me a private look—one of pure, venomous jealousy.

Honey, you can have him, truly!

Miss Moreland discreetly closed the door behind her. She wasn't gone five minutes before we heard her bloodcurdling screams.

CHAPTER 42

Blood, Sweat, and Paper

It is only when you open your veins and bleed onto the page a little that you establish contact with your reader.

—Paul Gallico, *Confessions of a Story Writer*, 1946

JACK AND HARRY were on their feet and through the door in two shakes of a duck's tail feathers.

Unfortunately, I was delayed by the sunken leather couch, too-high heels, and a skirt that only allowed for baby steps. When I finally reached the secretary's desk, I found a trembling Miss Moreland cradled in Harry Macklin's arms, sobbing into his lapels.

"It's horrible, just horrible!"

"Please, Miss Moreland," Macklin cooed. "Tell me what's wrong."

Like an Olympic-class precision hugger, the girl released Macklin's suit and latched onto his neck. If I were scoring, she would have gotten a perfect ten.

"Oh, Mr. Macklin, it was awful! I went to the file room to retrieve the Pinkerton report. When I returned to my desk, that box was waiting for me. I knew it was important, so I opened it, and . . ."

She began sobbing all over her boss again.

Jack observed the scene with cool concern. He caught my eye, tipped his head, and together we turned our attention to Miss Moreland's tidy desk. A large cardboard box sat in the middle of it. The parcel was unwrapped, brown paper still gathered around its edges. With the tip of a pen, Jack carefully lifted off the cardboard lid.

Inside sat a manuscript. I cringed at the sight of dried red blood on the neatly stacked pile of typed pages. Whoever splattered the gore was considerate enough not to obscure the title.

DAMES DON'T DIE
A NOVEL BY MICKEY SIZEMORE

With his secretary still clinging to his neck like a sea lamprey on a herring, Macklin cautiously peeked into the box. His eyes lit like blue neon, and he pushed Miss Morehouse aside so quickly she nearly bounced off the wall.

"Mickey, you magnificent bastard! You came through!"

Only after a quick victory rumba around his secretary's desk did Macklin take note of the bloodstains. He glanced up at Jack Shepard.

"They say a writer has to bleed on the page. But this?" Macklin jerked his thumb at the box. "I'd say it's overkill."

"Be grateful Sizemore delivered," Jack replied. "Though it looks like this could be his final opus." He picked at the brown wrapping paper. "There's no postmark and no stamps. Though it's addressed to you, Harry, this package wasn't delivered by the post office."

He turned his steel gaze on the mousy secretary. "Miss Moreland, answer me straight. You claim you found this box on your desk?"

"It was right there when I got back from the file room."

"Did you see anyone drop it off?"

"No. No one. It just appeared!"

"Like magic?" Jack stepped closer to the suddenly nervous secretary—so close Harry Macklin felt the need to step between them.

"Back off, Jack. Dorothy's just an innocent child. She can't help you. I'll call the mail room. They'll know how that box got delivered."

As Macklin went back to his office, Jack focused his penetrating gaze back on the secretary.

"Excuse me. I took a fright. I need to put myself back together!" Miss Moreland announced before fleeing to the ladies' room—though it was clear enough she was running from Jack and his questions.

"Now what?" I asked.

Jack folded his arms. "You tell me, sweetheart. What's next?"

"I see. This is another test, right?"

Jack cocked his head.

Thinking fast, I stepped into the hallway, not to follow Miss Moreland, but to check for any sign that her story was true.

"Jack, look, there's a mail room boy near the elevator. He's pushing a cart."

"Hey, pal!" Jack whistled, stopping the mail boy. "Did you just deliver a brown paper package to Macklin's office with a manuscript inside?"

The boy shook his head. "Nothing like that. Only a stack o' bills and some perfumed letters. Manuscripts always go to Mr. Macklin's lady editors first."

Now I did my bit. "Do you know everyone on this floor, everyone who belongs?"

"Sure, miss, I been working here a year. Deliver to every office, and I know every pair of pretty legs." He didn't bother hiding an open leer at mine. Then he winked.

Jack stifled a laugh at my outraged expression. Wrestling with my desire to lecture the boy on sexual harassment, I focused instead on the case at hand.

"Answer me this, young man," I demanded, voice stern. "Did you see anyone on this floor who doesn't belong—man or woman?"

"No, lady. I didn't see nobody like that." Then he shrugged

and with one last leer at my legs, turned, and ambled his cart away.

"So, you thinking what I'm thinking?" Jack asked.

"What you *thought*, you mean, back when you worked this case. Yes, I think Miss Moreland might have put the manuscript on her own desk. And if she did, she might know Mickey Sizemore—or, at least, where we can find him."

"That's what I thought. So, sweetheart, what's our next move?"

"With Macklin so protective, I say we find out where Dorothy Moreland lives and question her at home."

"Good." Jack nodded, and the two of us returned to Macklin's office. While he went into the man's lair to pick up the Pinkerton report, I pawed through the secretary's purse, looking for anything with her home address.

In her wallet, I struck gold, and not just because I discovered where she lived. I'd discovered something even more important to this case. After some quick scribbling, I tucked everything back the way it was, nice and tidy—everything but one small item, which I slipped into my own purse.

"Okay, Harry. You're the boss . . ." I heard Jack loudly declare (to warn me, no doubt) as he walked out of the publisher's office. "That is, *if* you still want me to find Mickey Sizemore."

"Sure, Jack! I want you to find him. Now more than ever. I need to know if he's alive in case I need rewrites!"

Ten minutes later, Jack and I were back on Manhattan concrete. Jack carelessly folded the Pinkerton report and tucked it behind his lapel.

"Something stinks like old fish," he muttered. "I never liked that smell, yet it's always tickling my Jimmy Durante."

He whistled for a taxi.

"Where are we going?" I asked.

"We got some time before Miss Moreland's off work." He checked his watch. "How about you and I have a nice romantic dinner? I know a little Italian joint, down in the Village—candlelight, fruity Chianti, veal pounded so thin it'll melt on your tonsils. What do you say?"

"I could eat."

"Good. We can talk over the case. There's something off about Macklin's ding-dong girl. Did you notice?"

"Sure, I noticed. Did you see that jealous look she gave me?"

"Maybe it's no more than a crazy crush on her boss," Jack said. "Harry was right about one thing. She's practically a child."

"That's the impression she likes to make, but that look of jealousy wasn't from a babe in the woods. More like a she-wolf. Hard, tough, a real fighter—and I found out how she got that way."

Jack gave me a sidelong glance. "You found out?"

With puffed-up pride, I handed Jack the card I'd pinched from her purse.

"Yowzah!" he cried. Jack pushed back his fedora and shook his head. "Yeah, this is real dynamite, baby. It changes everything—"

We both heard a squeal of tires as a big brown DeSoto hopped the curb. This wasn't the cab Jack whistled for. It was a weaponized ton of steel and gasoline.

For a split-second, I caught sight of the driver. His cap was pulled low, his collar up, but I recognized the gritting grin of his golden teeth. They belonged to the street brawler Jack had bested.

Behind the wheel of hurtling metal, the Tiffany shark laughed as he steered right for us.

CHAPTER 43

Paint the Town Red

I don't need an alarm clock. My ideas wake me.

—Ray Bradbury

FINGERS CLAWING THE bedsheets, I opened my eyes in a breathless state, still believing I was on a Manhattan sidewalk, facing a tank-sized DeSoto with a homicidal shark of a driver bent on flattening me.

Then my alarm rang in my ear, and I nearly screamed. Heart pounding, I slapped the ringer off and sank back against the pillows.

"Jack?!" I called in anger. "You never pulled a trick like that before! Why did you do it?"

Silence was the only reply.

The ghost was gone. For how long? I couldn't know. After that dream, his energies were probably sapped. Well, mine were, too. Maybe some quiet time would do me good.

KNOCK! KNOCK! KNOCK!

This time I did scream. The sharp rapping on my door completed my scares for the morning.

"Mrs. McClure?" called a little girl's voice. "Are you all right? It's Amy! Amy Ridgeway!"

"Yes?!" I called. "Come in, Amy!"

Her curly-haired head popped through the door. "Ms. Thornton sent me to get you. Your oatmeal is ready. It's almost time to open the store! I can't wait!"

The girl was gone as fast as she came. Her bubbly enthusiasm *almost* gave me the energy to feel good about rising. Shining? Not so much.

BY NOON, AMY had learned all about restocking, and I was taking stock in the dream Jack gave me.

For hours, I asked myself why he'd left me in that terrified state. And then, working with Kevin Ridgeway's young daughter, it struck me. Jack wanted me to know what it felt like, standing helpless in front of a hurtling piece of machinery, facing down your demise from a driver set on vehicular homicide.

My gumshoe ghost was trying to make me focus on the death of Professor Ridgeway.

Okay, Jack. I'll do what I can.

First, I called Chief Ciders to let him know Kevin's daughter was staying with us for the week—in case he wanted to speak with her. Using that pretext, I asked about his investigation of the hit-and-run.

Ciders was in a good mood for once, and willing to talk, but there wasn't much to tell. They'd made no progress on finding the vehicle that struck and killed Amy's father.

When I suggested that it might have been intentional, even premeditated, he gave me the same reply his deputy chief presented to Amy. In the opinion of the police, it was a terrible accident, nothing more.

They would try their best to keep looking for the vehicle that committed the "manslaughter," but so far, none of the local garages or auto-body shops had turned up any probable suspects. Ciders was out of leads and short on manpower. The trail had gone cold, and the case would likely close that way.

Next, I tried to contact Brainert—three texts and two voice mails, all of which he ignored.

Eddie Franzetti was at the courthouse for hours, testifying on two cases of drunk driving. So I spent the afternoon waiting on bookshop customers, and (in between) calling animal shelters in the area, looking for Emma's missing Yorkshire terrier. (Jack's first dream, of that missing Manhattan dog, still resonated, too.) If a shelter could remember who brought the dog in, we'd have a lead. But none had a Yorkie in their care. No luck there.

When Eddie finally called back, I asked for a progress report on Emma Hudson's mystery friend, the one Mr. Brink mentioned.

"Sorry, Pen, nothing to tell. I talked to her building's landlord again, and he didn't know a thing about the woman. Neither did the meth heads or any other neighbors. Except for Mr. Brink, no one else knew about her."

When Spencer got home from school, I put him to work in the store beside Amy, which made them both deliriously happy. After supper and homework, I thought they'd earned some fun, and allowed them to play *Avenging Angel* until bedtime.

When my own bedtime came, Jack was still missing, but I didn't mind. After that nightmare, I was looking forward to sleeping like the dead.

THE NEXT DAY, I *finally* heard from my ghost.

Amy was spending time with Sadie, learning how we processed online orders; Bonnie was taking care of customers; and I took charge of the Community Events space, making sure it was ready for our sold-out signing with the Bentley Prize winner taking place this very evening.

I had just finished stocking our displays with copies of Dr. Leeds's acclaimed work, *Fiction Enslaved: Literature and Colonialism*, when a familiar cold breeze washed over me.

We should be making tracks, doll, not stacking books.

"Oh, so now you're back and giving orders? You know you've been gone for twenty-four hours—and after giving me that terrible nightmare, too!"

But I steered you in the right direction with that careening car, pardon the pun.

"If you mean you got me to thinking about Kevin Ridgeway's accident as not being so accidental, you're right."

So, what did you do about it?

I gave Jack the rundown (pun intended) of the previous day's activities, including calling shelters about Emma's missing Yorkie.

My gumshoe ghost was not impressed.

You're barking up the wrong tree. If you're looking for answers, you've got to cage your cagey friend, and give him the third degree!

"I've been trying! But Brainert's been ghosting me—"

He's dead, too?

"No, Jack—don't even joke about that! It would kill me if anything happened to him. 'Ghosting' just means he's been ignoring my texts and voice mails."

The way I ghost you, sweetheart, is a lot more fun.

"I've noticed. As far as Brainert is concerned, I'm done putting up with his pouting. Tonight, after Dr. Leeds's lecture, I plan to camp out on his doorstep. He'll have to talk to me."

Why wait? Call your pal and invite him to listen to his colleague gas on, gratis.

"He won't come. You saw how Brainert reacted when he saw our promotional materials for Leeds. My friend has a bad case of professional jealousy. And, I'm sorry to say, after the awful way he left the Quibblers meeting, he's been avoiding the bookshop completely—"

Just then, Bonnie Franzetti crashed through the front door, her short black curls bouncing around her head. Like her tall, darkly handsome older brother, she had long-lashed brown eyes, and they were as wide as I'd ever seen them. She was panting, she could barely speak, and her olive skin was flushed.

"Bonnie! What's wrong?"

"Oh, Pen! It's your friend, Professor Parker. Just now, he

was hit by a truck speeding down Cranberry Street! There's blood everywhere!"

I raced by Bonnie and out the door.

Morning rush was over, and the streets were quiet. But at the crosswalk just past Koh's market, a knot of fifteen or twenty people gathered in a tight circle. More emerged from the surrounding businesses and rushed to the scene.

There was no truck in sight, no cars on Cranberry—nothing that wasn't parked, anyway. But there *were* splashes of crimson. Lots of them. An almost impossible amount of red stained the pavement, the sidewalk, and even a storefront or two.

"It was a hit-and-run!" Bonnie's heart-shaped face was twisted with anguish as she caught up to me. "The van just kept going, until it accelerated around the corner."

I was accelerating, too. Though I dreaded the horror I was about to encounter, I had to know the fate of my lifelong friend.

"Oh God," I prayed. "Oh God, please, no . . ."

As I approached, I could hear people tittering nervously—not everybody, mind you, but more than a few. Then someone actually laughed out loud!

Suddenly, I heard Jack in my head. He was appalled by the laughter.

Mother Machree! I thought the boys at Murder, Inc., were soulless. But these rural rubes chuckling over a fresh stiff really burns my bacon!

I pushed through the giggling gaggle to find a moaning Brainert flat on his back. Like some deranged Red Sox fan on game day, he was stained from head to toe in crimson.

As he began to stagger to his feet like a zombie in a horror movie, I realized my friend had not been resurrected from the dead. He was simply covered in red paint! A battered can lay in the roadway, while a dazed Brainert still clutched its metal handle.

Because of the toxic mess, people were reluctant to get too close. I didn't care! I rushed right up to him.

"Can you hear me? Are you okay?"

Staring straight ahead, Brainert blinked and shook his head. Then his near-vacant eyes met mine. "Oh, hi, Pen. I'll have to purchase another gallon of Sherwin-Williams Heart-throb. The lobby needs a new coat. There's such wear and tear . . ."

He spoke in a shell-shocked monotone that made me fear he had actually been zombie-ized. Then his head lolled back as he fainted dead away.

Fortunately, Bonnie helped me keep him upright, though we both became sticky with red goo in the process.

"Hey, lady! That guy spilled paint all over my car!"

Nearby, Fred Kelly clutched his bald head. "Look at my Laundromat. The windows are ruined!"

Move it, doll. You better get Professor Paint-Can out of here before this hayseed mob grows ugly.

"I'll call Bud Napp for an emergency turpentine delivery," I told Bonnie.

Then we walked my semiconscious friend back to my bookshop.

CHAPTER 44

Eyewitness

Girls can see all kinds of things that boys miss.

—*Sally Snoops and Her Curious Kitty: The Car Crash Caper*

IT SEEMED LIKE a Stooges gag more than a life-threatening event, but when Officer Eddie Franzetti learned that Brainert had been doused with a gallon of paint, he called Poison Control, and then Dr. Rubino.

The situation was so dire that Quindicott's resident physician actually made a house call. After Brainert cleaned up in Buy the Book's utility closet, he absolutely refused treatment at an emergency room. So Deputy Chief Franzetti drove him back to his home, where Dr. Rubino ambushed Brainert at the door.

The professor reluctantly submitted to the doctor's care, along with a question-and-answer session with the deputy chief.

Meanwhile, Bonnie and I took our turn in the utility room.

After a lot of scrubbing and too many rolls of paper towels, I was running a brush through my auburn hair when Sadie appeared, offering fresh clothes with one hand, while clutching her nose with the other.

"This place reeks like a turpentine factory and looks like an abattoir!"

"I wouldn't know," I moaned. "My eyes are watering too much to see anything but a blur, and my sense of smell is pretty much shot."

"Mine, too," Bonnie said. "But that might be a good thing."

Sadie went around opening all the windows. Soon there was a steady flow of refreshing autumn air—and a whole lot of street noise.

"What's going on outside?"

"Mr. Koh and Fred Kelly are stripping paint off their businesses, and Bud Napp is power washing the street and sidewalk at the request of Chief Ciders."

"Do you know what the police think?"

"You can ask Eddie yourself. He's finished with Brainert. Now he's on his way back here to speak with both of you."

Bonnie simply shrugged. And why not? How intimidated could a girl be when the cop about to grill her was her own big brother?

Five minutes later, we found a frowning Eddie beside my newly stocked Dr. Leeds display, hands rested on his gun belt.

"Sadie told me what happened." He shook his head at his little sister. "You scared poor Pen half to death when you ran in here screaming about blood and making Pen think that Professor Parker had been killed."

"That's what it looked like to me!" Bonnie returned, eyes still watering from the turpentine. "I saw a panel van run the red light at the end of the block just as Dr. Parker stepped into the street. I heard a smack and saw a huge splash of red. What was I supposed to think?"

"You didn't think. If you'd waited another second, you might have seen that Professor Parker was just shaken up."

Bonnie threw up her hands. "But it *looked* like a hit-and-run!"

"Yeah . . ." Eddie glanced away and out our front window. "A hit-and-run by a dark-colored van. That's a nice generic description I'm hearing from everybody who witnessed the incident. But no one managed to get the make, model, or license number."

"There were no plates," Bonnie said. "And the van was black. As for the model, I'm pretty sure it was a Ford Transit. Maybe a 2012."

Eddie's gaze whipped back to his sister so fast I thought he would need a neck brace.

"Don't be so surprised, *Officer*." She glanced my way. "Since my older brother's a cop, I know enough to memorize things like license numbers and any other pertinent details."

Eddie scratched under his cap. "But how did you know it was a Ford Transit?"

"I've been dating Ben Stuckley, Junior, for almost a year, remember? He works part-time at his dad's used-car dealership, and I've chilled with him enough to pick things up."

Cri-man-ee, Jack cried. *She's a Wanda Clark in training. These salesmen must talk cars more than bookies talk horses.*

"Did you see the driver, sis?"

"Sorry, bro. I can't help you there. The windows were tinted."

"Probably a teenager," Eddie said. "First-time drivers have been trouble around here since the school year started."

Aunt Sadie stepped forward. "What about those traffic cameras? You must have gotten a good picture of Brainert's hit-and-run driver with them."

Eddie frowned. "Those cameras won't be fully installed until the end of next month. But don't worry. That truck has got a new bright red paint job. It shouldn't be hard to identify. We've already put out a BOLO."

Sadie hummed skeptically. "You know what I don't understand? Traffic cameras are something that would make this town safer. Yet that project gets put on a back burner, while we business owners have all been saddled with a touchy alarm system and petty violations. Can you explain that to me, Eddie?"

The poor guy actually hung his head—and it wasn't his fault.

"Let's not get off topic," I quickly said, and not just to save Eddie from embarrassment. I couldn't stop thinking about Kevin Ridgeway's hit-and-run. "It sounds to me like someone deliberately tried to run Brainert down. Will you be investigating this incident as an attempted murder?"

"I told you what I'm looking for, Pen. A teenager behind the wheel of his daddy's van."

"With no license plates? Who drives around without plates?"

Eddie's frown deepened. My stressed-out accusation finally broke his patience.

"You know what, Pen? *We're* the police in this town, law enforcement professionals. We know what we're doing, whether or not you think we do!"

This from the cornpone cops who are too busy writing littering tickets to catch a killer. Don't buy into it, honey.

I took a breath to calm down. I hoped Eddie would, too.

This man is my friend, I assured Jack, *and I do trust him, even if he does sound like he's starting to drink the Chief Ciders Kool-Aid.*

What's a fruity kid's drink have to do with police work?

No, Jack, I didn't mean he's actually drinking Kool-Aid! It's a modern term. It means, I don't know, swallowing the chief's malarkey.

That I get!

As I spoke my thoughts to Jack, my expression must have morphed into a mask of pure frustration, because Eddie took one look at my face and shook his head.

"All right, Pen, I give up. If you don't believe *me*, then ask Professor Parker if *he* thinks someone tried to kill him."

"You know what, Eddie? That's a brilliant idea. And don't worry. I'll be asking Brainert *plenty* more questions, too."

CHAPTER 45

The Impatient Patient

The art of medicine consists in amusing the patient
while nature cures the disease.

—Voltaire

"HYDROCARBONS ARE HIGHLY toxic," Dr. Rubino
said in a whisper, so as not to wake my friend in the next
room.

I was standing in Brainert's sunny yellow kitchen, listening to Quindicott's favorite bachelor physician explain
his prognosis. While the doctor spoke, I peeked around the
corner.

Brainert was stretched out on the living room couch,
eyes closed, wrapped in the handmade quilt Sadie and I
bought for him at last year's church Christmas market. He
wasn't wearing much else, and his scrawny, naked chest
looked pallid and too bony. But at least he was breathing.

There was an IV tube inserted in his arm, and a bag of
clear fluid dangled from the hook of an antique coat stand
moved from the corner. Though Brainert was paint-free,
the taint of turpentine still hovered around him—or was
it me?

"Paint also contains lead, mercury, cobalt, barium, and

other heavy metals. The infusion of IV fluids will flush his system of poisons."

"Are you sure he'll be okay?"

"No paint got into Professor Parker's mouth, lungs, or eyes. He would be in quite a bit of trouble had that occurred."

"What can I do?"

"Force fluids. The IV will run for the next two hours, so don't touch it. By this evening we'll know if he's suffered any side effects. We should be alert for blurred vision, swelling in the throat, difficulty swallowing, or mental confusion. If he exhibits none of those symptoms, I believe Professor Parker will be fine."

"What about a headache?" Brainert muttered weakly. "I have a doozy."

I followed Dr. Rubino to my friend's side.

"Nothing to be alarmed about," the doctor assured Brainert as he took his pulse. Then, from his doctor's bag, Dr. Rubino produced a vial of painkillers and ran off to fetch a glass of water.

"How do you feel?"

"Like a Jackson Pollock, Pen."

Pollock? Isn't that some kind of fish?

Quiet, Jack.

"Can you tell me what happened?" I asked.

"A stupid, careless accident."

More like a deliberate act of attempted murder.

"Give me the details, Brainert."

He took a deep breath. "I went to Napp Hardware and bought the paint I'd ordered. Sherwin-Williams Heartthrob."

"I remember."

"I waited for the green light at the crosswalk. I'd just stepped off the curb when I saw the van coming toward me, and I lurched backward in time to save myself. Unfortunately, the paint didn't make it, so I very un-comically re-enacted a scene from Charlie Chaplin."

"Did you see the driver?"

Brainert shook his aching head. "I barely saw the van."

Dr. Rubino returned and fed Brainert two pills and lots of water. Though he had to leave for another emergency, he planned to return in a few hours.

"Don't worry, Doctor, I'll stay with him," I said.

You better, Jack warned. *Somebody has to make sure the button doesn't get pushed on your pal*.

Once Rubino left, I sat beside Brainert.

"Listen. I want you to consider something, but I don't want you to think I'm crazy. Do you think it's possible that someone was trying to kill you?"

"Oh, for goodness' sake!"

"Think about it. Emma Hudson claimed a connection to *Shades of Leather* and ended up dead. Kevin Ridgeway was killed, too, and you as much as admitted his involvement at Monday night's Quibblers meeting. Now someone tried to run you down, and I think—"

"Stop! You're reading too many thrillers, and reading too much into everything!" Brainert squeezed his eyes shut and massaged his head. "Can we speak about this later? Go back to your shop, and I'll—"

"No! I promised the doctor I'd stay until he got back, and that's what I'm going to do. Or would you prefer I called Seymour to come over and babysit in my place?"

Brainert sighed. "Let me sleep until Rubino's painkillers give me some relief? Then we can talk."

"Okay, get some rest." I pulled the quilt up to his neck, tucked it tight around his body, and headed back to the kitchen. On the way, I noticed the door to his study was ajar. I pushed it open and entered, searching for a book to pass the time.

The selection was vast, the room literally lined with bookshelves. The little bit of empty wall space was taken up by framed diplomas (three of them), old photographs of his now deceased family, even pictures of Seymour and me in our misspent youth.

Defying the cliché about eccentric academics and their messy offices, Brainert's work space was as tidy as a military school bunk. His laptop sat in the center of his desk, positioned like a contented cat between two sets of student papers—one stack corrected, the other waiting. And right behind the computer, I found *six* pristine copies of *Shades of Leather*.

Hurriedly, I flipped to the copyright page of each book. Every one carried a little 1.

"Jack, all of these copies are first printings!"

What a co-co-coincidence.

"And as you once pointed out, coincidence is as rare as rain in Reno."

CHAPTER 46

True Confessions

"Villains!" I shrieked. "Dissemble no more! I admit the deed!"

—Edgar Allan Poe, "The Tell-Tale Heart," 1843

"WAKE UP, KNUCKLEHEAD!" Seymour bellowed in his best Moe Howard imitation. "I hear you pulled a Three Stooges gag right in the middle of Cranberry Street!"

Shocked out of a sound sleep, Brainert's peaceful expression turned to one of horror at the sight of the postal uniform.

"What are *you* doing here, Tarnish?"

"I heard you were feeling low, so I thought I would cheer you up."

Brainert blinked, surprised. "Really?"

"Nah. As Ricky Ricardo said to Lucy, 'You got some *'splainin'* to do!'"

I stepped into Brainert's line of sight, holding *Shades of Leather.*

"Seymour and I would like you to explain why you have six copies of this, every one of them a first printing."

Brainert frowned, but his lips remained sealed.

"Come on, Brainiac. Admit it. You wrote at least some of

Shades of Leather. Remember what I said at the Quibblers meeting? The truth is, I went to my attic and dug out that old Xerox of your junior high story. Then I compared it to chapter 34. Lo and behold, you pulled a Raymond Chandler and plagiarized yourself."

"You actually kept a copy of my story?" Brainert asked, more touched than annoyed. "From when I was fifteen?"

"Sure!"

There was a moment of silence between the friends; it was a nice moment, which Seymour finally broke. "So, if you didn't write *Shades of Leather*, I'll eat my mailbag."

Brainert sat up, only to get tangled up in the IV tube. In a fit of pique, he tore the needle out of his arm.

"Okay, you win! It's clear you two won't leave me alone until I confess. So, *yes*, I worked on *Shades of Leather*. But I certainly didn't write it all." Brainert wrapped the quilt tighter around his naked form. "Mostly, I shaped what was a chaotic manuscript into a coherent story."

"But why all the subterfuge?" Seymour's voice was earnest. "Buddy, if I wrote a bestseller, I'd be announcing it through my ice cream truck speakers!"

"That's because you don't have to worry about your academic reputation. Kevin and I do—that is, he did, before he died . . ." Brainert's voice gave out, his face looking so forlorn that I nearly cried. "Anyway, I still have to protect my academic standing. Especially now. If it came out that I wrote that . . . drivel"—he shook his head—"even tenure wouldn't save me. With a Bentley Prize winner on the faculty, and the administration demanding cuts, what would St. Francis want with a . . . a subliterary *hack*?"

"How did this all come about?" I asked.

"You really want to know, Pen?"

"Hey, me, too!" Seymour waved his big hand.

Brainert sighed with resignation. "All right. One of you make us a pot of tea, and I'll tell you. We might as well get comfortable. It's a story."

CHAPTER 47

A Tale of Two Rewrites

> I always start writing with a clean piece of paper and
> a dirty mind.
>
> —Patrick Dennis

"A YEAR AND a half ago, Kevin told me he'd written the
perfect potboiler . . ."

Brainert paused to take a sip of the ginger-lemon tea I'd
made us. Seymour passed on the tea, preferring a giant mug
of hot cocoa with double whipped cream.

"Did your friend write any fiction before this?" I asked.

"Two political thrillers, which were rejected. That's why
he wanted my advice. He sent a formal proposal to an editor, and she was interested in reading the entire manuscript.
Before he submitted, he wanted me to look it over and sug-
gest any improvements."

"And you had *mucho* suggestions, am I right?" Seymour
taunted.

"Yes, *mucho* is putting it mildly. While the basic story
was intriguing and salacious, the execution was dull, the
prose turgid. Kevin had a habit of abandoning a scene, just
as it was getting . . . *interesting*. I recommended added
material—"

Seymour raised an eyebrow. "What sort of added material?"

"I suggested more, you know, *exploits*."

"You mean *naughty bits*?"

"I merely suggested that Kevin should pull back the curtain. To capture the jaded imagination of the modern reader, the writing had to be more explicit."

"So, Kevin Ridgeway rewrote it?"

"Alas, his second draft was no better than his first."

Seymour peered skeptically over his cocoa mug. "I can't imagine you wrote the naughty stuff, Brainiac. You're not exactly a playboy."

"This from a man who still eats Froot Loops for breakfast and didn't have a steady girlfriend until he was thirty!"

"I was saving myself. And what do Froot Loops have to do with sexual exploits?"

"Let's keep our focus! And try to behave." I felt like I was chiding Spencer, but it worked, though both men assumed a sulking silence. I broke the deadlock with a firm question. "Brainert, answer me straight. If Ridgeway didn't write the erotic scenes, *who* did?"

"Pen, I'm sorry. I don't have a clue."

Seymour threw up his hands. "How can you *not* know who put the smut in *Shades*?"

Brainert explained, "About a week after Kevin handed in his second draft, he began giving me inserts. These were the erotic scenes. I knew they weren't written by Kevin. The prose was polished, descriptive, sensual, and even emotional, with wonderful turns of phrase. Each scenario built on the one before it, heightening the erotic tension."

"And you have no clue where they came from?"

Brainert sipped his tea in thought. "I can give you one clue. No, two. I remember when I complimented him on the new pages, Kevin said something about working a *woman's touch* into the prose, and that's what improved the book."

"Sure sounds like he got a woman to write for him," Seymour said. "That confirms my own analysis of your third mystery author. I thought it was a woman all along."

I only knew of two women in Kevin Ridgeway's life—and one was far too young to write, let alone read, parts of *Shades of Leather*.

"Could his ex-wife be the mystery writer?" I pondered.

"I don't think so," Brainert said.

"Why?"

"Because of clue number two: the way the inserts came to me. Kevin always gave me hard copies, which meant I had to type the pages into the manuscript myself."

"I don't follow," I said. "Why is that a clue?"

"It means the author really wished to remain anonymous. There are lots of markers on an electronic file. *And* each batch came tucked inside an old-style St. Francis University folder, one that featured the logo with our original student union, before it burned down. That folder and that logo have not been around for twenty years—and they weren't handed out to students, either. Only faculty members got them."

"How do you even know that?" Seymour asked. "You weren't teaching twenty years ago."

"I saw a stack in Dean Pepper's office, and I asked about them."

"So you think the mystery author is a female senior faculty member?"

"That's right, Pen. But there's one more thing. I found a bunch of photocopies packed in with the final insert."

"Photocopies of what?" Seymour asked.

"They appeared to be entries from a diary. A woman's diary."

CHAPTER 48

The Paper Chase

I never travel without my diary. One should always
have something sensational to read . . .

—Oscar Wilde, *The Importance of Being Earnest*

I WAS SHOCKED by Brainert's revelation. The more he
shared, the more I realized *Shades of Leather* was not
fiction—or at least not all of it.

"Are you sure the pages were from an actual woman's
diary?"

Brainert nodded. "There were eleven pages of entries,
all written in the same flowing cursive. The copies themselves were a copy of a copy that was old and faded. The
basic contents of the diary entry were the same as the insert. It's as if someone handed over the diary pages and
instructed the author to dramatize, enhance, and embellish
the scene for fiction."

"Which could have been the case with every insert," I
said. "Did you ask Professor Ridgeway about those photocopies?"

"No. Midterms were coming, and the whole process had
gone on far too long. I just wanted the project to end. I

honestly thought nothing would come of it, but three months ago, Kevin handed me a bank draft for ten thousand dollars and those six copies of the first edition."

"Ten thousand dollars? Is that all?" Seymour burst out laughing. "You came cheap, Brainert, considering *Shades* has been on top of the hardcover bestseller lists for a month."

"It didn't seem so at the time," Brainert sniffed. "My theater required a wheelchair ramp to make the bathrooms code compliant, and the city council was threatening to shut us down. That check just about covered the cost of the installation—and that was enough for me."

The money wasn't what concerned me. I still couldn't get over the fact that *Shades of Leather* was based on a real woman's diary.

"Brainert, do you have any idea who wrote that diary?"

"No, Pen, I have absolutely no idea."

"Do you still have those photocopies?"

"I do. But they won't help you."

"I'd like to see them anyway."

"Fine. Look in the bottom right-hand drawer of my desk. You should find them there, along with the vintage folders and hardcopies. But there are no names. No dates beyond the day of the week; no clue to the author's identity."

"We'll see about that!" I hurried to Brainert's study.

Minutes later, I was scanning the diary pages and handing them off to Seymour.

"Ooh la la. I remember this scene! Proves the old adage that two's company and three's a party!"

"And there *is* a date," I cried. "The heading is Monday, and three paragraphs down the diarist writes that it's the seventh day of June. We can approximate the year with a universal calendar!"

"That's something," Brainert acknowledged. "But it won't reveal much."

"There are a few more pages," I said gamely, but I was beginning to lose hope. And then I saw it, two innocent little words.

"Look! Right here!"

Seymour squinted at the words next to my pointing finger. "Coffee milk?"

"Yes! Coffee milk!"

Brainert leaned over to read the passage with Seymour:

I woke up and stretched my young body like a satisfied feline. Orgasms all night long. Coffee milk in the morning. I stir the Eclipse into the milk and it is oooh sooo groovy! It is an orgasm for my mouth. I made a glass for him. I take it to his bedroom. He yawns and stretches his long hard body. Like a cat looking for his cream, this is what I said. Here it is! Here is your cream! With my pink tongue, I licked my lips and am slowly unbuttoning my shirt . . .

"Hubba-hubba!" Seymour cried. "Forget the coffee milk. I need a cold shower!"

"Ugh," Brainert cringed. "It's a grammatical nightmare."

"Oh, for heaven's sake, don't you two see? *Shades of Leather* is set in New York City. Justine, the main character, was born and raised in Manhattan. But in these diary pages, the girl mentions *coffee milk* and she makes it with *Eclipse*—as in Eclipse coffee syrup! That's a local Rhode Island brand, and I can tell you from experience, New Yorkers don't know about Eclipse syrup, let alone coffee milk, not unless they grew up around here!"

Brainert met my eyes. "You're right, Pen. I missed that. Eclipse wouldn't have been sold in New York stores. It appears you've found a connection to this region."

"Unless there's some other explanation for why she has the syrup," Seymour said. "Like maybe one of her lovers gave it to her. And what does a connection to this region actually get us? We still don't know the identity of the other author, never mind the girl who wrote this diary. According to the Brain here, the only guy who might know got planted in Old Q."

As the three of us sat in silence, I recalled the last time

I saw a bottle of Eclipse coffee syrup. It was on Emma Hudson's counter the day I found her body.

Emma's ex-husband said she grew up in California, so why did she have the coffee syrup? Sure, she could have developed a taste for coffee milk. Or maybe she'd bought it to please a local friend—maybe the very friend who Mr. Brink mentioned. And could that friend have been the diarist of *Shades of Leather*? Or the third writer of the book? Or both? That would certainly explain how Emma Hudson's old photo ended up on the book jacket.

While I considered the big picture, I suddenly remembered something small. "Guys, I can think of one brain who might know the name of the mystery woman."

"Who?" asked the two like brother owls.

"Waldo."

Brainert frowned. "Who's Waldo?"

"Emma Hudson's pet parrot."

"And how are we supposed to find a dead woman's pet bird?"

"Easy!" Seymour grinned. "At the moment, he's perched in my living room."

CHAPTER 49

The Unusual Suspects

I have had a perfectly wonderful evening, but this wasn't it.

—Groucho Marx

WE OUGHT TO be giving Waldo the third degree right now, Jack complained an hour later. *As goofy as it sounds, bracing that stool pigeon makes more sense than greeting gawkers and passing out dead wood.*

Our bookshop was filling up fast. Sadie and I were waiting for all the ticket holders to arrive before we locked the shop doors. Until then, the register would remain open for last-minute buys, and Bonnie would continue to ring up purchases.

"Sorry, Jack. This book signing takes precedence. I do have a business to run."

Your business is murder, baby, and you can take that two ways! We're looking for a dame, not a wheezy old professor.

Jack was right about that.

Evidence pointed to the third writer as a woman. And because of that vintage folder, Brainert concluded that she was a senior member of the faculty.

I wasn't so sure.

What if this female writer found those vintage folders in a forgotten supply closet, or a faculty office she'd inherited from a retiree? The more I thought about it, the more I was convinced there were better suspects right here at this signing.

So instead of enjoying an event that I'd been looking forward to for weeks, I found myself acting like Jack Shepard in the flesh, suspiciously scanning each female faculty member in the crowd, wondering if one of them could be the mystery ghostwriter of the biggest bestseller of the season.

Helen Frye was a candidate. Her course on human sexuality was as popular as it was controversial. At the moment, the attractive thirty-something doctor of applied psychology was perusing our true crime section.

Another possibility was Donna Copeland. The no-nonsense economics professor shopped our store for used romance novels—the racier the better, she said. From experience, I knew that many women who read romances also aspired to write them. Did Donna dip her toe in the perfumed pool and produce the erotic scenes?

There were others—Marta Simone, an education teacher whose tastes ran to the most extreme and sadistic thrillers. Jennifer Strawn, of the Women's Studies program, who wrote a thesis on *Story of O*. Mina Goldberg, whose course on the French Revolution tipped a hat to the Marquis de Sade.

While I considered those suspects and more, my aunt appeared at my shoulder. "Have you seen Dr. Leeds?"

"Ichabod Crane with muscles? Not yet."

"He is quite fit for an older man, isn't he?" Sadie remarked. She sounded a bit smitten, but then everyone here was giddy with excitement. "Did you know Dr. Leeds went to Columbia University on an athletic scholarship? He mentioned it on NPR."

I glanced at my watch. "I hope he gets here soon."

"Don't fret," Sadie said. "We're selling a lot of books in the meantime. In fact, Bonnie seems a bit frazzled. I'm going to open the second register."

"I can think of worse fates," I said absently.

"Will you be able to handle the door alone?" Sadie asked, and I nodded.

"Spencer finished the sound check, with Amy's help," she added. "They make a cute pair, don't they?"

"I know your proclivity for matchmaking, but I'm not ready to be a mother-in-law just yet."

Sadie laughed, eyes sharp. "Don't worry, dear. I can think of worse fates."

"Good evening!" Shirley Anthor greeted me with enthusiasm.

As I took her ticket, I couldn't help adding her to my suspect list. The petite, vivacious, and outspoken fifty-something taught medieval history at St. Francis. I remembered Brainert mentioning her film series lecture comparing the Arthurian tropes in *Excalibur* with *Monty Python and the Holy Grail*.

"Is the store section still open for business?" she asked, tossing her frosted curls.

"Only until our event begins."

"Great! I'm looking for a replacement. It's an out-of-print book I loaned and have no chance of recovering."

I nodded. "We hear that all the time. Was it part of your film lecture at Professor Parker's theater? I always enjoy Arthurian stories. I'm sorry I missed it. How did it go?"

"Oh, it was a great success, but this book's quite different, a history of weapons in the Middle Ages. I read choice passages to my freshmen class about how they sliced and diced one another on the battlefield. It gives them a sense of medieval brutality in ways they won't easily forget."

"Sounds like your course should come with a trigger warning," I joked.

"It does," Shirley said flatly. "My next lecture is on campus this Friday, if you're interested."

"I might be. What's the subject?"

"Feminist Jurisprudence and the *Malleus Maleficarum*!"

I cleared my throat. "Well, if you don't find the book

you're looking for, leave the title with Sadie. I'm sure she can locate a copy for you."

"Why, Shirley, you're looking lovely tonight."

We both turned to find a grinning Dr. Wendell Pepper, dean of communications at St. Francis University—and Brainert's partner in the Movie Town Theater.

Pepper was looking dapper this evening in his tailored suit and favorite burgundy tie, the one bearing the coat of arms for Lodge House, Quindicott's exclusive country club.

Since his recent divorce, I noticed the "salt" had disappeared from the dean's formerly salt-and-pepper hair. Like Brainert, he'd shed a few pounds, too. But unlike my friend, he'd replaced that fat with muscle.

"Are you alone tonight, Shirley?" Pepper pressed. "It so happens that I am, too. We could certainly find a cozy spot together."

"That would be nice," Shirley replied. "Right now, I'm looking for a used book—"

"Splendid! Perhaps I can help!"

"You can certainly do the hauling," Shirley said, looking him up and down. "You're fit enough."

"Tennis at the country club has done wonders for my waistline—as well as my energy," he replied, eyes sparkling. "Perhaps you'll join me for doubles at the club, or at my practice court at home, as long as you don't mind spending time with my new Yorkie."

"A Yorkie?" Shirley replied, her own eyes sparkling. "And here I would have guessed an Irish wolfhound."

They both laughed. Then together they headed off.

Meanwhile, my mind raced. So, Pepper has a Yorkie? A new Yorkie, at that. Is that a coincidence, or is Brainert's business partner the one who tried to off him today?!

A moment later, my aunt reappeared. "I've closed the registers, and Leeds is waiting. We should begin moving people to the event space."

Herding a hundred chattering, book- and phone-distracted people into the event space was a logistical challenge that took ten minutes to overcome, even with help from an enthusiastic Amy and Spencer.

Just when everyone had taken their seats, the man of the hour tapped me on the shoulder.

"I see someone has brought an infernal dog to this event."

Dr. Roger Leeds followed his rude remark with a noisy honk into a well-used handkerchief. He swiped his prominent nose and tucked the cloth behind his lapel.

"You're allergic?" I asked, forced to look up to meet the six-foot-five professor's lofty gaze.

"Terribly so, Mrs. McClure. *Please* see that the beast is *nowhere* near the front row, or I shall be unable to give my lecture."

The doctor's haughty tone took me aback. Just six months ago, at our first signing, Dr. Leeds seemed polite, though distant. At that event he spoke for over two hours, and stayed another hour to answer audience questions.

Brainert was right. As usual!

The professor's attitude really had changed since he went from Bentley Prize nominee to winner. Now Dr. Leeds scanned the room with an expression of hostile impatience.

"I'll give them the short version tonight. My full lecture would be lost on them. And signing all of their books and fielding the same puerile questions will be trying enough."

What's gotten into him? I thought in disgust.

I'll tell you what's gotten into him, Jack replied. *The big time. Because of some pumped-up piece of paper, he's become a very large wheel on a narrow little road.*

That very large wheel just ordered me to move Mrs. Hiller and her Seeing Eye dog to the back row!

That's the way the world works, baby. Dare to get in a big wheel's way, and you might just get run over.

I approached Mrs. Hiller and apologetically explained the situation. She graciously traded seats with a grad student in the fourth row. I returned to Dr. Leeds with the good news. He didn't bother thanking me. He merely signaled to Sadie that he was ready, and she introduced him.

"One last dance," he muttered as he approached the podium.

As the Bentley Prize winner took the stage to enthusiastic applause, I returned to the bookstore, deciding I'd rather tally the registers than listen to anything this disdainful man had to say.

CHAPTER 50

A Little Bird Told Me

When the murders are committed by mathematicians, you can solve them by mathematics. Most of them aren't and this one wasn't.

—Dashiell Hammett, *The Thin Man*

"WELCOME TO TARNISH Mansion!"

It was after ten P.M. when I arrived at Seymour's house, a grand Victorian on posh Larchmont Avenue. Ever the lucky duck, Seymour had inherited the estate from the town's eccentric spinster, Timothea Todd, who'd taken a shine to her friendly mailman before departing the earthly plane.

My blunt, socially backward best friend, the geeky *Jeopardy!* champ and part-time ice cream truck entrepreneur, was now an official resident of Quindicott's most exclusive lane; his neighbors were among the town's most accomplished, uber-educated elites.

Brainert had yet to get over it.

"He's still decorating in late-American garish," the professor sniffed in my ear as I entered the large living room.

The Victorian furnishings Miss Todd bequeathed Seymour, along with her portrait, framed in silver, were still in place, along with the flat-screen TV. His lava lamps were still slowly undulating, the gobs of neon goop rising and falling in glowing color.

But since I last visited, Seymour had added life-size cardboard standees of the original *Enterprise* crew from *Star Trek*, and landscape paintings had been replaced with framed portraits of the Universal monsters—Karloff as Frankenstein, Lugosi as Dracula, and Chaney as The Wolf Man.

He'd emptied the glass display cabinet of Miss Todd's Dresden dolls, and replaced them with resin statues of the tripods from H. G. Wells's *War of the World*s, a scale model of the Time Machine, and an action figure–sized Claude Rains as the Invisible Man.

A massive, lighted replica of Jules Verne's *Nautilus* from *Twenty Thousand Leagues Under the Sea* dominated an entire shelf, and below that stood an army of vintage *Star Wars* figures.

In a cage flanked by cardboard cutouts of Captain Kirk and Mr. Spock, Waldo the parrot proudly preened his blue feathers and warbled happily.

"Beam me up, Scotty! Beam me up! Squawk!"

"We're in luck!" Seymour grinned. "Waldo is in a talkative mood tonight."

When I first explained to Brainert that Waldo was a witness to Emma's life, as well as her death, and he might give us a valuable clue, he stared at me as if I were crazy. But Seymour took my side.

"It's not *that* crazy. Whenever I delivered PetMeds to Mrs. Hudson, the bird always greeted me by name. And this mystery ghostwriter must have known Emma, at least well enough to swipe an old photo."

"And, Brainert, you still believe the ghostwriter is a member of the St. Francis University faculty, right?"

"Yes, Pen. Those vintage folders are a dead giveaway. No one else is likely to have them."

"So it makes sense." I turned to Seymour, who'd been looking after the bird for days. "If Waldo hears a woman's name that he recognizes, he'll likely repeat it, right?"

Seymour nodded, but Brainert still voiced doubts.

"Oh, come on," I coaxed. "I know you have a copy of the faculty directory on your mobile phone. You can read the women's names out loud and see if Waldo responds to one of them."

"I still think it sounds crazy."

"Yeah," Seymour cackled, "about as crazy as a few stuffy professors writing the hottest erotic thriller of the year!"

"Speaking of which, I had an encounter with Dean Pepper tonight that made me think he might be the secret writer we're looking for. While he was hitting on Shirley Anthor, he mentioned he'd just acquired a Yorkie—"

Brainert raised a hand to stop me.

"Sorry, Pen. I don't know where he got the Yorkie, but there is no way he's our mystery writer. The man's literary ability is limited at best. He insists on writing the movie descriptions for our features, and I always revise his pedestrian prose before the public sees it. He's a fine teacher and administrator, but Wendell could never have made those flamboyant contributions to *Shades of Leather*."

"But didn't you say it was Dean Pepper's office where you saw those vintage folders?"

Brainert frowned. "That's true . . ."

Seymour clapped his hand. "So why don't we start Waldo out with the dean's name? What do you say?"

Despite his misgivings, Brainert loudly recited Dean Wendell Pepper's name to the caged bird. Waldo gave no reaction.

"I told you, Pen, we're looking for a woman."

Turning to his phone, Brainert began reciting female names from the faculty directory. Twenty minutes later, he'd only reached the letter F.

"Tracy Anne Fritz, Ph.D. Department of Biological Sciences."

Waldo whistled, squawked, and looked away.

"Come on, Brainert. Hurry it up! You don't have to read their degrees and departments, just the names."

Seymour's tone was exasperated, and I sympathized. At this glacial pace, we'd be here for another hour.

Worse than that, Waldo showed no interest, never mind a reaction.

"Kay W. Frolla, Ph.D. Department of Computer Science."

Waldo chewed his feathers and dipped his beak in the water dispenser—a sure sign he was bored, according to Seymour.

"Go faster, Brainiac. He's waiting for the next name."

"How do you know what he's waiting for? Are you a bird whisperer?"

"Guys, will you stop bickering!"

"Very well, Pen." Brainert leaned back in one of Seymour's massive lounge chairs. "Helen Frye, Ph.D. Department of Psychology."

Seymour covered his ears. "You're a *psycho* if you keep reading their credentials."

"You're a psycho!! You're a psycho!" Waldo cried.

"See! Now you're confusing him!"

"Me!" Brainert was incensed. "You're the one who called me a psycho!"

"Read the next name," I begged.

"Mary Frances Giordano."

"Wait," Seymour whispered. "He seemed to react to that name. Read it again."

"Mary Frances—"

Waldo bobbed his head and dropped a fresh one on the *Quindicott Bulletin* lining the bottom of his cage.

Brainert blew his stack. "The only reaction I get is bird guano!"

"Technically, bats drop guano," Seymour said. "If it's from a bird, it's just crap. Or if you prefer the vulgar plain old birdsh—"

"Next!"

"Anupama Gupta—"

"Gupta! Gupta!" Waldo cried.

"Eureka!" Seymour jumped to his feet. "Read it again, but slower this time."

"Anu . . . pama . . . Gupta."

"Sanjay Gupta! Sanjay Gupta. Squawk!" Waldo's voice dropped an octave. "This is CNN."

Seymour sighed. "Sorry, guys. Waldo always watches the news with me."

Brainert grit his teeth and went back to reading.

"Henrietta Hollister, Ph.D. Department of Mathematics—"

"Yeah, sure, a mathematician is going to write bestselling erotica," Seymour cracked.

"Caroline Linden has a Harvard math degree," Brainert sniffed. "And she writes romance novels."

"Okay, you got me," Seymour said. "But do her books have naughty bits? And how naughty are they?"

"For the *last time*, Seymour, let him read!"

"One last dance! One last dance!" the bird cried.

I blinked. "Where did I just hear that phrase? I know! Dr. Leeds said those words tonight, as he approached the podium."

"Except we're looking for a woman," Seymour said.

"And that arrogant ass is about the last man on earth who'd participate in putting together a potboiler," Brainert added.

"Jealous, much?" Seymour goaded.

"It's not jealousy. It's pure dread. Can you imagine what that Bentley Prize winner will do to me if he finds out I've cowritten a piece of literary trash?"

"Stop being so dramatic," I told him. "Plenty of people are enjoying the book, and it's certainly helping our shop's bottom line."

"That won't help my case in the department."

"I think you're selling your colleagues short."

"Not Leeds. At departmental meetings, he routinely ridicules choice passages from *New York Times* bestsellers—as a form of amusement."

"Amusement is right," Seymour snorted. "'Cause if he read 'choice passages' from his idea of literature, he'd put the room to sleep!"

"Enough! I don't care about Leeds and his awful, pompous attitude. What I care about is solving this mystery."

"Oh, very well!" Brainert went back to reading names. "Jessica Pardy—"

This is *Jeopardy!* This is *Jeopardy!* Squawk!"

"Melissa Hunt, Ph.D. Department of Theater Arts."

Waldo preened his feathers and glanced away.

And so it went, seemingly forever. When we finally finished, it was well past midnight.

"What do you think?" Seymour asked. "Who's our most likely culprit?"

I glanced at my notes. "CNN's Sanjay Gupta. But I'm guessing he has an alibi."

CHAPTER 51

The Way We Were

The past is whatever the records and the memories agree upon.

—George Orwell, *1984*

DECLARING THAT "FAILURE made him hungry," Seymour went to the kitchen to whip up snacks. Dejected, I sank into the oversize Victorian couch.

The bird was no help at all, Jack. The stool pigeon was just another dead end.

A draft swirled around me. *Given your pal's close call with a paint can, you better find a way around this detour. Or that dead end may turn into a dead friend.*

The spirit's words chilled me more than he did.

"We still don't know the identity of the other writer, Brainert. How am I going to protect you?"

"Protect me? Who says I need protection?"

"I do. Emma Hudson stumbled upon her stolen image, used to help sell *Shades of Leather*, and she was dead in a matter of hours. Kevin Ridgeway worked on the book, and he was brutally run down on a dark road. You helped write it, too, and the same thing almost happened to you—and in broad daylight. It seems to me this killer is becoming more desperate, maybe even unhinged."

"What happened to Kevin and to me could have been random accidents. Emma Hudson was probably an accident, too. Didn't you read your *Quindicott Bulletin*?"

I wanted to scream. "Fine. Believe what you want, but I say we need to find this other author and determine whether she's behind this string of so-called accidents."

"All right. I'll indulge you. What would be her motive?"

"Remember what you said about how she turned in her pages? No electronic trace. Maybe she wasn't counting on the book getting so much attention, and now she's obsessed with keeping her identity secret. And don't forget the money. That novel stands to rake in millions now that it sold to Hollywood. She may want to keep it all."

"But I have no contract, no legal recourse. With Kevin gone, I can't even prove I was involved."

"You could muddy the waters. If you spoke up about the truth behind the book, there would be demands for Jessica Swindell to step forward and answer the charges."

"But Jessica Swindell doesn't exist. It's Ridgeway's pseudonym."

"No, Brainert, it's Ridgeway's and *your* pseudonym, along with this third writer, who Ridgeway brought in. With one ghostwriter turned into a ghost, you *nearly* sent to the spirit world, and the subject of the book's author photo sent over a balcony—all in the space of one week—it seems to me the third author could very well be a murderer!"

In the long silence that followed, the professor's pale skin went even paler.

Either he's ghosting you again, sweetheart, or you finally cracked the egghead.

Just then, Seymour returned in his lord-of-the-manor wear: maroon ascot and gold smoking jacket (even though he didn't smoke). Proud of his hosting abilities, he set down an antique silver tray laden with sizzling, preprocessed microwavable foods.

"I spread this repast before you. 'Tis my Hot Pockets combo."

Brainert made a face. "What's that bowl in the middle?"

"The house dipping sauce, prepared by yours truly."

"So, there's something actually made in a kitchen and not an industrial facility?"

"Hey, it's hot and it's free. Plus, I've got root beer. You're lucky I didn't serve Tang."

Despite Brainert's snipe, he was the first to dig in, and he ate quite a bit. After a few minutes of munching, Seymour waved his phone.

"I used a universal calendar to find all the Monday, June sevenths, and I've concluded the diary was written in 1971."

"How did you determine that?" I asked.

"The diarist wrote that a song on the radio reminded her it was Monday. The song she's referring to is 'Rainy Days and Mondays' by the Carpenters, which topped the Billboard charts in June of 1971."

"And she did use the term *groovy* in her diary," I pointed out.

"Technically, the term's been in use since 1937," Brainert said.

"But it did dominate youth slang through the late sixties and early seventies," I countered, and then calculated in my head. "Given Emma Hudson's age, she would have been in her late teens or early twenties in 1971. Could she have possibly been the diarist as well as the model for the author photo?"

Not likely, I thought as soon as I asked it, recalling Philip Hudson's description of his ex-wife . . .

"Emma Royce was a California girl, through and through. She was raised by a wealthy family in Pacific Heights, and only left San Francisco to start her own New Age spiritual center in Venice Beach . . ."

Jack grunted at my memory of Philip's words. *You're kidding, doll, aren't you? That boozehound was crying to the police about his ex-wife's death the same morning he chirped like a canary on the phone to you. He told the coppers he was in New York and you he was in Providence. He said he lived a life of "leisure" in California while his ex gives a list of his failed business ventures to her neighbor downstairs. You really want to rely on what Philip Hudson says?*

I get your point. But why lie about Emma's upbringing—and so specifically? Unless she lied to him. That seems more likely. People like to remake themselves—that's not uncommon. Either way, she might have grown up around here. And Philip did claim she was an expert in tantric sex, which also suggests she might have written the diary.

Doll, when are you gonna learn? Why rely on "might" when hard evidence can tell you whether you're wrong or right?

Hard evidence of what?

You know what. You got the dead dame's handwriting!

I nearly dropped my Hot Pocket. "Guys, listen! We should compare the handwriting in those diary pages with Emma's handwriting!"

Brainert blinked. "You have a sample of her handwriting?"

Nodding like mad, I called up my mobile phone photos of Emma's mileage logbook, the one Eddie retrieved from her car on the day she died.

"Brainert, did you bring the diary pages?"

He produced them, and we all studied the evidence.

"Check it out," Seymour said. "Notice how the letter S is larger than the other letters in both the mileage logbook and in the diary?"

I pointed. "And see the way both writers put a slash through the number 9. That's unique . . ."

Brainert found similarities, too, enough that he finally agreed with me and Seymour.

"The handwriting looks the same."

Progress at last! If you were alive, I would kiss you, Jack!

And I would pucker up.

CHAPTER 52

Get Out of Jail Free Card

Very few of us are what we seem.

—Agatha Christie

LYING IN BED that night, my heart was still pounding.

My friends and I had uncovered a shocking secret about the most talked-about book in the country. *Shades of Leather*, a supposed work of fiction, *wasn't* fiction, not entirely, anyway. An old diary of Emma Hudson's had served as the basis for the tale.

Come on, sweetheart, there's a bigger shock than that behind your bogus bestseller.

The cool whisper of Jack's arrival gave me a shiver.

"You're talking about Emma's murder?"

How many authors do you know who toss the subject of their book over a balcony?

"None, and that's the problem. The most important piece of this puzzle is still missing."

The piece with the killer's name on it.

"And other pieces, too, ones that might help us see the whole picture. Like why did Emma move to California and lie about her past?"

That's not a hard nut to crack.

"True. Lots of women make changes in their lives, start over someplace new."

"Make changes"? Jack snorted. You still don't get it, do you?

"Get what?"

Lots of Do-Right Janes start over, sure. You did it your-self, when you moved back here to Cornpone-cott. But you never lied about your past, did you? You never tried to cover it up.

"No . . ." I said, stifling a yawn. "Why would I?"

You would if you had something to hide.

"And what did Emma have to hide?"

When I was workin' the meanest streets of Manhattan, as a flatfoot and then as a gumshoe, I only knew one kind of bird who wanted to erase her past—a jailbird.

"Jailbird . . ."

I repeated the word. It knocked around my brain until my eyes drifted closed.

I WAS NO longer in my quiet bedroom, snoring the night away. I was back on that crowded Manhattan sidewalk, traffic horns blaring as I faced down a car the size of a freight train.

In crippling heels and a long, tight skirt, running wasn't an option. Before I even tried, a strong arm circled my waist and yanked me into a doorway.

The thug behind the wheel was forced to turn, missing us by a hair. Then the DeSoto veered off the sidewalk, clip-ping a fire hydrant as it bounced into the street and sped away.

For a moment, my body went limp. When I came to, I found myself looking into Jack's steel gray gaze. His face was so close to mine I could feel his breath on my cheek.

"Where am I?" I sputtered.

"Exactly where I want you, baby. In my arms—minus that horrified look on your face."

"Sorry, Jack, but my heart is pounding!"

"Don't worry, doll. I got the universal cure for that."

"What is it?"

He lifted an eyebrow. "A good stiff one."

TEN MINUTES LATER, I accepted the glass of Scotch from Jack's rough hands.

"You're still shaking, sweetheart. Better shoot it."

Throwing back my head, I swallowed the amber liquid and squeezed my eyes shut, figuring if the burning liquor didn't wake me from this dream, nothing would. But when I opened my eyes again, I was still in a smoky, dimly lit, oak-lined gin joint, circa 1947.

No ESPN playing here, just a radio announcer calling horse races; a scarred wooden bar; and a big tattooed guy standing behind it with a ball bat and .38 within reach.

I was one of maybe three women in the entire place. Nobody here noticed. They kept to their own business, which was mainly hard drinking—and reading their racing forms.

As for me, my ridiculous, cork-shaped tower of a hat was gone, but my red suit and white gloves were back in place, along with those pinching underthings. I fidgeted on the barstool, trying to adjust my armor-like girdle without ripping my skirt off.

Despite the Scotch, I was still feeling breathless, still seeing certain death bearing down on me.

"I thought it was curtains for both of us."

Jack poured me another and offered a wry smile. "We both know a runaway DeSoto ain't what stops my clock. It's just not in the cards."

"The card! Oh my gosh! Have you still got the card? I pinched it out of the purse of Harry Macklin's secretary."

"Got it right here." He patted his lapel. "And I'm impressed."

"I knew there was something suspicious about Dorothy Moreland. Now we know that's not even her name. It's Doris Sizemore—some coincidence, right? Same last name as Macklin's missing star author, Mickey."

Jack pulled the card out of his pocket and turned it in his hand.

"New York State Training School for Girls," he read.

"Is that a prison?"

"It's a couple of birthday candles shy of one. It's a place to house incorrigible girls, until they grow up to be incorrigible dames."

"How do you think she ended up there?"

"Any doll between twelve and seventeen can do time there if she got on the wrong side of the law. This card shows that Macklin's mousy secretary did her time and is ready to return to society."

"It also says she's a trained stenographer."

"They teach the girls skills, so they won't go back to doing what jammed them up in the first place."

"I see—and I can guess why Doris Sizemore changed her name."

"Why's that?"

"She probably couldn't find work on Publisher's Row, not with a criminal record. So, she took the name Moreland. How she got Macklin to hire her is a mystery to me, but it's clear she developed a terrible crush on her boss; and with her real last name the same as the missing author's, I'd say Mickey Sizemore is her father or uncle—someone who's a born storyteller and had some hard knocks in life."

I told Jack what I knew about the author, and it wasn't much.

"Sizemore's books are pretty dated, as I recall, and he died sometime in the 1950s. But he wrote colorful characters, and I can see why his books were bestsellers in his day. He knew the truth about the seamier side of the city, including prison life, and I'm guessing he wrote from experience."

"I know a lot of miscreants and ex-yardbirds, but they *got* booked. None of them ever wrote one. And why all the drama, do you suppose? The bloody manuscript, the disappearing act?"

"I don't know. Maybe Mickey Sizemore never thought his books would do so well. Now the pressure is on to write more, but he doesn't want to. He's out of ideas, or he's just tired."

"Why not just say so to Macklin?" Jack scratched the scar on his chin. "Why use Doris to deliver a bloody manuscript?"

"You got me there."

"What about this mug with the gold dentures? The guy who doesn't want Mickey Sizemore found? Who do you think he is?"

"Best guess? Someone the author hired to scare Macklin—and us, too—from trying to find him." I took another sip of Scotch for courage. "So now what?"

"I've heard your theory, partner. You tell me."

"That's easy. I saw Dorothy's gas bill in her purse, so I know where she lives." I glanced at the horseshoe clock on the wall. "I say we stick with our original plan and pay her a visit. She should be heading home from work soon. With the right pressure, I'm sure she'll tell us how to find Macklin's missing author."

Jack finished his Scotch in one gulp. Then he slid off the barstool and donned his fedora.

"Just remember, Penny. Theories are fine to start, but the case don't end till you find hard evidence."

"All right, Jack. Then let's go find it."

CHAPTER 53

Family Feud

When I type "The End," it's like being paroled from prison.

—Clive Cussler

JACK AND I tailed Dorothy Moreland from the subway station. We watched her buy groceries and a paper before turning onto a quiet street in Canarsie, Brooklyn.

We planned to confront her on the front stoop of her three-story walk-up, when somebody beat us to it.

"Trouble," Jack said, jerking his thumb at a too-familiar brown DeSoto speeding down the block.

The car braked hard, the door opened, and out popped Gold Teeth. He left the vehicle idling, the door wide open, as he charged up to a rattled Miss Moreland.

"Doris!" he bellowed.

"I told you not to call me that," the frightened woman shot back. "It's Dorothy."

He brushed off her complaint. "I need three yards, right now—"

"Three hundred dollars!"

"And maybe another grand next week."

Miss Moreland—or should I say Doris Sizemore—

backed away from the big man. "I don't have that kind of money! Honest, Mickey."

Mickey?! Gold teeth is Mickey?!

Gobsmacked, Jack and I exchanged astonished glances.

"You're my sister, so you gotta help," Mickey Sizemore growled. "You're getting paid for that new book, ain't ya?"

"You took the advance, Mickey. There's no more money until publication—"

"Let's see what you got, then!"

Horrified, I watched Sizemore push his sister to the stoop, and the groceries scattered. He slapped the cowering woman's hand aside and reached for her purse.

Jack cursed low. His long legs and rapid stride carried him right up to Mickey Sizemore. Gold teeth flashing, Sizemore reached for his gun—only to remember the PI had relieved him of his iron in Hell's Kitchen.

By then, Jack was on him. There were no niceties, no exchange of snappy patter this time. The gumshoe slugged Sizemore, and the man went down.

Jack quickly helped Miss Moreland to her feet.

"Move your Mary Janes before the mug gets up again!"

Heels clicking, I caught up with Jack as he pushed Miss Moreland into the idling DeSoto. I dived into the back seat beside her, and Jack took the wheel. As Mickey Sizemore began to stir, we sped away, his curses echoing after us, down the Brooklyn block.

ON THE DRIVE to Manhattan, the former Doris Sizemore tearfully told us her story.

Orphaned at fourteen, Doris was left in the care of her delinquent older brother. When he and his punk friends were caught knocking over a liquor store, he was given a choice by a criminal court judge. He could join the navy or face eight years in Sing Sing. The war had just begun, and Mickey figured the draft would have gotten him anyway, so he opted for a long sea voyage.

Alone, with no job and no skills, Doris did what a lot of

young women were forced to do to survive—until she was
arrested and sent to reform school. While learning stenog-
raphy, she penned a story and sent it to Macklin's short-
lived mystery magazine *Dark Façade*.

"It was rejected," Doris confessed, "but Mr. Macklin
wrote me such a nice letter. I knew that I wanted to work
for him someday."

Years passed, the war ended, and Harry Macklin turned
from magazines to books. Doris finished her time served
with a secretarial degree, a smoothing of her Brooklyn
rough edges, and a permanent stain on her record.

Doris told us she'd been a voracious reader since she
was a little girl. Once incarcerated, she read even more. She
also became the fastest typist in the entire school.

"One of my instructors helped me land a job at a print-
er's office. Turned out my boss was an ex-con himself. So
when I asked if he'd sign a letter of reference for me as
'Dorothy Moreland,' he said, 'Sure, kid, I'll do it.'

"That's when I started applying for jobs on Publisher's
Row. Mr. Macklin liked me from the start. I told him things
about how his books were printed that he didn't even know.
I read enough to converse with him about writers, too:
Dash Hammett and Chandler and James M. Cain—I so
loved *Mildred Pierce*. Anyway, he hired me as his personal
secretary . . ."

Unfortunately, as Doris told it, Harry had the same luck
with books as he had with magazines—very little. His
company was floundering when Doris brought him a manuscript that she claimed she'd found in the slush pile.

"The plot was based on a story my brother told me when
he was running with his gang of street punks, so I put his
name on it," the tearful girl told us.

"Next to the jam that landed me in reform school, it was
the worst mistake I ever made. When Mickey found out, he
threatened to tell Mr. Macklin the truth. I paid my brother
to shut him up, because I knew if Harry Macklin found out
his innocent secretary was a . . . a criminal, he'd fire me on
the spot."

"How much did you pay your brother?" Jack asked.

"Plenty, but Mickey wanted more. I wrote a second book, then a third. He took all the money, and it still wasn't enough."

Jack passed his hankie to her, and Miss Moreland dabbed at her tears.

"When Harry hired detectives to find Mickey, I wanted it to end. So I splashed the manuscript with pig's blood from the butcher to convince everyone that Mickey Sizemore was dead."

Once again, tears filled her eyes as Miss Moreland turned to me.

"What do I do, Mrs. McClure? As a woman, you know no decent man would have anything to do with me, not after learning how I got by on the streets. But Mickey knows my secret. He can ruin everything for me!"

I took her hand. "Doris, they say the truth will set you free—and in your case, you need to get free of your abusive brother. Remember, Harry Macklin hired us to find the truth, so he's going to learn it anyway. You might as well be the one to tell him. Come clean and confess, that's my advice, whatever the consequences."

WHEN WE KNOCKED on the door of Harry Macklin's plush Park Avenue apartment, he answered with a whiskey in one hand, a Cuban cigar in the other.

"Jack! Penny! What brings you here?"

"You wanted Mickey Sizemore?" Jack said. "Well, here she is."

Harry Macklin blinked, then donned the spectacles he'd tucked into his smoking jacket. "Miss Moreland? I don't understand."

Jack removed his fedora. "I figured you liked Sizemore's stories so much, you'd want to hear the latest from the horse's mouth. It's a doozy."

"Come in, come in."

Harry's vast apartment was a real bachelor pad with a

mirrored bar, a gorgeous view, and a large couch for entertaining the ladies. Like his office, the man's living space was in total chaos. Despite the mess, Harry found more whiskey and cigars, and for the next hour Dorothy Moreland confessed all.

She told her boss about reform school, her identity switch, her felonious brother, and how she wrote the books under his name. She even told Harry she tipped her brother off when he went to meet Jack Shepard.

"I wanted him to scare you off, Mr. Macklin, not hurt you," she explained. When her confession was over, the woman set aside her glass, rose, and straightened her skirt.

"I'll be going now, Mr. Macklin. You'll have my resignation on your desk tomorrow morning."

Harry jumped to his feet so quickly he spilled his whiskey.

"You poor kid," he cried. "You're not going near Canarsie, not even after I deal with your brother! You're staying right here with me from now on, so I can look after you."

With that, he wrapped both arms around his secretary.

"I'm willing to write a few more books for you, Mr. Macklin, if you can find a way to control my brother—"

"Harry! It's Harry! And I swear I'll put your brother on a leash. We'll make a deal with him to shut him up and leave you alone. If I have to, I'll hire muscle to make sure he sticks to it."

"The truth is, Harry, what I really want to do is help you find better authors than the ones you're publishing; new authors, who we can afford, but who have sensational stories to tell. I know your business inside and out, and I know what real people want to read. I know what will sell!"

"I'll bet you do, Dorothy!"

"It's really Doris, you know."

He put a protective arm around her frail shoulders.

"Doris Sizemore is dead, and so is Mickey," Harry replied. "You're sticking with Moreland until you get hitched—and maybe after that. We'll stick a hyphen in there or something."

"What are you saying, Mr. Macklin?"

"It's Harry. Just Harry!"

Harry-Just-Harry was still cooing to his star author—
and, most likely, future editor in chief—as Jack hooked my
arm and pulled me out the front door.

"Hey, aren't you going to collect your fee?"

"Sure, I'll settle with Harry next week." Jack shook his
head and set the fedora on top. "Some things are worth
more than twenty bucks and expenses."

I touched the big man's shoulder and smiled. "Like reuniting another lost puppy with someone who cares for her."

CHAPTER 54

Jack in the Box

I do not believe they've run out of surprises.

—Larry Niven

THE NEXT DAY, I woke with a smile on my face. Quite a change from the heart-pounding terror Jack had left me with the last time he shared his memories of a case.

I was glad things ended well for Dorothy Moreland and Harry Macklin. It started my day on a bright note. Pushing aside my window curtains, I let in the morning sunshine.

While the warmth was pleasant, it was empty.

Jack was gone again.

Since I had no new leads, a son to get off to school, and a bookstore to run, I decided (for once) to trust Deputy Chief Franzetti and his fellow officers on the QPD to do more than write citations for every business on Cranberry Street.

Maybe the "professionals" would actually track down the driver of the van that nearly killed my friend. Until they did, however, my worries would continue.

I wasn't the only one concerned for Professor Parker's safety. Last night, Seymour insisted on his old friend sleeping over at Tarnish Mansion. Typically, Brainert would have declined such an offer (in a microsecond), but last night he actually accepted the invitation.

Obviously, Brainert was shaken up by the mounting stack of evidence that someone had intentionally run over Kevin Ridgeway, tossed Emma Hudson over her balcony, and was now out to "disappear" him.

Though our bookshop wouldn't open for another thirty minutes, Aunt Sadie was already working at her computer, Amy by her side.

Today's lesson was how to process book returns.

After getting Spencer off to school, I brought down a fresh a pot of tea and a plate of toasted English muffins with jam made from locally grown raspberries. The ladies grinned when they saw the goodies.

While we all munched, Amy continued her schooling, and I called Brainert and Seymour. Turns out they were having breakfast, too.

"Hey, Pen. Hold on a second . . ." In a muffled voice, I heard Seymour speak to Brainert. "If you don't like what's on the table, there's more cereal in the cupboard!"

Then Seymour put us on speakerphone.

"How are you two doing?" I asked.

"Great, Pen," Seymour replied. "Brainert's still selecting his breakfast—"

"There's nothing in this cupboard but two more boxes of Froot Loops!"

"Sorry, buddy, I must be out of Cap'n Crunch."

"We'll have to stop at the student cafeteria," Brainert huffed, "so I can eat something *nutritious*."

"We?" I said.

"Yeah," Seymour admitted, "I took some stockpiled personal days to bodyguard Professor Parker, twenty-four seven."

"And he's letting you?"

"We'll see how it goes," Brainert replied. "The mailman has already thrown me off schedule. I haven't eaten breakfast and I have a ten o'clock class."

I knew the day might be trying for Brainert, but I was

relieved that Seymour would be with him, watching his back.

As the day progressed, the sunny sky grayed and clouds rolled in. Winds kicked up, stirring the trees, as intermittent drizzle streaked our store widows.

Just after lunchtime, I noticed Amy pulling boxes out from under the front counter. "Ms. Thornton," she called to Sadie. "There are three boxes of returns here. Not two."

"Let me take a look, honey." As I checked each box, I realized one did not contain returns. It held books from the personal library of Amy's father. Of course, I didn't wish to upset the girl, so I said nothing.

Instead, I sent Amy back to Sadie with one of the other two boxes. When she was gone, I had a thought—and decided to check Kevin's box more thoroughly.

The gold mine of first editions was still there, along with the six copies of *Shades of Leather*. A strip of brown paper lined the bottom of the box, and I pulled everything out to see if (crossed fingers!) a vintage St. Francis folder was underneath with maybe a stack of photocopied diary pages.

Alas, no luck.

I did notice a Post-it note in the stack, flagging a page in one of the books, so I pulled the volume out.

As thunder rumbled in the distance, I scanned the title of the out-of-print hardcover by Daniel P. Maddox, *Arms and Armor of the Middle Ages*, its ominous black dust jacket well-worn and partially torn.

I didn't expect to find anything of use, but I checked the flagged page anyway, and found a note, written in an unfamiliar hand, tucked inside:

Kevin,

The villain is too easy on our heroine. The scene is a dud. He wants Justine dead and plans to do it with a sharp blade. On this page you'll find illustrations of a few dirks, stilettos, and daggers. Pick one, and I'll run with it. I'll also revise the previous erotic scene to include your weapon of choice.

Holy cow! I wanted to cry out, but with Kevin's daughter in the shop, I held my tongue. *Justine* was the name of the heroine in *Shades of Leather*, and I remembered the scene with the dagger. It came early in the novel.

Unfortunately, this telling note wasn't signed.

As I flipped around the pages, looking for more evidence, I realized this volume carried a bookplate. There, in bold, black print, was the name of the book's owner, and it wasn't Kevin Ridgeway, though it was a name I quickly recognized—SHIRLEY ANTHOR.

"Professor Shirley Anthor," I whispered. The same petite, middle-aged medieval scholar who'd given the Arthurian lecture for Brainert's film series. The same Shirley Anthor who last night mentioned an out-of-print book she had "no chance of recovering."

Was it this very book?

Suddenly, I was enveloped in a swirling cocoon of cold air.

That's some co-co-coincidence, baby—if I believed in coincidence.

"It's about to rain outside, Jack, but I think it's already raining in Reno! Professor Shirley Anthor just might be our third ghostwriter."

MIGHT is right, because it's not a fact yet. That note ain't signed. Remember what I taught you?

"I remember, Jack. Theories are fine to start, but the case don't end till you find hard evidence."

That's right, sweetheart. So let's go find it.

CHAPTER 55

Death Takes a Joyride

Objects in the mirror are closer than they appear.

—Mandatory warning on car mirrors

FIFTEEN MINUTES LATER, I was heading out to see Professor Anthor.

Before I left the bookshop, I called Shirley's university office, but she wasn't in. According to her teaching assistant, she had no afternoon classes and was working at home.

"Then I can catch her there?"

"I'd call first," the young woman warned, giving me her mobile number. "I just talked to her, and she was packing up books to donate to the local library."

Perfect, I thought. If I can get into her house and innocently peruse her bookshelves, I might just spot the same literary evidence that gave away Professors Ridgeway and Parker—multiple first printing copies of *Shades of Leather*.

When I phoned Shirley, I already had the perfect excuse to see her. "I found that out-of-print book you mentioned last night. It came in a box of donations. Your bookplate is still inside it. I'd be happy to return it to you."

"Great!" Shirley said. "When should I come by the shop?"

"Tell you what. I'm driving by your neighborhood this afternoon. Shall I drop it off?"

"Sure, I'll be here for the next two hours. Then I'm heading to the library and meeting a friend in Millstone for dinner."

As I started the engine, cool air swirled inside my car.

Let's roll, sweetheart—

Raindrops exploded on my windshield almost as soon as I pulled onto Cranberry Street. Soon the car was being pelted. With the afternoon sky nearly dark as twilight, I switched on the headlights as well as the wipers.

The weather service predicted light rain, but the flash storm, blowing in from the Atlantic, proved the forecasters wrong. A sudden downpour turned my windshield into a waterfall. Getting off the road for safety, I made a stop at the Metro Mart for some caffeinated courage: a super large (and scalding-hot) coffee with three sugars.

By the time I checked out, the worst had passed. The rain was still steady but negotiable, and I didn't want to miss Shirley. Her house was near the ocean, and I had to get going.

As I got behind the wheel, my phone buzzed with a text message.

I assumed it came from Seymour or Brainert—though I'd told them my plan, I had yet to hear back from them. Not unusual, since Brainert had a strict "All phones off!" rule during his classes.

But the text was from someone else. Philip Hudson—

I need 2 C U about Emma's death.

I know U R asking Qs.

I have answers. It is urgent we speak.

"I don't like this, Jack . . ."

The lush is full of surprises.

"Why does he want to talk so urgently?"

He either knows something, like he claims, or he has something to hide.

"Like maybe he really did get rid of his troublesome ex, and he wants to stop me from looking into it?" I shook my head and pulled back onto the highway. "I suppose it's possible Kevin's death was an accident and Brainert's near miss was, too, and I've been reading too much into both."

And how do you explain the dead woman's reaction to her photo on the bestseller? Or her diary being in the hands of the ghostwriters who wrote it?

"I can't—" And that's when it struck me. "Shirley mentioned meeting a friend in Millstone. Philip Hudson lives in Millstone. Do you think it's possible the two know each other? That Philip gave Emma's diary to Shirley?"

Remember what I said about theories? You don't know for sure this Shirley dame is the third ghostwriter. You need more. You need evidence—or a confession.

At this point, I doubted it would be a confession to murder. The fact was, I couldn't see bubbly, friendly, enthusiastic Shirley Anthor offing her colleagues for money or fear of exposure. But I *could* see Philip Hudson—with his drinking and duplicity—doing exactly that.

"If Philip is the killer of the ghostwriters, then Shirley's life may be in danger right now. And after that text message from the man, it looks like mine may be in danger, too!"

So what are you going to do?

"For now, ignore Philip's message and get to Shirley."

No, doll, I'm talking about that hearse that you've glanced at once or twice in your mirror. It's been following your car for the last several miles.

"Really?"

Jack was right. Now that I took a closer look, a dark panel van, one that fit the description of the vehicle that nearly killed Brainert, was pacing me. I didn't see splotches of red in my rearview, but paint stains were easy to cover up. With the rain still steady, wipers moving, and a heavily overcast sky, I couldn't tell who was driving—just a man with a collar up and a ball cap pulled down.

"Jack, I hope you have a suggestion."

Take it easy. Drive casual. Like you don't think the driver might be a wiper.

"A wiper?"

A peg-out artist.

"Huh?"

A violin player. A widow-maker. A hit man—

"Hit man!"

Sure. You sang like a canary to the local flatfoots about Phil Hudson's false alibi and his "Federal Hill" money. Button men come with the territory.

I nearly skidded into a ditch. "If he's an assassin, I shouldn't be driving 'casual'; I should be driving faster."

No. Stay in control. That's the ticket. Whoever's up your tailpipe is not aggressive, just a little too close for comfort.

"It's only a few blocks to Montrose Place and Shirley's house."

Go. But if the hearse follows, don't stop. Drive on until you find a red-blooded American copper.

"What if that truck pulls a *Christine* and runs me off the road!"

Six days a week I'm aces with your lingo, but you'll have to clue me in on this dame Christine.

"It's a book by King."

King who? King of what?

"Stephen. King of horror," I whispered, glancing over my shoulder.

Black as the Grim Reaper, the van edged closer. Then the driver flashed his headlights. There was a ten-second interval, and the lights flashed again.

My eyes lingered too long on the mirror image and not on the road, so I almost missed the turn. I cut a sharp right onto Montrose. Tires squealed on the slick pavement, but I regained control after a scary fishtail.

The black van made the turn with me. Its headlights flashed a third time.

Use your Dick Tracy radio to call the law!

As I fumbled for my smartphone, I realized Shirley's house was on a cul-de-sac, and I'd driven myself into a trap!

I spied a late-model BMW idling in the street, trunk open. The front door of Shirley's tidy brick house was open, too. She must have been loading her car, so she wouldn't be far away!

Though it made me feel safer, as I rolled to a stop, I speed-dialed the Quindicott Police anyway. Meanwhile, the black van pulled up beside my car, close enough that our side mirrors nearly touched, close enough to box in my driver's side door.

With a shaky hand, I reached for my coffee. As weapons go, it wasn't much, but I planned to dash the hot beverage into the driver's face at the first hint of trouble. And if there was a second—

Don't worry, partner. I've got your back.

CHAPTER 56

Down the Up Staircase

In Greek tragedy, they fall from great heights. In noir, they fall from the curb.

—Dennis Lehane

AS MY FINGERS tightened on the coffee cup, the passenger side window descended, and a familiar face peered at me.

"Larry Eaton?" I lowered my window, and a blast of rain hit my cheeks. Only then did I realize I was already damp from a cold sweat.

Who's Baby Face?

He's the town plumber, Jack.

We got spooked by a pipe-pusher with slippery pants?

Larry's cherubic smile dominated his round face. "When you left the Metro Mart, I noticed your taillight wasn't working."

"Do tell," I rasped, my heart still racing.

"Bull McCoy wrote me a ticket for that same violation last week. Cost me fifty bucks! I wanted to give you a heads-up before you got nailed, too."

"You're a guardian angel, Larry. I'm sorry about the chase. I would have stopped, but I didn't recognize the van."

He nodded excitedly. "It's new. I took my old clunker over to Stuckley's to get that taillight fixed, and Kent Clark talked me into this beauty. I'm on my way to get my business logo stenciled on the side."

Larry made a U-turn and drove away. As he gave me a final wave, I heard an irritated voice speaking through my smartphone. My frantic and forgotten emergency call had been answered by dispatch, who sent it right to Chief Ciders.

"So sorry, Chief. It was a false alarm."

"Then get off the line!" he roared. "I've got a smashup near the college that's turned the campus into a parking lot!"

I ended the call and took a breath. "Okay, Jack, let's forget this happened, find Shirley, and get some answers."

I reached into the back seat to retrieve Shirley's lost book, my hand brushing the bag where I'd put Emma Hudson's leather gloves. I couldn't help cringing, remembering her terrible end.

That made me pause.

I had misjudged Larry and his van.

What if I misjudged Shirley, too?

"Jack, what if Philip Hudson really is innocent, and Shirley is not only the third ghostwriter, but the killer, as well? It's possible, right?"

Almost anything's possible, kiddo, in theory.

"I know, I know. Get hard evidence."

I checked my phone again but still hadn't heard from Seymour and Brainert. I could wait for them to join me here. By then Shirley might be off to Millstone . . . *Millstone?* I frowned, remembering—

"Philip Hudson lives in Millstone. What if Shirley is meeting Philip for dinner? What if Shirley is innocent, just an anonymous writer, and Philip is the real killer, maybe working with hired help? That would explain why he had an alibi on the day of his ex-wife's death. What if Hudson plans to end Shirley the same way Emma and Kevin Ridgeway were ended?"

Slow down, baby, or you'll "what if" yourself into the cackle factory.

"Fine! I've decided. I'm pressing forward. Shirley knows I'm coming to return a book. I won't present a danger or threat, so I should be safe. If I see those copies of *Shades of Leather*, I won't say a thing. I'll simply tail her to Millstone. If her meeting is with Hudson, I'll call Eddie."

On my way to the house, I passed her car with the wide-open trunk and spied boxes of books inside. Obviously, Shirley was in the middle of moving her donations to the library. But so far, there was no sign of her.

The front door stood open, but I rang the bell anyway.

"Dr. Anthor? It's Penelope McClure!"

Silence followed. A spooky silence. I shivered—and not because of Jack's spiking energy.

Keep your peepers open, baby.

I pulled out my phone, thumb ready to press the 911 button, and carefully entered the house. The foyer was flanked by a plant on one side and a deer-antler coat hanger on the other. When the corner of my eye caught a bulky male figure, I let out a shout.

Cool your heels, doll. It's just a steel scarecrow.

Feeling stupid, I moved passed the suit of faux medieval armor guarding the hall, and called out again. My voice echoed back to me.

The foyer ended at a flight of stairs to the second floor. Doorways stood on either side. One to the library and one to the kitchen. I headed for the library, assuming Shirley would be there.

I was wrong.

Alone in the room, I decided this was my chance to snoop. The walls were covered by heavy oak shelves. Most of the books were focused on medieval studies.

Everything was tidy, except the antique desk, facing the curtained window. Its surface was layered with student papers, lesson plans, and textbooks—stratified by semester instead of geologic age.

Glancing over my shoulder, I began my excavation, worried Shirley would come upon me at any moment. The first thing I uncovered was an old electric typewriter. I slid more layers of papers aside, until I found books, the kind that would have provided, *ahem . . .* inspiration for a writer penning *Shades of Leather.*

On top was *Story of O*; then a Grove Press paperback of *My Life and Loves* by Frank Harris; and *The One Hundred and Twenty Days of Sodom* with a broken spine. Under those I found a coffee table book with illustrations of all 245 *Kama Sutra* positions.

Beneath that, I counted six copies of *Shades of Leather*, all first printings and in pristine condition.

"Eureka, Jack!"

Looking around the room, I saw no other copies and quickly did the math. "Six copies were with Kevin, six with Brainert, and six here. That leaves six of the twenty-four copies still unaccounted for."

Who has the final six, do you think?

"I don't know, Jack, not yet."

Buried under the hardcovers, I found a vintage St. Francis University folder, and inside that, an old diary. I hurriedly flipped through the diary pages, skimming enough to be certain of what I was holding—

"Jack, this is Emma Hudson's diary!" (Now I had no doubt.) "I found our third author!"

Sorry to rain on your parade. But you haven't found anyone yet. That Shirley dame is missing.

"She must be here . . . somewhere."

I crossed the hall to the kitchen, which was empty of all but plant life. There was a closed door near a breakfast nook, which I assumed would lead to a dining room.

Wrong again.

Behind the door I found a flight of rough wooden steps, leading to the basement and something else—Shirley Anthor. She was sprawled at the bottom of the steps, a burst cardboard box and dozens of hardcovers piled on top of her.

I descended the stairs, carefully stepped around the woman, and kneeled beside her. I could not feel a pulse at her wrist, but the flesh was warm, and I held out hope that she was still alive.

It was only after I'd cleared away the heavy hardcovers that I realized Shirley was lying on her stomach, yet her dead eyes stared up at me.

"Her head. It's twisted around. Her neck is broken, Jack. Could that happen from a fall down a flight of stairs?"

Not like that. This was no slip and fall.

I tried to quell the revulsion welling up inside me, but I started shaking uncontrollably at the sight of her corpse.

Take a deep breath before you shoot your cookies.

Fortunately, I didn't shoot my cookies, though I did hurry to get out of there—

Slow down! Jack counseled. *Go back to the library.*

"Jack, I have to call the police!"

Listen to me. Remember Doris Sizemore? To solve this case, you've got to pinch something, too—and not a reform school card.

"You want me to take the diary?"

It's the key to the case, honey. You need to see what's in there.

"But this is a crime scene!"

Sure it is. But you know and I know the local yokels won't understand how to read that evidence. Not for a while. Maybe not ever. And the clock is ticking down on your egghead friend—and you, too.

"Okay, Jack, you win." I grabbed the diary and got out of there. "I'll read it fast. Then the evidence is going to the police!"

On the way to my car, I hit 911. Dispatch gave me Ciders.

"Is this another false alarm?!" he barked.

"No, Chief. It's another corpse."

CHAPTER 57

Wrong the First Time

A doctor can bury his mistakes but an architect can
only advise his clients to plant vines.

—Frank Lloyd Wright

GOOD NEWS, THE Keystone Cops arrived.

"Bad news. Look who's driving."

The first officer on the scene was none other than Chief
Ciders' ham-handed nephew, Bull McCoy. Though less
than half his uncle's age, McCoy already had the body of a
high school athlete gone to seed—so out of shape that exit-
ing his police car made him wheeze.

After I told Bull I discovered Shirley dead in the basement, he ordered me back in my car until Ciders showed up
to take a statement. Then he went inside the house.

A few minutes later, Ciders' police car loomed in my
rearview, and the top cop was not alone. I didn't recognize
the man in the passenger seat, but I knew an argument
when I saw one, even in mime.

*Looks like there's some sort of a beef grilling in that
donut wagon. Hackles are up and feathers are fluttering.*

"I'd like to know what they're fighting about. But I doubt
they'll tell me."

Open the window and get out of sight, Jack ordered. *Next to a gat in your pocket, eavesdropping is a gumshoe's best friend.*

Too curious to argue, I followed Jack's advice. Though the pedals dug into my ribs, I managed to squeeze my body close to the car floor before the squad car braked beside me.

Nice move, doll. Now keep those ears wax free and listen.

The chief made it easy. He was practically shouting. Then I heard the words "death at Pine Tree Avenue," and I listened even harder.

"I wish Quindicott could afford its own medical examiner. I'm sure any country doctor could do a better job than your Statie lab did with this."

"Be reasonable, Chief. I came all the way out here to deliver the news personally."

Ciders snorted. "Good thing, too. We've got more work for you and your so-called experts. I only ask that you don't blow it this time."

"I did warn your deputy that our initial assessment might change, pending the results of our autopsy. And so it has."

"What I don't understand is why."

"There was a considerable amount of soft tissue damage to the victim's throat, along with evidence of a powerful blow to the thorax. The bruises around the neck and shoulders indicate the victim was assaulted, but the blow came first and likely rendered the victim unconscious, if it didn't kill her outright."

"Why didn't I notice any bruises? I examined the corpse, too."

"Her head was smashed against that rock. The subcutaneous bleeding was easy to miss under all that blood and brain matter."

"Then the woman was dead before she went off that balcony." Ciders' tone was glum. "How many days did I lose worrying about scofflaws when I should have been hunting a cold-blooded killer?"

"Chief, the cause of death is the least of our worries. Turns out the dead woman is not who we thought she was."

What! I cried—almost out loud.

What? Jack echoed in my head.

"What!" Chief Ciders roared. "Are you sure?"

"We had a positive ID from her ex-husband, so we *thought* we were in the clear. But fingerprints don't lie. The dead woman is not Emma Hudson. Her name is Mae Stuart, a retiree who served the Providence, Rhode Island, library system for thirty years." The doc paused. "We both made a wrong assumption and a big mistake."

"Maybe," Ciders said. "Or maybe someone wanted us to *think* Emma Hudson was dead . . ."

As the chief continued talking, my mind raced.

"Jack, did you hear? Now it all makes sense . . ."

I thought back to the day I went to Emma's apartment and the things I noticed at the crime scene: the open suitcase in the second room; the missing mobile phone; even the missing Yorkie.

"That mystery friend of Emma's, the one who Mr. Brink was supposed to meet for dinner, the booklover. She was the woman who was murdered and tossed over the balcony—not Emma Hudson!"

Emma must have asked this woman to stay with her and catalog the valuable book collection, which meant those footsteps I heard may not have been the killer. That might have been Emma fleeing the scene.

"I don't think Emma is the killer, do you? There's no motive. And how could she know about Kevin Ridgeway and Shirley Anthor and Brainert Parker?"

She couldn't, Jack agreed. *The bird took flight in fear. That's what it looks like.*

"Fear for her own life." I agreed with that theory. "Otherwise, she would have stayed to talk to the police."

It certainly explained why her little dog was gone, along with its bowl and leash and other doggy items. It explained why she took the *Shades of Leather* book, too.

"But, Jack, how did she get away? Eddie found Emma's car parked on the street."

Easy, sweetheart, she probably used the dead dame's car. That's how she beat the heat!

I heard the voice of Bull McCoy call from the house. "Hey, Chief, you comin' in?"

"Yeah, we're comin'. Show us what you found . . ."

As Ciders and the doc moved toward the house, their voices faded. When I was certain they were out of sight, I started my car and got out of there.

I knew Ciders would want my statement, and I would give it to him soon. Right now, I intended to examine the diary in my handbag.

Jack was right. The clock was ticking down on a murderer at large, and I didn't trust the locals to solve this in time. Not before the killer made certain Brainert and I ran out of it.

CHAPTER 58

Pretty Little Scribbler

Fiction is based on reality unless you're a fairy-tale artist.

—Hunter S. Thompson

I TURNED THE page on the final diary entry and swallowed another gulp of cold coffee.

Outside, the last of the rain pattered against the windshield. The thunder and lightning had ceased, though the late-afternoon sky still roiled with storm clouds. My thoughts were roiling, too. The truth behind the bogus bestseller was wilder than any fiction. The heat of the diary alone seemed to steam up my car windows.

"It's just as I thought, Jack: *Shades of Leather* is a true story, and this is the hard evidence!"

I waited for my gumshoe's reaction, but silence was my only reply. "Jack? Jack! Don't abandon me now!"

The fog on the windows cleared up as the temperature quickly dropped.

Sorry, honey, I lost track of time . . .

I didn't blame the ghost. After I fled the crime scene at Shirley Anthor's house, I drove to Silva's Seafood Shack, got a fresh cup of coffee, and returned to my car. Then I sat in the parking lot, riveted for well over an hour by the events of the diary. Jack, not so much.

That little girl sure did get a kick out of making the springs sing. Me? I'd rather make whoopee than write about it. Give me the highlights, will ya?

"Okay, let's start with the basics. This diary was written by a girl in the 1970s. She was orphaned and put in foster care in her early teens. Her name was Stacy Baylor; and, according to the shocking things I read in this diary, she had good reason to flee Rhode Island, change her name to Emma Royce, and make up an entirely new history for herself."

What did she do, kill one of the fellas she slept with?

"No—and keep in mind that she was legally still a child, only seventeen, and technically underage. At a dance club one night, she met a young man who she called 'Dodger' in the diary. He was a grad student, good-looking, on an athletic scholarship. They slept together often, and he introduced her to a lot of kinky stuff. He also brought her to private parties. This was a time period known as the 'free love' era—"

Like I already told you, no such thing as free love.

"The girl in the diary hooked up with at least a dozen different men, two of whom were dealing drugs and one of whom was a crooked politician. She never writes their full names, only nicknames and occasionally some physical characteristics."

Physical, right, since she knows how their hambone's boiled.

"Their what? NO, don't tell me. I get it."

Go on, doll.

"Two of these drug dealers sweet-talked her into dropping out of high school to take a job at a furniture store. They rented her an apartment above it. She partied with these guys, after hours, and they did plenty of drugs. Then they told her their 'brilliant idea' of using the couches in the store to move large amounts of drugs around the region without detection. At that point, Stacy was enthralled by these men, and addicted to the drugs, which they supplied to her. So, of course, she agreed to help them commit these crimes."

This ain't gonna end well. Give me the skinny.

"She wrote that she finally wanted out. The men started treating her badly, and she was desperate to be free of them, but she knew too much. She started obsessing about Marilyn Monroe and was sure if she tried to say *no* to any more criminal activity, these men would kill her, probably make it look like a fatal overdose. So she decided to kill herself first. That's how she ended the diary. She wrote, 'I'm going to end this. Not like Marilyn. I'm going to die my way.' And I believe she did kill herself by killing the identity of Stacy to become Emma."

I drained my coffee cup. "What I'd like to know now is how this diary ended up on Shirley Anthor's desk."

And how did the perky professor end up at the bottom of her basement steps?

"I don't know who killed Shirley. But I'll tell you who didn't: Philip Hudson."

Why not?

"Because I believe whoever killed Shirley also killed the librarian at Pine Tree Avenue—and did it by mistake. Philip knows what his ex-wife looks like. He wouldn't have killed the wrong woman. And we know he was in Providence at the time."

Unless he hired an idiot thug to do it, and the killer got confused.

"I don't think so, Jack—and I'll lay out why in a minute. First, think about this. The morning after Emma's death, Eddie Franzetti described Philip as 'broken up' when he got back from Providence and heard the news. Then, only a short time later, Philip is chipper as a canary on the phone with me."

And you don't think he was playing the violin for the yokels?

"I think between the time he heard Emma was dead and the time we spoke on the phone, Emma contacted him for his help. I think that's why he intentionally misidentified the dead woman and why he fed that false story to the *Quindicott Bulletin*. I think he still cares about his ex-wife and is trying to protect her."

That's a pretty sentimental view. You could be wrong. And if you're wrong, honey, you could be dead.

"I could be dead soon anyway, and I've got to trust my judgment. I read enough of your case files to know you played your hunches, too, didn't you?"

You got me there. So, what's your hunch?

"That an academic colleague of Shirley's and Kevin's and Brainert's is the man behind these murders—this Dodger character. I'll bet he's the one who had the diary for all these years. How did he get it? Why did he keep it? I don't know. But I'm thinking he had it. And he used it to create a bestselling erotic thriller. He even used an old, sexy photo of Emma to serve as the image of the author, which tells me he thought she was dead . . ."

Go on, baby, this theory has potential. Sounds like all the pieces are finally fitting.

"When Emma ran out of my shop in a state of hysteria, she nearly ran over Wanda Clark, remember? Wanda said Emma was on the phone with someone, arguing violently. And she heard Emma shout the words, 'Sorry isn't enough!'"

"Emma's librarian friend was killed only a few hours later. According to the medical examiner, the woman was attacked before she was sent over the balcony. As I said, Philip was in Providence; and a few hours is hardly enough time to hire an assassin and arrange a hit. No. It's more likely that whoever murdered Emma's friend thought he was getting rid of Emma, which means he hadn't seen her in years."

Wrong place. Wrong time. I saw that enough in life— and come to think of it . . .

"I know, Jack, the big chill is no joke. And I think it was Dodger who gave it to that poor, innocent woman. Dodger was the only man in the diary who the girl routinely confided in. He kept sleeping with her, and sweet-talking her, but he didn't care enough to help her, even after she begged him. She described him as a tall, muscular guy, an athlete—yet he continually claimed he was afraid of the drug dealers and their friends. In the diary, she started referring to him as Dodger the Worm. And he's the most likely person in her circle to have kept a picture of her and landed a job at a university like St. Francis."

It makes sense to me. But it's still just a theory. What are you gonna do about it?

"Find the evidence to prove it. But I'm going to need help."

Not the Keystone Cops.

"No. Emma's ex-husband."

I called up the text from Philip Hudson. The one I never answered. Hitting reply, I typed my message:

Philip, I have the diary. We need 2 talk.

Want 2 know all that U know.—Pen

I waited for a reply. It came within five minutes:

Pen, want 2 trust U. Must ask 4 proof.

If U really have diary, meet me at the Beach House 2 night.—Phil

I quickly opened the diary to one of the entries. "I found it!"

Lay it on me, honey.

"The Beach House was owned by a wealthy family who bought furniture from the store where Stacy/Emma worked. The family used the house only a few months in the summer and kept it closed the rest of the year. That's when she would go out there and squat. It was her place to be alone and 'get herself together to think,' as she put it. She was at the Beach House when she made the decision to break free of the men who'd effectively enslaved her."

And where is this beach house? On the Atlantic coast,

I'll bet. That only gives you a thousand miles to comb through.

I flipped through the diary, looking for another reference, and noticed a sticky note on a page near the end. I'd been so gripped by the diary, I hadn't stopped to read it.

"Jack, this note is in Professor Anthor's handwriting . . ."

*Kevin, I finally worked out who "Dodger the Worm" is.
You know, too, don't you?—S*

"Shirley knew, Jack! Before she was killed, she figured out who Dodger was, and she believed Kevin knew, too!"

And now you're close to knowing, sweetheart, so keep your peepers open tonight, wherever you're going. Or you could end up like they did. Where are you going, anyway? Got a clue yet?

"Here it is—I found the reference. The Beach House is in Denton Cove. That's not far from here!"

You better bring backup.

"I've got you, don't I?"

For this you need more than a willing spirit. Ring that postman again—and his puny professor pal.

I DID AS Jack suggested (I'd planned to anyway), and Seymour put me on speaker with Brainert.

I filled the pair in on everything that happened, including Shirley Anthor's "fall" down her steps, my pinching of the *Shades of Leather* diary, and my hunch on the identity of the killer.

Brainert approved of my guess, and so did Seymour, who even recognized the location of Denton Cove.

"Been there," he said, "but not for years. The locals call it Dead Teen Cove."

"Why?"

"It's an urban legend, Pen. A teenager drowned herself there decades ago, and now her ghost supposedly haunts the place. It's private land, anyway, and very few people go there."

"Do you remember a beach house?"

"Sure, but you can't see it from the shore. The place is in the woods, above the cove."

"We'll find it," I assured them. Then the postman and his professor pal sent me a map, and we all agreed to meet there.

CHAPTER 59

Pleasure Victim

She'd been too eager, too trusting, too hungry for love. Now she knew too much, and her life had turned cheap. These men she'd slept with would snuff her out as easily as a spent cigarette.

—Jessica Swindell, *Shades of Leather*

THE MAP PROVED less than helpful. A wrong turn had me driving in a big circle. Finally, I spotted the muddy lane and followed it. A quarter mile later, I reached the cove.

White waves crashed against jagged beach rocks on this curving line of rugged coast. Tangled woods ringed the shoreline. In the stormy winds, the ancient trees swayed like dark giants.

I saw no sign of the beach house. Seymour said it was located in the woods above the cove, so I followed the tree line until I found a path marked with a warning.

PROPERTY OF HUDSON DEVELOPMENT
NO TRESSPASSING

"This has to be the right place, Jack."

I hurried along the path, until I emerged from the trees in front of the rickety old house.

The sagging structure was still fenced in, but in such disrepair, no one could possibly live there. So, I was surprised to see a single guard dog present—if you could call the tiny thing that. On the other hand, the angry Yorkie, leashed to the front porch, did bark like it hated all humanity. Seymour was right!

Jack, we did it. We found Emma!

"Who are you?!" a hysterical voice demanded. "What are you doing here!" Something hard and metallic poked my spine.

Sorry, doll, but I think she found you.

I faced Emma Hudson—and the gun she was waving.

"Don't shoot! I'm Penelope McClure, from the bookstore. I'm not here to hurt you."

Her eyes blinked in recognition, but she didn't lower the weapon. "What are you doing here? What do you want?"

How about the thirty smackers for that book you pilfered?

"I came to see you, Emma."

"How did you know I was here?"

"Philip told me, after I told him I found your diary. I know your real name is Stacy Baylor. I know everything. You can trust me. Philip does."

Emma lowered the gun. "He texted that someone might be coming . . ."

"Why are you hiding, Emma? What are you afraid of?"

Her laugh was brittle and cut off abruptly. "I suppose you thought I was crazy. The way I went off in your store like that. But the book you handed me had my picture on the cover, and if you read my diary, then you know that bestseller exposed my whole past to the world. I panicked, Mrs. McClure, and I had a good reason to be afraid."

"Of being found out. I understand—"

"No. You don't. Because it wasn't in the diary. You see, Mrs. McClure, when you steal two million dollars from a pack of ruthless gangsters, fear is just common sense."

Two million smackers! See, doll, I told you she could afford to buy your book!

For a moment, I couldn't find my voice. "You stole two million dollars from those drug dealers?"

Emma nodded. "You better come inside."

She led me into a house so run-down it made Whitman Brink's digs look like the Taj Mahal. Forget fading paint and peeling wallpaper. There were missing floorboards and walls without plaster, where the rotting frame was exposed.

Emma was holed up in the first-floor study—a drafty room with a bay window, now curtained by shabby velvet. A cot, a tiny refrigerator, a space heater, and a hot plate completed the poverty row decor.

The shabby surroundings didn't bother Yummy, Emma's Yorkie (named after *Yab Yum*, a tantric pose, she informed me). The angriest dog in the world was content with a cardboard box, a blanket, and Emma by her side.

In the harsh illumination from bare bulbs, Emma looked haggard—not the stylish, confident woman who came into my shop last Saturday; more like Miss Havisham, forlornly waiting for her lost lover.

We sat on wobbly chairs. Between us, a rickety table held her gun and the battered copy of *Shades of Leather* (the one she took from my shop).

Now that she knew I'd spoken to Philip, Emma opened up.

From her mature perspective, she recounted her past, telling me she'd been a wild, promiscuous, very stupid seventeen-year-old, impressed by rich men twice her age, and drawn in by easy money—plenty of it.

The couch smuggling worked well for the men who were using her, and they became even richer. Then they started moving more than drugs. Laundered money and weapons entered the picture, and her life with these criminals became a nightmare. She wanted out, and she feared going to the police. She knew cops were being paid off to look the other way, but she didn't know which ones. She didn't know who to trust. She wanted to be safe again, away from all of it.

Suddenly alert, the dog sat up. Emma patted the Yorkie's head.

"So, you stole some of their money to fund your getaway?"

"You're darn right I did. That decision saved my life. I intercepted one of the shipments, stashed the money and some personal things in a storage bin in Salem, and drove to this very cove to fake my own drowning."

"You mean, you're the 'dead teen' in Dead Teen Cove?"

Emma's eyes widened. "Is that what they call Denton Cove now?"

"They used to, so I'm told. People even believed it was haunted."

Quivering, the Yorkie began to bark. Emma was apologetic.

"Yorkshires are high-strung, Mrs. McClure. And very aggressive. They were actually bred to corner barn rats."

At her mistress's insistence, Yummy quieted, but she continued to emit low growls. I thought the dog might sense the presence of Jack or the approach of Brainert and Seymour, but I didn't want to spook Emma by mentioning them (the living men, that is). Not yet.

"Why did you come back, Emma?"

She explained that it was necessary to secure Philip Hudson's inheritance. Over the years, Philip's failed business ventures had depleted every last dime she had. Now that she was destitute, she was desperate for her share of his inheritance. After so many years of supporting him, Philip said he honestly felt he owed her the money.

"And you trust him?" I said. "Even though he's dealing with the mob?"

"The mob?"

"He told me he secured a loan from a Federal Hill moneyman."

Emma bit back a laugh. "You mean the hedge fund? It's based in Providence and run by one of Philip's old school chums. His friend agreed to make the loan."

"That's the moneyman?"

She nodded. "Philip had big plans to revitalize Millstone. He was bitter about my refusal to support his vision. But once I finally confessed my whole ugly past to him, he finally understood *why* I refused to settle here permanently. Now that he knows my story, he's going to give the money back—and after he gets his share of his father's inheritance, we're remarrying and getting out of here together."

I could certainly understand her desire to get clear of her past once more. But I couldn't help questioning her decision to come back here in the first place.

She admitted now that it was a mistake. But at the time, she believed enough years had passed that no one would recognize her. She'd been declared dead, after all. Still, as a precaution, she used an Internet search engine to learn how many of her former associates remained in the area. She couldn't confirm the whereabouts of the drug dealers, but she did find a local address for Dodger the Worm, and she planned to avoid him.

After seeing *Shades of Leather* in my bookshop, however, she placed a panicked, half-hysterical call to the man.

He apologized, but quickly defended himself. Like everyone else, he thought she was dead. When Emma phoned him, livid and almost crazed over what he'd done, he agreed to meet her at her apartment the next day and pay her off to stay silent. He promised to hand over the diary and enough cash for her to flee a second time.

After the call, Emma parked at Quindicott Pond to calm down and quickly read the book. Hours later, she returned to her apartment, and found the librarian brutally murdered. Emma had hired the woman through an Internet ad to help her catalog and sell the valuable Hudson book collection. Since the woman resided in Providence, she agreed to live with Emma while she worked.

"I knew it was a case of mistaken identity. But was it the drug dealers I'd robbed? Had they finally tracked me down? Or was it the man I'd just spoken to? I didn't have a clue, so I grabbed Yummy, took the librarian's car and phone, and ran."

"Why did Dodger even have your diary?"

"I gave it to him, Mrs. McClure. Before I faked my own death, I made him *promise* to turn it over to the police. Obviously, the worm never did. I suppose he didn't want to take any risks. I never used his name in the diary. But, at the age I am now, I can see he was afraid of being recognized—and being made to answer for the way he took advantage of an underage girl the way he did."

By now, I had guessed who the culprit was, but I needed this woman to say it. To say his name, out loud.

"Who was he, Emma?"

"I called him Dodger because it rhymed with his first name. In those days, he was a grad student in literature at a local university, on some kind of athletic scholarship. He graduated from Columbia and thought of himself as a tough guy because he was from New York. But he wasn't tough at all, Mrs. McClure, not where it counted."

Lit major. Columbia University. Athletic scholarship. Jack, I was right! It's—

AHHHHH-CHOOOOO!

The dog allergy had gotten the better of Bentley Prize winner Dr. Roger Leeds. The tall man stood in the doorway, swiping at his runny nose with his right hand.

In his left, he held a gun.

CHAPTER 60

The Rat Came Back

Dogs never bite me—just humans.

—Marilyn Monroe

"ROGER DODGER." EMMA grimaced. "I knew I should have bolted that door. What do you want from me?"

"You know. And it's not to return that stupid diary."

Emma lurched for her gun. But the move was desperate and clumsy, and she knocked it off the table. Rushing forward, Leeds quickly kicked her weapon into a hole in the floorboards.

Meanwhile, the room was becoming steadily colder, and the naked bulbs in the ceiling began to dim.

"A fire sounds about right, don't you think?" Leeds said with a grim smile. "This place is a three-alarm blaze waiting to happen."

Jack, what do I do?

Don't break my concentration, doll. I'm working on it. But we're running out of time.

This guy loves to gas on. Get the blowhard to talk about how smart he is, and he'll flap his gums till you'll wish he'd just pull the trigger.

"How did you *ever* find us, Dr. Leeds?!"

"Genius, really. Before I paid Shirley a visit, I found your car behind your store and broke a taillight, so I could follow you after dark. That's what I was waiting for. I intended to lure you onto the highway and run you off the road."

"The way you killed Kevin Ridgeway?"

"Exactly. When you showed up at Shirley's house, I waited in my car, outside the cul-de-sac, and followed you to that dump of a restaurant . . ."

We never saw him tailing us, Jack!

He's no happy plumber, honey. This rat knows how to tail without getting made.

"Then I saw you heading to this godforsaken firetrap," Leeds went on. "So I waited to see what would come of it. I thought maybe I could kill two problems in one night. I expected Professor Parker to show. This discovery is even better."

Dr. Leeds sneezed again. "All right. Time for this to end. How about it, Stacy? One last dance . . ."

I could almost hear Waldo repeating the phrase as Leeds raised the gun, aiming it at Emma's heart.

Jack! Do something!

Suddenly, the room dropped twenty degrees in temperature. It became so cold I could see my breath.

Then three things happened at once. The bay window exploded in a shower of glass as a man leapt through it.

A shot rang out.

And a rotting two-by-four flew out of a hole in the ceiling, knocking the gun out of Leeds's hand.

Philip Hudson, entangled in the velvet curtains—after his leap through the window—took the bullet. It knocked him back a step, but it didn't stop him, and the two men grappled.

The Yorkie barked madly as Emma held it back. I snapped up the fallen board and used it to smack Leeds in the back of the head. The professor pitched to the floor.

"Sic him, girl!" Emma cried.

For a split second, I thought the former dead teen was

talking to me. Then I realized: It was the mailman's scourge she'd commanded.

And Yummy obeyed.

With teeth bared, the tiny dog with the heart of a lion went for Leeds. The man on the ground howled as he tried to fend off the dog. But there was no stopping the little Yorkie. Growling, ripping, and tearing, Yummy had cornered her sneezing rat!

Hearing the shot, Brainert and Seymour burst through the door.

Realizing what had happened, they took their time pulling the vicious dog off the whimpering Leeds. I'm certain I saw a glint of pleasure in Brainert's eyes as he helped Seymour hog-tie the Bentley Prize winner with the dog's long leash.

"Sorry we're late, Pen," Seymour said. "Because of Brainert, we missed the turn."

"You're the nincompoop who can't read a Google map!"

While the frenemies bickered, Philip Hudson's eyes glazed and he sank to the floor. A tearful Emma rushed to her ex-husband.

"You brave, foolish man," she sobbed, cradling Philip's head.

Brave? The ghost chuckled. *He was pumped up on the kind of courage that comes out of a bottle. But she's right. It sure turns a man into a fool!*

"I came to your rescue, darling, armed with my trusty flask!" Philip declared to Emma as he struggled to place the alcohol to his lips.

"He needs a doctor!" Emma cried.

"On it," Seymour said, smartphone to his ear.

"Don't worry, love. I can't feel a thing," Philip rasped.

Maybe not when you're sloshed to the gills, hero. But you'll be whistling a different tune once you dry out.

CHAPTER 61

Debriefing

The answer is always there. You just have to put it all
together. Sometimes you need a little help.

—*Sally Snoops and Her Curious Kitty:*
The Girl Who Was Lost and Found

"ONCE A WORM, always a worm," Deputy Chief Franzetti said.

"Dr. Leeds?" I presumed.

Saturday meant cinnamon buns in Quindicott, and Eddie and I were sitting inside the Cooper Family Bakery,
polishing off a few. We were alone—not literally, the place
was as busy as ever. But Jack was out of the picture, still
sapped by all the excitement from two nights ago.

"You would not believe the elaborate excuses and ratio-
nales Roger Leeds had for everything," Eddie confessed.
"He swore he had nothing to do with the attempted murder
of Professor Parker. When we found the paint-stained van
in his locked garage, Leeds insisted it had been planted
there to incriminate him."

"I guess we know how he got his nickname."

Eddie sipped his coffee and nodded. "Leeds claimed he
was 'nowhere near' Shirley Anthor's home when she fell

down the stairs, even though his mobile phone tells a different tale. He said he didn't bring a gun to the beach house. That it was Philip Hudson's gun—and Hudson attacked him—even though we have sworn statements to the contrary by you, Emma, and Philip. When I asked him why he was at the house in the first place, he claimed he was simply out for a walk and came upon the place."

"What about Professor Ridgeway's death?"

"He denied his involvement. So I showed him a picture of the broken taillight on Ridgeway's car, and the Usher Security recording of Leeds breaking the taillight on yours."

Eddie laughed, the way Jack does when he's cornered some thug and is ready to dispense justice.

"Leeds was shocked by the recording. He didn't realize there were any cameras around. But within two minutes he was claiming that the NSA or CIA was framing him. It only got crazier as the night went on. By the end of the interview, Leeds was ranting."

Eddie fixed me with his gaze. "I've heard the term *psychopathic liar*, but I had no experience with one until my evening with Roger Leeds."

"So what do you think really happened?"

"It's clear Leeds was desperate to turn that lurid diary into a novel. He has three ex-wives breathing down his neck for alimony, and he's in deep trouble with the IRS. But Leeds discovered writing a novel wasn't so easy, and he brought Professor Kevin Ridgeway aboard. Then Ridgeway found he needed help and hired your friend Brainert and Professor Shirley Anthor. After the book became a big bestseller, Ridgeway threatened to expose Leeds if he didn't hand over more of the profits. In Leeds's sick mind, poor Kevin had to die."

"And Shirley?"

"You already told me she'd figured out Roger Dodger's identity. That was reason enough to kill her. But I suspect she was pressuring Leeds for more money, too."

"But why try to kill Brainert? He didn't want money. And he didn't have a clue Leeds was involved."

"After Kevin Ridgeway's death, Brainert was upset. He

started asking questions at the university. Leeds figured it was only a matter of time before Brainert would start unearthing answers."

"And how did Leeds know I was involved?"

Eddie lowered his voice. "It was Brainert, Pen. He showed up on campus the day after that van nearly killed him, talking about how you and Seymour were protecting him, and you were searching doggedly for the culprit behind the wheel."

"So I had to die, too?"

"Roger Leeds was feeling big enough to roll over anyone he wanted. And, frankly, I think the man did so many drugs in his youth that it damaged his brain. He was becoming more unhinged and reckless as time went on. By the end, I think he was looking for excuses to kill people. It gave him a thrill. The way I look at it, Waldo the Parrot got off lucky."

"You know, from the start, that talking bird tried to warn us. He gave a telltale phrase, but we didn't listen."

"How could you know the bird wasn't spouting nonsense?" Eddie stretched his long legs and finished his coffee. "I mean, who listens to a parrot? You might as well talk to the dead."

A chilly draft suddenly swept through the bakery, making the whole joint shiver. I simply smiled. By now, I was used to it.

"You know what, Eddie? You may have put the cuffs on the killer. But the parrot and a dead teen solved this case."

Don't forget Sally Snoops, sweetheart. She helped, too.

EPILOGUE

"We are the dead," he said.
"We're not dead yet . . ."

—Julia's reply to Winston in George Orwell's *1984*

"LOOK, AN E-MAIL from Emma and Philip Hudson!"
Sadie said.

I glanced up from refilling the *Sally Snoops* display at
the front of the store. "Have they decided where they want
to live yet? They've been dithering about it since they got
remarried."

"They've put aside thoughts of Seattle and decided on
Hawaii," Sadie read. "Now, they're trying to decide which
island."

"I thought for sure they'd go back to California."

Why be haunted by the ghosts of failures past? Jack
whispered as a cool breeze caressed the nape of my neck.
*The lovebirds want a fresh start, and that means a fresh
place to start.*

*You're right, Jack. Just like your own case—and little
Miss Moreland, the reform school girl turned publishing
professional—they need to remake themselves.*

It would be a long road to Philip's recovery from his alcoholism, but Emma was now committed to walking every step of the way beside him, just as he'd hidden and protected her.

The man certainly had his faults, on that I could testify, but he had his virtues, too, enough for Emma (and me) to forgive him.

Unfortunately, Philip's false identification of the librarian's body was a crime the authorities refused to forgive. Lucky for him, the grand jury decided not to charge him with perjury, not after hearing his whole tearful story.

There was a final irony that Jack appreciated. Though Emma hadn't been able to confirm the whereabouts of those drug dealers—the ones who would have taken vengeance on her—Eddie stepped up to investigate, using police resources. His conclusion: "Their last breaths were as spent as the money Stacy Baylor pinched to escape them."

The bad guys were gone. As far as the world was concerned, Stacy was gone, too, nothing but a ghost of a story haunting Dead Teen Cove.

And *Shades of Leather* was complete fiction.

"Goodness!" Sadie clapped her hands. "Philip writes that he wants us to keep all the money from the sale of his book collection—as a thank-you for all you've done! His father's inheritance finally came through. He says it's more than enough for him and Emma and Yummy to lead a comfortable life."

"And a calm one, I hope. Now that Emma has shaken her past, and the court has sealed her records."

"And now that Philip has stopped drinking," Sadie added. "That night at Chez Finch, I thought that man had a hollow leg!"

Ha! Your auntie's pretty savvy, doll.

"Excuse me, Aunt Sadie, but if I remember correctly, you were in matchmaking mode that night."

Sadie slipped off her glasses. "I thought you liked him, Pen. You seemed interested in everything Mr. Hudson had to say, and you asked so many questions—"

Jack? Should I tell her I was interrogating a suspect, not hunting for a potential boyfriend?

Nah, you don't want to tip the old gal off. You might have to throw yourself at another suspect someday.

Hey! You know I didn't "throw myself" at Philip—

Just then, deafening cheers erupted from our Community Events room. Whitman Brink had been talking about his *Sally Snoops* series to a packed house for the past two hours, with no end in sight. The last time I'd checked on things, Mr. Brink was posing for pictures, surrounded by a dozen adoring women.

When I'd scheduled this event, I'd figured on a modest audience of preteen girls, and there were plenty here. But at least half the attendees were women of a certain age, who'd read Sally's adventures in their youth.

Soon after a burst of loud applause, Amy and Spencer emerged from the community room.

"What was that ruckus about?" Sadie asked.

"Mr. Brink read a chapter from his new *Sally Snoops* adventure, the one that's going to be published soon," Amy replied.

"But we already heard it," Spencer noted. "He read it on NPR and *Tina Talks*, too."

Amy checked Sadie's computer screen. "Ugh, you're processing returns again! Ms. Thornton, there's got to be a smarter way to do business than wasting fossil fuels shipping books back and forth!"

"You're a clever girl, Amy. Maybe you'll finally figure out a solution to the problem that's plagued this trade for decades."

Jack moaned at Sadie's words. *This kid escaped academic prison to get to her pop's funeral. Then she snuck a peek at his police file. A gal like that has my admiration. She'd be completely wasted shilling wood pulp and ink— just like you are, sweetheart.*

"Thanks, Jack, but I'm perfectly happy giving new life to dead wood. And speaking of the dead—"

Hey! Whatever you do, baby, don't speak ill of me . . .

Whether or not Amy Ridgeway transformed the book

business, or enforced the law, I knew she'd have a bright future.

The legal dispute over the monies earned by *Shades of Leather* was solved in record time. With Shirley gone, and Brainert accepting a onetime contributor's fee, Kevin Ridgeway's daughter would be the primary beneficiary of all those royalties.

In the months since the settlement, Amy used her newfound financial (and emotional) clout to change some of her domestic rules, with Mother Bergen's reluctant agreement. Among other things, gluten was a go, video games were permitted (for one hour after homework was done), and Amy was allowed to visit with us one weekend a month.

Roger "Dodger" Leeds was excluded from the settlement when it was revealed that he did absolutely nothing to create the novel beyond handing over Emma's diary and a modest payment to Kevin Ridgeway. Leeds even considered the job of editor beneath him, which is why he convinced Ridgeway to bring Brainert aboard.

"Leeds was monumentally arrogant in his disdain for popular fiction," Brainert told me later. "He thought he could toss off a potboiler and make a quick buck. But writing one wasn't as easy as he thought."

When news of the settlement was published in the trades, Sadie marveled at how quickly the legal quagmire was cleared up.

Jack and I weren't surprised at all.

The cofounder and chairwoman of the board at Salient House stepped in personally to fix the problem. The esteemed elderly publisher, Mrs. Dorothy Moreland Macklin, was widely quoted in the company press releases.

Aw, well, Jack remarked, *if anybody knows how to deal with a bogus bestseller, it's little Miss Moreland.*

Of course, the legal machinations exposed Brainert's involvement with *Shades of Leather*. But the reaction from his peers was not what he expected—just as I told him. He should have had more faith.

Many of his colleagues, afraid to speak with a bully like Leeds dominating meetings and discussions, now expressed admiration for aspects of popular fiction, and for Brainert's accomplishment.

Me? I was happy to see the last of Leeds, though that would take time since the man had become a local Internet sensation. Someone duped the security footage of the Bentley Prize winner breaking my taillight and made a meme out of it.

"Now, who could have done such a thing?" I wondered when I first saw it.

"Yes, who?" Brainert replied, none too convincingly.

I didn't blame my old friend for the digital prank, given the awful red paint van incident and the years of literary bullying, not to mention Roger Dodger's other crimes. And on the latter matter . . .

St. Francis University's administration quickly detached the school from Professor Leeds. They mourned the loss of their literary light—and knew they had to find another, fast. Why not the man who helped write one of the most popular thrillers since the *Millennium* series? And behold, a new curriculum was born, one that focused on popular fiction, its rich history, its place in today's culture, and how to write it.

This week, Brainert's undergrads would be attending two of his lectures at the Movie Town Theater, along with screenings of *Peyton Place* and *Valley of the Dolls*.

So, all's right with your little, living world now?

"The Quibblers are still at war with the city council, Seymour can't decide on whether to adopt a bird friend for Waldo, I heard Bull McCoy may get a promotion, and Spencer's obsessing far too much about reaching Level Five of *Avenging Angel*. But I think you can rest assured that things are good."

Rest sounds good, baby. For now, anyway. I'll see you in your dreams . . .

As a draft in the room made me shiver, I swore I saw the gumshoe flash a ghostly smile before fading back into the fieldstone walls that had become his tomb.

Ready to find
your next great read?

Let us help.

Visit prh.com/nextread